# LAST RESORT

Visit us at www.boldstrokesbooks.com

# By the Author

Mending Fences

Last Resort

# LAST RESORT

*by*

Angie Williams

2020

# LAST RESORT

ISBN 13: 978-1-63555-774-9

THIS TRADE PAPERBACK ORIGINAL IS PUBLISHED BY
BOLD STROKES BOOKS, INC.
P.O. BOX 249
VALLEY FALLS, NY 12185

FIRST EDITION: SEPTEMBER 2020

## CREDITS

EDITOR: CINDY CRESAP
PRODUCTION DESIGN: SUSAN RAMUNDO
COVER DESIGN BY TAMMY SEIDICK

# Acknowledgments

Thank you, BSB family, for the support, the laughs, and for welcoming me with open arms. A special thank you to Cindy Cresap for your guidance and to Kris Ridste for beta reading like a boss.

I'm very fortunate to have parents who enthusiastically support me and repeatedly tell me how proud they are. I may be an adult, but hearing your parents are proud never gets old. Thanks for always being two of my biggest fans.

I couldn't have done any of this without the love of my family and friends. This is especially true of the family I'm lucky enough to have with my wife, son, and co-parents. There have been many ups and downs over the last fifteen years, but I am so incredibly proud of the family we have created and the son we have raised together. We took a difficult situation and created a family full of love and support. That's amazing.

Finally, thank you, Meghan. Every morning I wake up and I'm so glad. (Inside joke we have from the movie *Best in Show*). You have exceeded all of my childhood dreams of the perfect partner to spend my life with. You make me laugh every single day. You're always happy to snuggle even when you're technically in the middle of doing something else. You're my biggest cheerleader and an incredible mother to our son. I hit the absolute jackpot when you proposed to me mere hours before my appointment with the jeweler to pick out an engagement ring (jerk). You are everything to me and I'll spend the rest of my life proving to you that even though I'm technically a Texan, I'm the one for you.

# Dedication

For Meghan, always and everything

## CHAPTER ONE

K atie's phone rang for the third time in as many minutes, pulling her once again from her work. She hated being interrupted while she was working but worried if someone was desperate enough to call her repeatedly it might actually be an emergency.

She glanced at the phone before answering and noticed the call was from her sister, Elise. "This better be important because I'm in the middle of a project."

"You're always in the middle of a project, and this is important. Are you bringing someone to Sunday lunch at Mom's tomorrow?"

The love-hate relationship with her family's Sunday lunch was something she both dreaded and looked forward to every week. She loved about seventy-five percent of the time she spent with her family but hated the twenty-five percent they spent harassing her about not being in a relationship. In all fairness, only part of her family harassed her. Katie's twin brother, Andy, prudently kept his mouth shut as their mother and Elise did their best to nudge her back into the dating jungle.

"Why would you think I would bring someone to lunch? It's a family thing." Katie couldn't restrain the irritation from creeping into her voice. Elise acted like being single was the worst thing to ever happen, refusing to accept she was perfectly fine with things as they were.

Katie heard chaos in the background as her niece and nephew argued enough to send their mother over her limit. "Give me the bucket. Give it to me right this minute," she heard Elise say to them. "Both of you get a five-minute time-out. Go to your time-out stools, now."

"Are they seriously fighting over a bucket?" Katie asked.

Elise sighed. "These kids would argue over anything. You and Andy were never like this. I thought twins were supposed to be cosmically connected in some way?"

"I was always a much more passive child who didn't fight Andy for anything. Your kids are not passive. They take after their mom." Katie was teasing her, but there was truth to her words. "Why are you asking me if I'm bringing someone to lunch? Please don't tell me you're trying to set me up with someone named after a Disney movie again."

"Fantasia was lovely. She was a bit quirky but totally hot."

"I'm sure Fantasia will make some granola lesbian a wonderful wife someday, but every time I took a bite of my pot roast she looked at me like I was a wild animal. Why would you ever think she was right for me?" Katie asked.

Elise sighed again. Katie realized Elise sighed a lot for a woman who was only thirty-seven years old. "You never make this easy, Katie. I'm running out of options because you're so freaking picky. You'd think I would be able to find one damn lesbian in San Francisco who's good enough for my baby sister."

Katie rolled her eyes. Elise almost made her feel guilty for not making this whole matchmaking thing easier, but Katie never asked or wanted to be set up with anyone. She wished her mother and Elise would worry about their own lives and leave her the hell alone. She was perfectly content just the way she was. She had a cat who was completely devoted to her but gave her the space she needed, she had a sixty-five-inch television with an endless library of entertainment on Netflix, and she had the best vibrator money could buy. Katie's life was pretty much perfect and a girlfriend would only add complications. She hated complications.

"Maybe you should just stop trying to fix me up with every lesbian you meet. I love you and I appreciate that you and Mom are worried about me, but I'm really and truly just fine. Why don't you guys hound Andy about being with someone? He's single."

"We nag Andy about other things. Besides, he was in a relationship for seven years that didn't work out, but he at least is out there trying to find someone he connects with. We harass you because it's been years and you don't even try. That worries us. You can't be alone forever, sweetie."

"I don't think that's true. Plenty of people live alone for their entire lives and are perfectly happy. Besides, I tried the love thing, it wasn't my jam. I have to let you go, Elise. I have a deadline and I've only finished three of the ten cards I have to do. To answer your question, no, I'm not bringing anyone to lunch, and as an added bonus, I don't want you to bring anyone to fix me up with either. Let me live my life, woman," Katie said. The last bit was with more humor in her voice than she actually felt.

"You can't shut yourself off forever, Katie." Elise sounded sad which made her feel guilty all over again. "Amber was a grade A bitch who didn't deserve you."

The mention of her ex-girlfriend still felt like a stab to her heart. "Hey, don't bash Amber. It wasn't all her fault." Katie hated it when she felt she had to stick up for the woman who after a four-and-a-half-year relationship left her for their mutual best friend. It had been almost three years since Amber moved out of their apartment, and she swore to herself she would never let anyone get that close again. Losing not only the person she thought was going to be her forever, but the friend she trusted more than anything, was too much for her to process. It had taken her months to pick up her life and learn to love herself and accept her place in the world. She wasn't about to just allow someone to waltz in and break her heart again.

"You're right, it was Heidi's fault, too. They better hope I never run into either of them in a dark alley."

"Elise, stop. What's done is done."

"But it's not done, Katie. Not even close. It may be done for them, but they've pushed you into this box you use to protect yourself from ever being hurt. The problem is you have to risk the hurt to be able to find happiness."

"Is this the 'you have to kiss a few frogs before you find a princess' speech?"

"You won't even go to the pond, Katie, let alone kiss any frogs."

"Hey, I kiss plenty of frogs. I just don't kiss the same frog more than once. Okay, we've got to get off this frog thing. It's really freaking me out."

"I love you, Katie."

"I know, I love you, too. Don't worry about me. I really am happy. You're losing more sleep over my lack of a relationship than I am, trust me."

"That doesn't make me feel better," Elise said. "I need to go. I have to put shoes on these two monsters and pick up the other monster from school. I need a break."

"Take care of yourself. Make that husband of yours stay with them while you do something nice for yourself. Why don't you and Mom go get facials or something? Her birthday is coming up. We have to talk about what we're doing for that. Let's talk Sunday."

"Sounds good. Love you, squirt," Elise said.

"Don't call me that, stilts." Elise could be a pain in Katie's ass, but she had always looked out for her younger siblings and Katie loved her dearly.

Elise was only a year older but always seemed much more mature. In high school, she was the homecoming queen, editor of the newspaper, head cheerleader, and the most popular girl in school. Andy never quite reached the social level Elise did, but he was an extremely attractive baseball star who was valedictorian of their class, so he did all right.

Katie had always just been Katie. She made good grades, had a few friends, and hung out with the artistic crowd. She was content with her place in the pecking order, but Elise had always tried to elevate her status somehow. It drove Katie crazy. Elise would drag her to party after party with the popular kids, setting her up with one boy after another before Katie finally confided in her that she liked girls. Elise didn't miss a beat and had been trying to force her into a relationship with every eligible lesbian in Northern California ever since.

Amber had been one of the lesbians Elise set her up with, and even though Katie had told her time and again that it wasn't her fault things didn't work out, Elise would never forgive herself. Of course that didn't stop her from trying to set her up with more women.

Finding her partner of four years in bed with her best friend had been so cliché, but at the end of the day, Katie wasn't as surprised as she should have been. Things with Amber had been strained for at least a year before, and if she were honest with herself, longer than that. Amber was the type of woman who liked to be the center of someone's universe, and as an artist, Katie just didn't have the energy required to satisfy that kind of need. It didn't help that Katie's life at that time was consumed by her father's death. The countless hours she spent grieving with her family were hours she wasn't at home tending to Amber's needs.

Katie sat at her drafting table forcing herself to focus on work long enough to finish the rest of the greeting card order she was contracted to design. With a deep sigh, she thought of Sunday lunch at her mother's and said a silent prayer to the patience gods that they be with her if Elise showed up with yet another poor woman who had been drug there as an offering.

## Chapter Two

The deafening noise of the chainsaw masked the sound of someone entering the shop floor of the Morgan Woodworks Company, so when Rhys felt a gentle touch on her shoulder she almost cut the head off the bald eagle sculpture she was working on. When she pulled off her goggles and mask, she saw the guilty party was her father.

"You scared the shit out of me, Dad. We need to have some kind of flashing light that can alert me if someone enters the shop. You almost caused a fatal beheading of my eagle friend here."

Rhys's dad sat in a chair at her work bench. "It's looking great, kiddo. The detail on the feathers is incredible. You're going to make master carpenter in half the time it took me if you keep producing that kind of work." The pride in her father's eyes was evident as he inspected her latest piece.

"Thanks, Dad. This is one of a matching pair that I'm making for a bird sanctuary in Alaska. The orders are coming in so fast I have a waiting list. I'm not sure what happened to put me in such high demand, but it's a good thing for the business so I'm not complaining."

The Morgan family had been carpenters and wood workers since Rhys's ancestors left Wales to escape the coal mines in the late 1830s. Watkin Rhys Morgan opened the Morgan Woodworks Company in San Francisco in 1850, and Rhys along with her sister, Max, would eventually be the seventh generation to run things someday.

"Max and I have had the same experience on the cabinetry side of things. It seems like our wait list is getting longer and longer every day. We appear to be out of the recession and people are building houses again."

Rhys removed her heavy apron and shook her hair to brush off the sawdust. "I've noticed when I've peeked at the books. I think this is going to be our best year since Max and I have been old enough to be involved."

He nodded as he smoothed his hand over the wing of Rhys's eagle sculpture. "This is really something, sweetheart. I know I keep repeating myself, but I just wish your grandpa could see how good you've gotten. He would be just as proud as I am of both you and Max."

Rhys stuffed her hands into the pockets of her jeans and smiled. She'd never been comfortable with compliments, but nothing in the world pleased her like her father's approval. "Did I ever tell you you're the best dad ever?"

He wrapped an arm around her. "You have, but I never tire of hearing it. This is turning into the mutual admiration society. I like it."

"You've earned it. You've set Max and me up with a viable future. I appreciate you and all you've done. I appreciate you letting me focus on my sculpting rather than the cabinetry side of things, too. I know it's not what you'd planned, but you put my happiness first and I can't thank you enough for that. You're just a good dad." Rhys turned away to pour herself a glass of water before her emotions had a chance to spill out anymore and contradict her carefully crafted rugged persona.

"Well, I'm just the steward of the company, as you and Max will be someday. With any luck, you'll both have kids who will carry on the tradition long past when you and I are gone." He stood and walked around her work, inspecting every detail she had painstakingly carved. "As far as the sculpting, you're incredibly talented. I would be a fool not to nurture your gift. Besides, it's become profitable and has pulled the company out of more than one slump when the cabinetry side has been slow."

Rhys finished her water and rinsed the glass in the sink. Her family business was run from a large warehouse on Bryant Street in San Francisco. Each generation had updated the facilities here and there, but much of it was just as it had been since her grandfather did a complete renovation in the 1950s. The structure survived the great 1906 earthquake, but the damage had been significant so her grandfather almost completely rebuilt the building to repair things the previous generations had just learned to work around.

"Is Mom back from her tour?" Rhys's mother was a professional violinist who played for the San Francisco symphony but would occasionally tour with other orchestras in her off season.

"She'll be back tomorrow. I'm ready for her to be home. I'm glad she's able to have these experiences, but I sure do miss her when she's gone."

Rhys's parents had always been a perfect example to her and Max of what a loving, respectful relationship looked like. When they were kids they'd been grossed out when their mom and dad would kiss or be affectionate with each other, but now that she was an adult she realized how wonderful it would be to have that kind of love for another person.

"I hope I have what you and Mom have someday," Rhys said. She walked over to a couch they kept pushed against the wall and collapsed, toeing off her boots and stretching out to relax.

"You will, sweetie. You'll find the right person. Have you been dating?" He sat in a chair across from her and put his feet up on the coffee table between them. "You know you have to get out there if you want to find someone. They won't just show up at the shop."

Rhys rolled her eyes. "I know. Why can't it be like in the movies where the girl of my dreams places an order and when she comes by to discuss what she wants our eyes meet and we live happily ever after?"

"It's rarely that simple," he said.

"It was for you and Mom."

Her dad smiled at the mention of meeting her mother. "I think we may have given you the wrong impression of how smoothly our courting went."

"Courting?"

"Hush."

"Why didn't your courting go smoothly? Was it because you called it courting?"

"You're a smart aleck. No, your mom was just a little more mature than I was at that age. She was driven and already an accomplished musician and I was a bit of a goof. In the end she couldn't resist the Morgan charm, but she took some convincing and I had to do some growing up."

"Well, I'm glad it worked out. I like having you guys as my parents."

"We think you're a little bit of all right, too. Hey, your uncle Gareth was telling me about a singles resort in Marin that your cousin Gavin went to a couple of months ago. He met several nice girls there and he's been dating one of them ever since. Maybe you could do something like that."

"If Gavin was able to find a girl who puts up with his crap they must have pretty desperate women at that resort. Besides, it's not like I'm interested in some straight hookup resort." Rhys knew she sounded like she was pouting and she couldn't deny that she might be having a pity party, but she couldn't help it. How could she live in one of the gayest cities in the world and not be able to find one girl she was interested in. It was infuriating.

Her father pulled his chair closer and patted her leg. "Hey, you'll find someone, sweetheart. Gareth said he thought they had a lesbian week which is why he told me about it. He thought it might be good for you to not only take a break from work but also a good way to meet people."

"What about the backlog of work? I'm backed up for months."

"You leave that to me. You may be more naturally talented, but I'm the one who taught you woodcarving. I'm sure I can hold the fort down for a week. Max and Gareth will take care of the cabinetry side. We'll make it work. You need this, honey. Whether you meet someone or not, you need to put yourself out there and interact with other humans for once. You've probably forgotten how to even talk to a girl." He jumped when she swatted at him for the comment.

She moaned her frustration and draped her arm over her eyes. "You're right. I'll give it a go if they really do have a lesbian week." "You make it sound like Shark Week." "You have no idea how true that is, Dad." Rhys got up to start her work again. She couldn't remember the last time she'd taken time for herself, and she had to admit her dad was right, burying herself in work wasn't going to get her any closer to finding someone to love.

"Will you ask Gareth for the details for me? I've got to get these eagles done."

He stood and scruffed her hair. "I love you, kid."

"Love you, too, Dad. Thanks for the chat and for opening up about that stuff with you and Mom."

"Thanks for listening. Now get to work, slacker."

Rhys watched her father walk out of the warehouse. She'd hit the jackpot in the parents department and hoped she'd one day be able to have that same type of relationship with her own kids. Who knows, maybe she'd meet the girl of her dreams at this resort. The thought made her smile as she picked up her tools to finish her project.

## Chapter Three

Katie waited by the curb in front of her apartment for Andy to pick her up for the drive to their mother's house just north of the Golden Gate Bridge in Sausalito. She worried about her mother living in the huge house all by herself since their father had died but didn't think her mother was ready to let go of the home where she had lived with the love of her life.

Anderson Fausch had been a force of nature when Katie and her siblings were growing up. The Fausch family had always been very close and the news that the patriarch had taken his own life shook them to their very core. Katie remembered the day Andy showed up at her apartment and told her the man who had always been their rock had taken his own life. Her world had been turned upside down in an instant and she wasn't sure any of them would ever truly get over the loss.

Included in his will was a note to his wife and each of his children. They discovered he'd been diagnosed with stage four pancreatic cancer. He had kept the information to himself and in an effort to not only unburden his family with his care, but to escape what seemed like an inevitable decline, he took matters into his own hands. The letters he left were meant to ease their suffering but did nothing to quell the pain they shared over losing the man that meant so much to them. Katie tried not to dwell on it, but the idea that he might have stolen time they could have spent with him broke something inside her. She knew his decision wasn't about her but the idea that he felt suicide was his only option was difficult to accept.

They all missed him, but her mother was the one she worried about the most. Their mother loved deeply and wanted everyone to experience the happiness she had known in her relationship. Unfortunately, none of her children had been as lucky in love.

Katie heard Andy's car before she saw the blue BMW roadster zip around the corner and stop in front of her. The top was down and her twin looked like a young 1950s movie star with his wavy blond hair and dark blue eyes. Andy, like their father, had always been the life of the party, which Katie appreciated since it took pressure off of her to be more social. She didn't consider herself shy, but she never liked being the center of attention like he did.

"Let's do this," he said.

Katie shook her head as she slid into the passenger seat and buckled herself in. "How in the world are you, my brother?"

"What kind of a question is that? I'm a great brother." He pouted for sympathy.

Katie gave him a gentle smack on the arm. "You're the best brother ever, but you're just so much cooler than I am. I don't know how we could have shared a womb for nine months."

"I've asked myself that same question many times, little sis," Andy said.

Although Katie was born only twenty-two minutes after him, he had always referred to her as his "little" sister. She hated it when they were kids, but now that he wasn't using it to establish dominance over her, she thought it was cute. Katie had always been the baby of the family and because of that, they treated her like she was just a kid. Even though she was in her mid-thirties she was still looked at by her siblings as someone they had to protect and look after.

The extra attention was sometimes a pain, but it also made her feel like someone always had her back. It could also be part of the reason why she didn't feel the need to be in a relationship. She thought she'd been in love before, and having her heart broken so thoroughly once was enough. She wasn't interested in reliving that pain. The first few months after her breakup she fell apart, but now she was finally in a space where she not only didn't feel the need to find someone, she didn't want to. She thought Amber was the person she would spend the rest of her life with, and when that idea was taken away from her, the dream of spending her life with someone lost its charm.

The only way she knew to put herself back together was to decide she didn't need anyone else. She cherished her independence now, and the thought of sharing her life with someone else was not something she was interested in reliving. She wasn't immune to the need for affection, but she had found there was no shortage of eligible ladies in San Francisco who were more than willing to scratch that itch when she needed it.

Her reclusive ways never satisfied her mother and Elise though. They made it a mission to get Katie married off before she shriveled up and became an old maid. The day she turned thirty-five it was as if some magical threshold had been surpassed and they were racing the clock to get her married and settled down before she met her expiration date. Katie thought her father's death and her mother losing the love of her life very likely had something to do with that urgency. She felt for her mother, but the more she pushed, the less Katie wanted anything to do with love and romance.

"You okay?" Andy asked. "You seem a little distracted."

Katie shifted in the leather car seat to look at him. "I'm okay. Just thinking about Dad. Tuesday will be three years since we lost him. Sometimes I feel like I don't remember what he was like. I do of course, but it feels like I was a kid when he was alive and now that he's gone, I'm an adult."

Andy gave her a sympathetic smile as he reached over to take her hand in his and give it a gentle squeeze. "I know what you mean. His death made us grow up in ways we weren't expecting or ready for."

"Do you think that's why Mom is so focused on me being in a relationship? I think Elise is obsessed because she's nosy and has to control every aspect of my life, but I wonder if part of it for Mom is that she wants me to have what she had before it's too late. She obviously doesn't realize that not only is it not that easy but I don't even know if I want it." Katie sighed as she turned back toward the window.

"Why do you think you don't want a relationship? You do realize not all women will cheat on you and leave you a brokenhearted mess, right?" Andy asked.

Katie watched the buildings and people pass as she gathered her thoughts. "I don't think I'm ready to give up who I've become to conform to what someone else wants me to be. I'm not doing that again. It ended badly the first time."

"First of all, you obviously have no idea how real, mature relationships work."

"I've been in a mature relationship," Katie said with annoyance in her voice.

Andy shook his head as he drove across the Golden Gate Bridge. "Don't take this the wrong way, but you haven't. I'm talking about being with someone who doesn't try to control you. Someone who loves you and appreciates the amazing woman you are, not the person they think they can force you to be."

"You think Amber was controlling?" Katie and Andy were very close, but they'd never really talked about Amber or the breakup. She'd avoided the subject and she wondered now if that was because she didn't want to admit the reality of the relationship she had.

Amber had been controlling, and now that she thought about it, so had Heidi. Katie never felt like she could be enough for either one of them. At the end of the day, she wasn't. They found something in each other she could never have given them.

"I'm not trying to dig up old wounds, but suffice it to say, you were a different person when you were with Amber. You lost yourself."

"That's exactly the part I don't want. I don't want to share my life. I like being able to do what I want to do and go where I want to go. If I want to stay up all night binging *Orange is the New Black*, I don't want someone to tell me I can't because I have to work the next day. It's my life."

"Easy there. No one is going to tell you when to go to bed, Crazy Eyes. I totally get not wanting to be in a relationship. They're messy and they're complicated and they take a lot of work, but there's also some great things that Mom worries you're going to miss out on. Just because it didn't work out with Amber doesn't mean it's not worth trying with someone else. The trick is to find someone who loves you for all your craziness and accepts you as you are. That person is out there. You just have to open yourself up enough for them to have a chance." Andy reached over and brushed Katie's hair behind her ear. "I love you, Katie. I support you with whatever will make you happy. I just hope you will someday allow someone else the chance to truly know the incredible woman you are. And by the way, I'm only this cool because I've always had you by my side."

Katie smiled. She knew he might be somewhat right about relationships, but she doubted she ever would be able to allow herself to let someone in long enough to find out. "I love you, too. I think you're a bit of a romantic like Mom, but I understand what you're saying and will take it into consideration."

Andy pulled into the driveway, turned off the car, and reached for her hand again. "Don't forget that Mom and Elise love you. We all do and we only want you to at least give someone a chance. You can't close yourself off forever."

"You're getting sappy in your old age." Katie knew he was probably right, but it was easier said than done. Katie took three deep breaths to center herself before braving what she knew would be a few hours of nagging from her family.

"Maybe I am, but it's only because I love you. Give Mom and Elise a break and humor them. You might accidentally find out they're right after all."

Katie gently shoved Andy's shoulder. "That sounds horrible. Why would I want to ever find out they were right? You're not very good at this. You know how I feel about being wrong."

Andy opened his door and unfolded his large frame as he climbed from the tiny vehicle. "Oh, I know how much you hate being wrong. I remember the time Dad grounded you because you sent Grandpa Fausch that article about single use plastic bags being terrible for the environment."

"Well, he was wrong. He thought I was ridiculous because he didn't want to be inconvenienced, but it's a small price to pay to cut down on the plastic that's ending up in our oceans and wrapped around sea turtles."

Andy wrapped his arm around her as they walked toward the house. "I totally agree, I just think calling your elderly grandfather a doddering fool might not have been the best way to get your point across."

"I know." Katie hung her head. "It wasn't my finest moment. Dad was pretty cool about it though. Did I ever tell you he came into my room later that night after Grandma and Grandpa left and told me how proud he was of me for having a well thought out opinion and sticking up for what I believed in?"

"No, but I'm not surprised. Dad was cool like that."

"He told me I needed to work on cooling my jets and respecting my elders but that he thought I was a passionate person with a good heart and he was proud that I was his daughter."

"He was right. You're the best person I know as long as I stay on your good side."

Katie snuggled closer into his side. "If only Elise would learn to stop poking the bear, we'd all get along just fine."

## CHAPTER FOUR

As Katie and Andy entered the side door into the kitchen, they checked each pot on the stove to see what their mom was making for lunch. Now that her mother lived alone, she only cooked big meals when the family visited on Sundays. When she did, she pulled out all the stops, making enough for each of them to take home leftovers.

"Roast beef and carrots," Katie told Andy as she checked the oven.

Andy used an oven mitten to open the pot on the stove. "Mashed potatoes. God, I love that woman."

Their mother entered the kitchen a few minutes later to find them picking at the chocolate cake she had hidden in the cabinet. "Step away from that."

"Why would you put this in the cabinet, crazy woman?" Katie swiped another finger of chocolate buttercream frosting.

"Because you heathens can't be trusted with chocolate cake."

The screen door slammed as Elise entered the kitchen. "Chocolate cake?"

"No, put it away or nobody gets any." Their mother pointed an admonishing finger at them.

"Wow, you're a mean cake hoarding lady." Andy placed the lid back on the cake stand and winked at his mother before giving her a hug. "Thanks for making us cake, Mom."

"Where's Jeff and the kids?" Katie hugged Elise and noticed she looked a bit ragged.

Elise rolled her eyes. "I can't keep making excuses for him. The kids are playing in the yard and surprise, surprise, Jeff is working. I appreciate all he does for our family, but sometimes I don't feel like he's actually part of it. He hasn't had a meal with his children in two weeks. They don't even ask where Daddy is anymore. He's this stranger who comes in to kiss them good night after they've already fallen asleep. He keeps telling me it's only for now, but only for now has been almost a year and it's getting more and more difficult to excuse it. I haven't had sex in two months. Mama needs some lovin'."

Andy snorted as the milk he was drinking shot from his nose. Katie tossed him a dish towel. She'd suspected things might not be good with Elise and Jeff, but this was the first time she had confirmed they had issues. The Fausches were typically a very open family, but Elise had always wanted a relationship that would emulate her parents' perfect marriage. Katie worried the need to maintain that illusion had kept her from talking to them sooner.

Their mother wrapped her arms around Elise and rubbed a comforting hand across her back. "I'm sorry, sweetie. He loves you and he's a good man, but you need to communicate with him until it gets through his thick skull that providing for his family is more than just making money. I wish your father were alive to have a talk with him."

"I'm not sure that would make things better, Mom, but I appreciate the thought. Things will be okay. I'm going to tell him he needs to at the very least have dinner with his children for an hour every night and I'm putting my foot down and insisting he spend Sundays with us."

Katie and Andy joined the hug circle.

"I knew things weren't great, but I had no idea it had gotten this bad. Why didn't you tell us any of this sooner?" Katie asked.

"I didn't want to bother you guys." Elise wiped a tear from her cheek. "You have enough going on to have to worry about my marriage."

Andy kissed her forehead. "You can always talk to us. Let me know if you need me to kick his ass." They laughed as they each began their designated jobs for lunch prep. Katie felt bad for being so irritated with Elise for meddling in her love life. It made more sense now that she knew her own situation wasn't what she had hoped it would be.

Sunday lunch was the typical family affair with a bit of teasing and a lot of laughter. After everything was put away, the kids went back outside while the adults relaxed on the back porch to watch the boats sail by.

Katie's mom excused herself as Katie, Andy, and Elise chatted about a party Andy had attended the previous Friday night. When their mom returned, she handed Katie an envelope and sat on the couch across from her. "What's this?" Katie asked.

Her mother and Elise looked a little too pleased with themselves for Katie's comfort as she opened the envelope and pulled out a colorful brochure. As she read the title page out loud, the meaning slowly sank in. "Last Resort, the last date you'll ever need. Join other local singles for a fun-filled week of meeting new people and falling in love. Last Resort's expert matchmakers will put you with a different partner every day until you've found your perfect match. After your morning excursion, you and your date will return to the resort to participate in one of our many activities or just relax and get to know each other better. Enjoy a week of fun, friendship, and romance as you get to know others who are also looking for that special someone to share their lives with. You and your dates will enjoy horseback riding, surfing, sailing, and many other activities as you make memories that will last a lifetime."

Katie let the brochure drop to her lap as she gave her mother and Elise a shocked look. "What the hell, yo? Why are you giving me this brochure?" Katie turned to Andy who shrugged as if he was just as shocked as she was.

Elise picked up the brochure from her lap and sat next to her on the couch. "I know what you're going to say, but hear us out. Your first instinct is going to be to resist, but Mom and I have already paid for the week so if you don't go, you'll be wasting tons of our money not to mention the fact that it would be rude to turn down a gift."

"Are you seriously trying to guilt me into going to that circus? Dude, first of all I'm a lesbian and I'm pretty sure the ladies at this resort are going to notice I don't have a penis. Second, I don't want to do this." Katie was in such shock she was having a difficult time even putting an argument together.

"Every six months they have a lesbian week and the week after next happens to be one. Mom's going to drop you off and I'll pick you up the following Sunday morning. Unless of course you find a ride with some handsome chick with a motorcycle," Elise said, wrapping her arm around Katie.

"I don't want you riding a motorcycle without a helmet," her mom said.

"Have you people lost your minds? I'm not going to some meat market resort and I'm not riding a motorcycle." She looked at Andy for support, but he wisely kept his mouth shut.

"I've seen some super hot chicks on motorcycles. If I was a lesbian I would totally go for a biker chick," Elise said.

Katie covered her face with her hands. "I can't believe this is happening. How long have you two been planning this intervention?"

"I was talking to Susan Carmichael the other day, you remember Susan don't you? Her daughter Tabatha is five years older than you and was having the same trouble finding a girlfriend so Susan sent her to the last lesbian week and now she's been happily dating the same woman ever since. She's a doctor," her mother said. This information seemed to be the key to her story.

"Tabatha or the girlfriend?" Katie asked

"What?"

"Tabatha is the doctor or the girlfriend is the doctor?"

"The girlfriend is the doctor. Tabatha is a piano teacher and still lives at home with Susan."

Katie did her best to keep the irritation from her voice, but she felt completely blindsided by her family's attempt to force her to go to a singles resort. "This is all becoming so clear. I'm not going to end up an old maid living with you, Mom."

Her mother sat next to her on the opposite side as Elise. "That's not what I think and even if you did, I'm your mom and I'll always be here for you. We aren't trying to upset you, sweetheart. We're trying to give you a little shove out of your comfort zone. It'll be good for you. I'll make you a deal, if you go to this resort, Elise and I will leave you alone about your love life for one year."

Well, that was intriguing. All she had to do was spend this one week dealing with people who were pathetically desperate for love and then she could live her life in peace for an entire year. "Deal," she said with a roll of her eyes.

"Yippee." Her mom and Elise said together like a cheer squad from 1952. "You won't regret it, sweetheart. Worst-case scenario you'll make some friends. Best-case scenario, I'll have more grandchildren someday."

"Holy crap, Mom, you're really going to freak her out."

Katie picked up the brochure and looked at the photos of women happily frolicking together. "This is nuts but if it keeps you guys off my case for a year, I'll do it. You guys have to promise you'll give me a break after this though. I don't want to do this and then show up at Sunday lunch to find Elise has picked up another lesbian she's trying to hook me up with. This is it."

"We pinky swear," Elise said, sticking out her little finger.

"Me, too," her mother said. She hooked her finger around Elise's in a pinky swear.

Katie rolled her eyes and pushed their hands away. "You guys are too much. How am I related to you weirdos?"

"Just lucky, I guess," her mother said. "Now, let's go see how much trouble those kids have gotten into."

They stood and walked toward the sound of kids' laughter. Katie dreaded the idea of the resort but knew she would do anything to make her family happy so she plastered a smile on her face and promised herself she would make the best of a ridiculous situation.

## Chapter Five

Rhys surveyed the clothing she had spread out on her bed. She didn't usually stress over what she wore but the wardrobe for her week at the resort felt more important than a typical week away. She'd never had a difficult time attracting attention from a woman, but she felt her wardrobe would determine the type of girl she wanted to attract.

"Knock, knock." She heard Max's voice as she walked into the loft where Rhys lived above the warehouse. "You here?"

"In the bedroom," she called back. She tossed a couple more shirts onto the shirt pile, bringing her count to ten, which was more than she needed for a week away from home.

Max bent down to avoid hitting her head as she entered the room. Rhys wasn't short at five foot six, but Max towered over her at five foot ten. She looked like a taller version of Rhys except she had their mother's blue eyes instead of her brown.

"What's up?" Rhys asked, collapsing into a chair in the corner of the room.

Max looked at the pile of clothes on her bed and then sat in the chair opposite. "Not much. Dad said you were leaving tomorrow for the resort thing so I thought I would stop by to check on you and make sure you didn't have anything you needed me to do while you're gone."

"Nope. If you could finish getting the eagle sculptures packed up for shipping, Clive will be by tomorrow to pick them up."

Rhys had put the final touches on the two large eagle sculptures that morning. She'd been carving for as long as she could remember, but she was particularly proud of the two almost identical birds that would stand guard outside a nature center in Alaska. These weren't the first birds she'd carved, but the detail she was able to get was something she'd never been able to accomplish before.

"Those birds look incredible, Rhys," Max said. She picked up a deck of cards from the small table between their chairs and began to shuffle.

"Thanks. I'm pretty proud of them. I hope they make it to Alaska okay. I've never shipped anything of this size that far, and the wing tips are pretty delicate."

Max tapped the deck on the table and started to deal each of them ten cards. "We'll get it packed up as tight as we can and the rest is up to them. There's only so much you can do."

Rhys picked up her cards once her hand was dealt. She studied them carefully before organizing them into melds. "I know. It's just hard to put so much into a piece just to turn around and send it far away."

"I get it. Your work takes so much out of you, I imagine it's hard to let them go." Max picked up a card from the stock pile and discarded another from her hand. "Dad was telling me about this resort thing you're going to. Sounds pretty cool. If it works out for you, I just might go myself."

Rhys smiled and knocked her knuckles on the table. She spread her cards out across from Max and counted the points she'd scored from the hand. "You don't seem to have any trouble finding dates. It might be a waste of your money."

Max documented her points in the notebook where they kept a running tally of their games. They'd been playing gin rummy since they were taught the rules of the game by their grandfather as kids. It always seemed to help them open up and communicate with each other more freely when they had something to occupy the part of their minds that typically kept them from talking about feelings with each other.

"I do all right in the dating department," Max said, flashing her a dimpled smile. "You don't do too bad yourself. What convinced you to go?"

Shuffling the cards for another hand, Rhys sighed. "I don't know. I think I'm just bored with the same girls I see every time I go out. I try to mix it up a bit and go to different bars, but girls in bars just aren't what I'm looking for. They're all too young, too high maintenance, and no matter what they say, none of them are looking for the type of commitment I'm ready for. I want the kind of love Mom and Dad have. I want to be with someone who lights up when she sees me and is just as happy to snuggle watching a show as she is going out to a fancy dinner."

Max picked up the cards she'd been dealt, and began grouping them in her hand. "I hear you. Sometimes I feel like I want that, too, and other times the idea of being with the same person every single day sends me into a state of panic. It's going to have to be a pretty spectacular person to convince me I'm ready to hang up my leather pants and settle down."

Rhys discarded another card. "You and those leather pants. Every time I see them I think of Ross being stuck in the bathroom on *Friends* where he sweated and couldn't get them off."

Max knocked and splayed out her cards to be counted. "Shut up. It's never happened, but I do think about that occasionally and get paranoid when I find myself trying to casually take them off when someone is lying in bed patiently waiting for me to rock their world."

"Rock their world?" Rhys shook her head. "You're such a dork."

Max winked at Rhys and jotted down her points. "I hope you find what you're looking for next week, Rhys."

"Thanks."

"Okay, enough sappy stuff," Max said. She crossed to the bed where Rhys had her clothes laid out in piles. "What look are you going for? Tough, brooding, mysterious lesbian or preppy chick who is the life of the party?"

Rhys welcomed the change in subject and stood next to Max to study the clothes. "I think maybe a combination of both. I am a tough, mysterious lesbian who's the life of the party."

Max pulled three shirts from her shirt pile, tossed them on the floor, and added three different ones from her closet. She studied the remaining clothes for a minute before adding a pair of dark jeans to the stack. "You can't only have shorts. I looked up information on the resort and it's on the beach. You're going to freeze your balls off if you only bring shorts. You'll need to pack a couple of sweaters, too."

"First of all, my balls aren't any concern of yours, they're very safely attached to the dick tucked away in a bag under my bed. Second, won't a sweater be too preppy looking? What about a hoodie?" Rhys rummaged through her drawers for her favorite hoodie.

"I'll make you a deal," Max said as she pulled a black sweater from the closet. "How about one sweater and one hoodie? That way you're prepared to impress whatever girl you're interested in at that moment."

Rhys nodded and tossed the hoodie in the shirt pile. "You're right, better to overpack a little and be prepared for anything."

"I'm counting on you to find someone who will help make Mom and Dad some grandchildren so they'll stop harassing me. Don't fuck this up. You've got all the tools to reel this woman in. Just don't make an ass out of yourself."

She pulled her suitcase from the back of her closet and started packing the clothes Max neatly folded and handed to her. "Wow, no pressure there. What makes you think I want kids?"

"Come on, Rhys. You've wanted kids since you were fifteen and you figured out you were a lesbian and could be a parent without actually having to give birth."

"It's kinda scary how much you know about me. It's almost like you pay attention, but I know that can't be true. If you did you would be better at buying me gifts."

Max rolled her eyes and tossed underwear at Rhys's face. "I'm just fine with my gift giving skills, asshole. Remember that time I got you the pickle grabber?"

Rhys loved the little tool Max gave her a few years before that allowed her to fish pickles from the jar without getting pickle juice all over her fingers. "That was an awesome gift. I'll give you that. I still use it all the time."

"See?" Max said. "Occasionally, I get it right. It's not my fault you're a bit of a weirdo and difficult to buy for."

"Having you as a sister is the best gift I've ever gotten," Rhys said dramatically, clutching her shirt over her chest.

"Yeah, yeah. Don't you forget it."

Rhys tucked the last piece of clothing into her bag and zipped it closed. "I'm serious." She wrapped her arms around Max. "I don't know what I would do without you. I'm really lucky to have you in my life."

Max kissed the top of her head. "Me, too. If you make me cry I swear to God I'm going to kick your ass."

She checked the time on her watch and sighed. "Well, I better take my bike down to get it gassed up and ready for tomorrow."

"How are you going to fit this big suitcase on the back of that bike?"

Rhys rolled the suitcase behind her as they walked out of the loft and down a flight of stairs to the warehouse where her motorcycle was parked. "I'm going to cinch it down as tight as I can and hope for the best. I don't have that far to drive, but the wind can get a little wonky going over the Golden Gate Bridge so I'm just going to hope for the best."

Max smiled as Rhys climbed onto her bike and put on her helmet. "That's comforting. You be careful up there this week. Relax and let yourself have fun but don't go and get your heart broken."

She slipped on her riding gloves and popped up the shield on her helmet so she could speak to her. "Geez, Max, thanks for the vote of confidence."

"That's not what I mean. I'm just saying don't pin all your hopes and dreams on this week. You don't half-ass anything, and I know you're going into this with your hopes up. My future sister-in-law is out there. Maybe she's at this resort, maybe not so don't put so much pressure on yourself that you fuck it up when she does come along."

Rhys adjusted herself on the motorcycle seat. "I hear you. I'm going into this with clear eyes and a full heart."

"Can't lose," Max said, rolling her eyes. "You're such a dork, Rhys. Really, you might want to tone down the dorkiness next week."

"The future Mrs. Morgan will love my dorkiness so mind your own business." Rhys started her motorcycle engine and flipped down the visor on her helmet as Max opened the large roll up door of the warehouse. With a wave, she drove out and onto the streets of San Francisco. She knew Max was right. She would have to keep her heart in check and not let herself get carried away.

# CHAPTER SIX

The parking lot was full of Subarus as Katie and her mom pulled up to the resort. "At least we know this really is lesbian week. Only a lesbian event would have all these Subarus." Katie watched out the window as women of all shapes and sizes drug suitcases toward the large wooden doors at the entrance.

"Look at all these beautiful ladies," her mother said, rubbing Katie's back for encouragement. Memories of the first day of high school filled Katie's mind as she watched people who seemed so much cooler than herself arrive.

"I know I'm your mom and I'm supposed to feel this way, but, honey, you're beautiful, smart, funny, and interesting. You have tons of friends. Don't think of the romantic aspect of this and just focus on the friendships you'll build. A romantic connection will either happen or it won't, but you've never had trouble making friends and I'm sure you won't this week. The only thing I ask is that you leave yourself open to the possibility of letting someone in. I know Amber and Heidi hurt you. I know it has taken you time to move on and you aren't keen to putting yourself out there again, but trust me, not everyone is like Amber. There's a wonderful woman out there that will make you so happy you won't know how you lived each day without her. Maybe that woman is here, maybe she isn't, but you have to open your heart and lower your guard long enough for her to prove to you that she's worth the risk. You can do this, my love. Now get out there and kiss some girls." She winked at Katie before giving her a gentle push toward the door.

"You're a crazy lady, but I love you to the moon and back. I promise I'll try. It's the best I can do."

Her mother squeezed her hand and gave her an encouraging smile. "It's all I ask."

"Okay, here goes. Wish me luck." Katie took a deep breath, grabbed her bag, and stepped out of the car waving to her mother as she drove off.

"You can do this, Katie." Katie gripped her bag tighter and followed the crowd of women through the front doors and into the lobby. Feeling a little lost, she searched the room for signage that would indicate where she was supposed to go.

Across the room, she noticed lines of women with luggage waiting to be checked in by staff sitting at tables. Behind the seated staff were papers indicating letters of the alphabet. Katie lined up behind the other E through Gs and searched her purse for the registration email she had printed out with her confirmation code.

When she reached the front of the line she was greeted by a very chipper redhead. "Hey there, I'm Linda. Do you have your reservation number?"

"Hey, Linda." Katie tried to match her enthusiasm but was afraid it came across as mocking. "Sorry." She handed her the paper and studied the room while Linda looked her up on the computer. "I can't believe how many women are here." The room was much more crowded than Katie had expected.

"Women come from all over the Bay Area, and since we only have a lesbian themed week every six months, we get quite the turnout. Is this your first time at a resort?"

Katie watched Linda check her paper and enter information into the computer. "My family vacationed at a resort in Mexico when I was fourteen but nothing like this."

"Oh, that sounds fun." Linda attached a luggage tag to Katie's bag. "You're going to love it, and with any luck, you'll find the woman of your dreams. Please leave your bag in the area to your left. It will be taken to your room once they're assigned."

Katie picked up her bag and stood on her tiptoes in an attempt to see over the crowd of women. "After I drop my bag over there, where do I…"

"Oh, I'm sorry, please follow the other ladies into the dining area and find a seat. Once everyone arrives the director will come in to give you more information."

"Thanks." Katie felt a little overwhelmed as she drug her luggage over to the designated area and then headed for the dining hall.

The sound of conversations filled the room. She chose one of the few remaining seats at the back and pulled out her phone to check her email. She'd finished her most recent order of greeting cards the day before and told her publisher she wouldn't be available for the next week, but she couldn't resist checking anyway. Her business ran via email and the habit of constantly checking her inbox had become an impulse.

"Is this seat taken?"

Katie looked up to find an adorable brunette pointing toward the chair next to her. "Nope." She sat up straight and scooted her chair over to make room.

"I'm Rhys by the way." The new arrival held out a hand for Katie to shake as she sat next to her.

"I'm Katie."

In an effort to pull her gaze from Rhys's soft brown eyes, Katie turned her attention back to the email on her phone hoping she would take the hint and do the same. She read through a new contract proposal for a project she was set to start the following week and discreetly watched her tablemate out of the corner of her eye. She thought Rhys was probably in her mid-thirties like herself and by the Alt-National Park T-shirt she was wearing, Katie guessed they were very likely politically aligned.

"Are you from the Bay Area?" Rhys asked.

The question startled Katie from her appraisal. "I'm sorry, what was your question?"

"I was just asking if you were from the Bay Area. I live in the City." People who lived in Northern California called San Francisco "the City" as if it was the only one worth the moniker. Katie thought they were right. The Bay Area had wonderful cities to boast about, but San Francisco had a special place in her heart.

"I grew up in Sausalito but live in the City now. Mission District." Katie pocketed her phone and turned her chair to face Rhys.

"We're almost neighbors," Rhys said. "I've never done anything like this. Have you?"

"Never. I was blackmailed by my overbearing family into coming this week."

"Blackmailed?" Rhys smirked. "I've never heard of anyone being blackmailed to spend a week at a resort."

Katie smiled, realizing how dramatic that sounded. "Maybe blackmail is too strong a word. How about coerced?"

"Wow, I can't wait to hear this story."

Before Katie could explain, a gorgeous woman stepped onto the stage at one end of the room. Katie shot Rhys an apologetic smile before turning her chair toward the speaker.

"Good morning. I'm Fran Taylor and I'll be your activities director for the week. I hope you are all as excited as I am." Whistles and hoots came from the crowd of excited women. "Well, let's get the paperwork out of the way first. My assistant will be coming around with a pen, an envelope, your room assignment, and an iPad where you will find a questionnaire. Please write your name and address on the outside of the envelope, power off your cell phone, and place it inside, sealing the flap when you're done. We will have a bin at each exit where you can deposit the phone on your way to your room. This week is about meeting new people and escaping the electronic leash that is your cell phone." More hoots and hollers came from the crowd mixed with a few groans.

Katie felt the blood drain from her face. What was this insane woman talking about? She couldn't give up her phone for an entire week. What if one of her clients tried to contact her? She knew her agent would tell them she was away for the week but still. This was unacceptable.

Katie gave Rhys a confused look as the woman continued. "Please complete the questionnaire to the best of your ability. We will use your answers to determine your matches and dates so be thoughtful when answering. Every morning, you'll find an envelope we've slid under your door containing the name of your date and where you'll be going. You'll have plenty of time to stop for breakfast before you need to find the van that will take you and your date to whatever exciting adventure you'll do that day. Once you're back from your date there are many activities we have available for you to continue getting to know each other or possibly meet someone new. Who likes karaoke?" Several women whooped and clapped while others shook their heads. "Our ballroom has been converted into Club Bump. You singers can join us for karaoke every evening to show off your skills, and after that, you can get up close and personal as you dance the night away. For the more competitive ones in the group, how about billiards, Ping-Pong, darts, bocce, board games, or beach volley ball?" The cheers were accompanied by high fives this time.

"Tournament signup sheets are outside the rec room. We can't forget those of you who simply want to relax and get to know each other better. That's what we're here for, right, ladies?" Katie looked at Rhys and rolled her eyes. Fran was quite good at getting the crowd excited, but Katie just wanted to know more about the cell phone issue.

"There's a pool, two large hot tubs, outdoor seating everywhere you look, and full access to our private beach. Everything you need to get to know each other a little better. You gals ready for this?"

The cheers were deafening as the ladies were in a near frenzy. "This is going to be such a fun week. Once you're settled into your room, we hope to see you at our mixer this evening after dinner so you have an opportunity to get to know some of the women you might end up on dates with this week. On that note, if at any point during the week you think you have found a real connection with someone, please stop by the office and we will schedule you with that person for the remainder of the dates. We'll need both of you to come in so we're sure both parties are agreeable to the match. If you have any questions at all, please don't hesitate to speak to one of us. Thanks so much, everyone, and I hope you all find love and happiness."

"What did she just say?" Katie asked Rhys. "Did she say she's taking our phone? I'm so not okay with that. I can't not have my phone all week." Her heart raced as she contemplated standing up and walking out right then.

"They mentioned it in the welcome packet that was sent to you last week," Rhys said. "They don't want phones or other electronics distracting you from interacting with people."

"That's insane." Katie realized she sounded like a crazy person, and the look on Rhys's face told her she needed to take it down a notch if she didn't want to embarrass herself even more. She could make it a week without her phone, right? It would be worth it to get her mom and Elise off her ass for an entire year...right?

"You okay?" Rhys asked.

Katie took a deep breath and checked her email one last time before powering off her phone. "I'm good. I just wasn't expecting it, and since I conduct my business through email, the thought of not having it available is a little unsettling."

Rhys smiled and powered her phone off as well. "I get it, especially when you obviously weren't aware of the rule. It makes me nervous too, but I'm also a little excited to get rid of it for a week."

She appreciated Rhys attempting to comfort her. Maybe her mom was right about making friends. When the envelope and questionnaire were dropped on the table in front of her she followed the instructions and sealed it up. She immediately felt a little adrift without her phone but also a little free. This week was going to be an adventure, and Katie knew she would need to keep an open mind if she was going to make it through.

Once the phone was securely tucked away, Katie reached into the envelope labeled room sixty-eight, and pulled out a key card adorned with the resort emblem. "What room did you get?" she asked.

"Looks like I am room..." A deep blush crept up Rhys's neck as she read the number aloud. "Sixty-nine."

Katie couldn't stop herself from cracking up at the embarrassed look on her face. "You're next door to me so keep it down over there, Casanova."

"I have no idea why that embarrassed me like I'm fourteen and someone said boob." They both pocketed their keys and powered on the iPads to complete the questionnaire.

Katie read through the questions on the first screen and was pleased to see they were all multiple choice. Glancing at Rhys she noticed she was already on question eleven. "You're whipping right through these questions."

"You aren't cheating off my paper are you?"

"I may have to so they don't escort me from the building. Question one, were you forced to come here against your will? Yes," she said.

"I'm pretty sure that isn't actually the first question unless they saw a worried look in your eye and gave you a different set of questions from everyone else. What's the story with that anyways?" she asked.

"My mom and sister are obsessed with finding me a wife and blackmailed me into coming here in exchange for not hooking me up with every lesbian in Northern California for a year. They can't accept the idea that someone could be happily single." Katie read the next question. "Are you a cat person or a dog person? Dog person, obviously."

"Me, too. Dog person all the way. Cats are okay, but I need the complete, unwavering devotion of a dog. Back to your purpose here, are you interested in making friends?"

"I'm totally open to friends. I'm not a monster," Katie said, giving her a wink.

"And you don't think there's any way you will find someone here who could possibly be more than a casual friend?"

"I promised my mom I wouldn't shut myself off completely, so I'll do my best to keep an open mind. If it happens, it'll happen, but she's going to have to be a pretty spectacular woman to get me to give up my ability to sleep diagonally across my bed." Katie moved onto the next question. "Do you hope to have children someday? Geez, they're getting personal."

"I'm pretty sure that's the point." Rhys finished her questionnaire and powered off her iPad.

Katie answered the last few questions and turned hers off as well before she stood to gather her things.

Rhys stood with her as they walked together toward the exit. "I just met you, Katie, but I think you're underestimating the charming women you'll meet this week. I have a feeling you'll meet the girl of your dreams."

"You're a romantic. I'm not trying to argue, but my chances of finding the girl of my dreams at some hokey resort are pretty slim."

"Interested in a little wager?"

"You're going to bet me that I will fall in love with someone in a week?"

Rhys smiled and Katie couldn't help but smile back. "I don't know about falling in love, but if you can't find at least one person you would like to date after this week, I'll give you a crisp one-hundred-dollar bill."

"You've really bought into this love thing, haven't you?"

Rhys shrugged and gave her a wink.

"Okay, you're on as long as you go to this stupid mixer with me tonight. I don't know anyone else and I'm scared of standing alone and looking like a complete loser."

"Are you asking me out already?" Rhys asked, giving Katie a sly smile. "This is going to be easier than I thought."

Katie rolled her eyes. "You wish. This is going to be the easiest hundred I've ever made." Katie stuck out her hand to shake on it.

Rhys smiled as she shook her hand. "Deal."

# CHAPTER SEVEN

R hys arrived at dinner ten minutes early hoping to scout out a good table before Katie arrived. She hadn't thought about much else other than Katie since they'd parted ways when they reached their rooms. After unpacking her clothes, she considered knocking on her door to see if she wanted to hang out, but before she could muster the courage to walk next door, she heard the shower running. Disappointed, she'd gone back to her own room and watched reruns of *Designing Women* before she had to get ready for dinner.

Once in the dining hall, Rhys did a quick scan of the room to make sure Katie wasn't already there. When she didn't see her, she looked for a table that would afford them a little privacy. Women were beginning to arrive and grouping off so Rhys settled on one in the back corner next to windows that looked out onto a beautiful garden. The table was large enough to seat four people so Rhys pushed two of the chairs under a surrounding table to ensure they were the only two seated at theirs. It wasn't that she didn't want to get to know other women, but she had really hoped to be able to spend some alone time with Katie before the week pulled them in different directions.

She wasn't exactly sure why. Katie had made her boundaries very clear and Rhys had no intention of crossing those boundaries, but there was something about her that drew Rhys in.

Growing up in San Francisco, Rhys had dated many women, but she'd never felt an instant connection to anyone like the one she found with Katie. Funny, beautiful, smart, she checked every box on her list of things she wanted in a woman. "Don't get ahead of yourself, you barely know the woman," Rhys said as she stared dreamily at the rose garden out the window.

"Barely know who?" Katie sat in the chair across from Rhys before looking out the window to see who she was talking about.

"No one, sorry. Ready to eat?" Rhys quickly stood and pointed toward the food line that had started to form near the cafeteria style buffet.

"Yeah, do you think we should go one at a time so we don't lose our table?"

Before Rhys could answer, two women approached them with trays full of food. "Mind if we sit with you ladies?" the taller one asked. "We can hold the table while you're gone."

"We're actually—" Rhys started, but before she could finish Katie gave her a questioning look. "Sure," she begrudgingly answered. "We'll grab something and be right back."

"Sounds good," the woman said before she set her tray on the table.

Rhys did her best not to show her disappointment as she walked to the end of the line.

"You okay?" Katie lined up behind her.

"Yeah, yeah, sorry. I'm just tired." She plastered on the best smile she could muster. "Did you get everything unpacked?"

"I did, did you?"

Katie stood close enough that Rhys could smell the honeysuckle of her shampoo which she found very distracting. "Huh?" Rhys asked, trying to remember what they'd been talking about.

"You asked if I got everything unpacked. I did get everything unpacked. The rooms are actually really nice. I asked if you got unpacked." Katie looked at Rhys like she wasn't sure what to think of her behavior.

"Yeah, I did. I'm sorry I'm being weird."

Katie gently squeezed Rhys's arm. "You're not being weird. You just seem really distracted. I know we just met, but if you need to talk, I'm a good listener."

The kind offer, even though she knew she could never take her up on it, made Rhys's heart warm and her stomach flutter. "Thanks," she said. "It's nothing some good food and sleep won't fix. I'm starving."

"Me, too. I wonder what they're serving us."

Rhys stood on her tiptoes to try to get a better look at people's plates as they exited the line. "Looks like…ohh…roast beef, gravy, potatoes, steamed carrots and peas, yuck, no thanks, dinner rolls, and oh my God, I think there's chocolate cake."

"Holy crap, that's like my favorite meal in the whole world," Katie said. She placed a hand on her stomach as if to reassure it food was on its way.

"Mine, too. My grandma used to make pretty much this exact meal every Sunday. She was born in Wales and moved to the States as a young girl, but she insisted the entire family get together for Sunday roast every week. It was always my favorite day of the week."

"My family does the same thing every Sunday," Katie said. "We don't have a huge family though. It's only my mom, my brother, my sister, her kids, and occasionally her husband."

Rhys handed Katie a tray from the stack. "That sounds nice." She turned to the woman behind the counter to ask for the items she wanted on her plate and they both headed back to their table.

"Hello, ladies," one of the women said in greeting when they sat down. "Thanks for letting us sit with you. This place gets crowded pretty quick." She pulled two chairs from another table so Rhys and Katie could sit. Rhys noticed the other woman indicated Katie should sit in the one next to her.

"No problem, I'm Katie and this is my friend Rhys." Katie set her tray down and reached a hand out to shake.

"It's a pleasure to meet you both. I'm Chris and this is my cousin, Amy."

Rhys sat in the remaining chair which was sandwiched between Chris and Amy, across the table from Katie. This wasn't working out like she'd hoped it would.

"Where are you guys from?" Rhys asked as she stacked her fork with roast, potatoes, and gravy.

Chris pulled her eyes from Katie so she could answer Rhys. "We're from Sacramento. Where are you guys from?"

"San Francisco," Rhys and Katie answered at the same time.

"Nice. So are you two together?"

"Nope, we're just friends," Katie answered.

Chris pushed her chair a little closer to Katie. "How is it possible you're single, beautiful?"

Rhys bristled at Chris's blatant flirting. Knowing Katie wasn't looking to be romanced, she formulated an escape plan so she could gracefully rescue her from the uncomfortable situation.

"Hey, Katie, you ready to—"

"Maybe I'm just too much woman for the average butch." Katie's flirtatious smile simultaneously confused and turned Rhys on. Why would she be flirting? Was all that she said to Rhys about not wanting more than a friendship only a nice way of turning Rhys down? No, from what little she knew of Katie, she seemed like someone who would be straight with how she felt.

"Lucky for you, I'm not your average butch." Chris placed her hand over Katie's where it rested on the table. Rhys watched the scene play out in front of her. She glanced at Amy who hadn't taken her eyes off Rhys since they'd sat down.

"I suspected as much. Unfortunately, I'm not looking for someone to settle down and play house with so we'll just never know." Katie popped a potato into her mouth and smiled. She glanced across the table at Rhys and gave her a wink as if she was part of this game.

Chris pulled Katie's hand up and pressed a kiss to her palm. "I could talk to the front office and make sure we get matched on a date. Maybe you'll find you're more interested in playing house than you think."

Katie smiled and pulled her hand from Chris's grasp. She stood and kissed her on the cheek. "Where's the fun in telling them to match us? Let's leave it up to the fates to decide." Katie picked up her tray and indicated to Rhys that she was ready to go. "It was a pleasure meeting you both. I hope you have a wonderful week."

Rhys scrambled to gather her tray and fell in behind Katie as she walked toward the garbage cans to bus her dishes. "What was that about?" Rhys asked.

"Have you ever watched a movie where a cocky guy goes to a nightclub and sits at the table and expects the waitress to sit on his lap and stroke his...ego because he's so sure she wants nothing more than his attention?"

"Sure, I guess." Rhys scraped the remnants of her meal into the compost barrel before placing her dishes in the plastic bin for washing. She took Katie's plate and repeated the same procedure with hers.

"I was getting that cocky asshole vibe from Chris and I wanted to set her up and knock her down a peg. I know it makes me a total bitch, but there was just something about her that rubbed me the wrong way."

They both pushed through the doors and into the cool night air. "That's...awesome. She rubbed me the wrong way, too. I was confused at first because I thought you were into her."

"Nope. Besides, I'm already hanging out with a studly butch this evening. My dance card is full." Katie gave her a wink that melted Rhys's heart. "I'll stop by the office tomorrow morning and make sure they don't match me up with her and hopefully that'll be the end of that."

Rhys let out a sigh of relief. "Good idea. Ready to check out this mixer thing?"

"Yep. Hopefully, we'll find you a lady who doesn't look at you like she wants to devour you," Katie said.

"Are you referring to Amy?"

"I don't think she pulled her loving gaze from you the entire time. She clearly wanted to skip dinner and head right to dessert."

"Right? It was a lot. I had no idea what to say to her when she was looking at me like that. She literally licked her lips at one point."

The path from the cafeteria to the room set up for the mixer wound through a Spanish style patio with a fountain in the middle. The sun had set while they were eating and the sculptures surrounding it were lit up. The stone benches that lined the area around the fountain held women chatting and obviously flirting with each other.

"Jesus, this is hormone central over here," Katie said.

"I guess that's what most women are here for so it makes sense."

Katie blushed and gave Rhys an apologetic look. "You know, hanging out with me isn't going to help you find the woman of your dreams. I think I might be cramping your style."

"It's cool," Rhys said, sitting on an empty bench. "Let's sit for a minute and enjoy the fresh air."

"Don't be all chivalrous, Rhys. I know why you're here this week and we both know you're not going to find that with me. I just don't want to stand in the way of you finding someone you really click with."

"Well, I really click with you and that's good enough for me right now. Tomorrow the date stuff will start, and unless they match us together, I'll have plenty of opportunities to meet other women. Besides, I have to protect you from the Chrises of the world."

"Hey, I'm might be little but I don't need to be protected."

"I have no doubt that's true." Rhys nudged her foot with her own. "I wouldn't want to piss you off. You seem pretty scrappy to me."

"You bet your ass I am."

Rhys sighed as she leaned back and looked up into the night sky. The light pollution from being so close to San Francisco left fewer stars visible than if they were in the country, but being as remote as they were helped. "I miss being able to see this many stars living in the middle of the city. My grandpa used to take us to Tahoe when I was a kid to stay in a cabin for a week every summer and we'd sit out under the stars searching for constellations."

"That sounds amazing." Katie looked up. "I wish my grandparents had lived closer so we could have known them better when they were alive."

"Where did they live?" Rhys asked.

"My mom's parents lived in Minnesota. They were nice people, but I don't think they ever really approved of my dad. We visited them once a year, but it always felt strained. My dad's parents were another story. They lived in Switzerland and were the best. They would come here one year, and we would go there the next so it's not like I didn't ever get to see them, but it wasn't the same as having them close."

"Why didn't your mom's parents like your dad?"

Katie sighed and stood, pulling Rhys up with her. "A story as old as time. He was a wild, long haired musician when they married, and they expected more for my mom. They were both doctors and assumed my mom would be one, too. Both of her sisters became doctors as well as her cousins except wild cousin Rebecca who's an attorney."

Rhys clutched her chest in mock shock. "Oh, the horror."

"I know. She's a rebel."

"Sounds like it," Rhys said.

The path to the mixer took them right by their rooms and Katie stopped in front of her door. "Would you be terribly disappointed if I skipped the mixer? I would really rather just get some sleep. It's been a long day and I feel like all the excitement has caught up with me."

"Sure." Rhys did her best to hide the disappointment she knew was written all over her face.

"I'm sorry, Rhys. I've had a really great time hanging out. Please don't think this has anything to do with you."

Rhys slid the key card into her own door lock. "I've had a great time, too. I get it. It's probably good for me to get to bed anyway. We've got an exciting morning and we better get some sleep."

"Hey, want to meet for breakfast tomorrow? I won't open the envelope with my date information until breakfast if you promise to do the same. It'll be fun." Katie slid her key card into the lock and opened the door.

"It's a deal. No peeks."

"I promise. See you in the morning, Rhys."

"Sweet dreams, Katie. See you in the morning."

Rhys waited for Katie to close her door before entering her own room and sliding the deadbolt. It had been one of the best and most frustrating days of her life. Why did the universe have to send her this girl who was so perfectly wonderful and so completely unavailable? Maybe her date the next day would help take her mind off of Katie. She knew that wasn't likely, but she could at least hope.

# Chapter Eight

Monday morning, Rhys showered and stood in front of her closet agonizing over what to wear to breakfast. She and Katie had agreed to meet so they could find out together who their dates would be, but now that the time had come, Rhys felt a little sheepish about discussing her date with the woman she was harboring a major crush for.

This week was quickly shaping up to be an exercise in frustration instead of the free-loving fun time she had envisioned. Not that she hadn't had a fun time the night before. Other than the two women who sat at their table at dinner, she'd had an awesome time getting to know Katie a little better.

She collapsed on the bed, closed her eyes, and pictured the woman she hadn't stopped thinking about since she saw her sitting alone in the banquet room. Katie was a few inches shorter than Rhys with a runner's body, compact and strong. She had beautiful blond hair and gorgeous blue eyes.

Rhys almost hadn't approached her the day before, deciding she was way out of her league, but after reminding herself the week was about putting herself out there and hoping for the best she asked to sit with her. The easy conversation they had was unexpected and there were actually moments when Rhys thought she saw genuine interest in her eyes.

She knew deep down she had to get those thoughts out of her head. Katie made it clear she was only looking for a friend and wouldn't be interested in anything more, but a girl could dream and although Rhys was fully prepared to respect her wishes, she wouldn't be upset if it turned into something. All she knew was she couldn't get Katie out of her mind and would take anything she was willing to give.

The lecture from Max about not getting her heart broken echoed in her mind as she rubbed her hands over her face and pushed out a breath. "Don't get your heart broken, dummy. You can't just fall for the first woman you speak to. Especially a woman who has made it very clear that she's not interested in anything you're looking for."

Rhys cleared her mind of negative thoughts. The yellow envelope concealing her date's identity, and the activity they would be doing that morning sat next to her on the bed. It had been difficult not to open it since she found it on the floor that morning, having been shoved under the door while she slept. She had promised Katie she wouldn't open it until breakfast when they would find out together, but it was torture to wait. She checked her watch and realized her daydreaming had wasted too much time. She was going to be late. She quickly stood and pulled on her favorite polo shirt, khaki shorts, and Adidas sneakers.

Rhys checked her reflection in the mirror as she finger combed her short hair and added a little dab of gel to force her soft curls to behave. She typically didn't do anything fancy to her appearance, but she wanted to look her best for her date and if she was honest with herself, mostly for Katie.

She would be late if she didn't get a move on, so with one last look in the mirror, she rushed out of her room en route to the place they agreed to meet.

As she neared the door, she silently sent a plea to the universe that Katie remembered their breakfast arrangements. Even though it was all she had thought about since the plans were made, she worried Katie had forgotten as soon as Rhys was out of sight. A sigh of relief escaped her lips when she found her sitting at a small table in the back corner.

"Sorry I'm late. I let the time get away from me." Rhys sat in one of the hard plastic cafeteria chairs.

Katie glanced at the clock on the wall to check the time. "You're like five minutes late, silly. Of course you know I'm going to have to dock your pay next time, but I'll let it slide for now." She touched Rhys's hand for just a moment before picking up her orange juice and taking a drink. The brief touch was enough to send Rhys's heart into overdrive, but she knew she had to keep it together if she wanted to convince Katie she could handle a friends only relationship.

"I like to be punctual."

"I see that. Don't worry about me, though. Ready to look at the torture they have planned for us this morning?" Katie picked up her envelope and ran a delicate finger along the crease to break the seal.

Rhys did the same as they both pulled out the paperwork and read its contents. "Looks like I'm with Gretchen and we're kayaking."

"That sounds fun." Katie read hers out loud. "Good morning Katie, you will be joining Tammy today on the ropes course. Enclosed you will find instructions and a map to show you where you can meet your date. Enjoy. Fran Taylor, Activities Director, Last Resort, Inc."

"Oh boy," Katie said. "This should be interesting. Please let Tammy be okay with heights. People think they're okay with it and then they get up on that platform and the reality of it freaks them out."

She had only met Katie the day before, but hearing about her date with Tammy made Rhys more jealous than she knew she had any right to be. She'd never been a jealous person, but something about Katie made her want to spend more time getting to know her, and the idea that Tammy was going to get that time, frustrated her.

"Poor Tammy, she might be an adrenaline junkie who is looking for a woman to go skydiving with."

"Ha, ha. I have no problem with heights, but she's going to be sorely disappointed if she's hoping that woman is me. For more reasons than one."

Rhys stuffed her paper back into the envelope and tossed it on the table. "I forgot, you're not into women."

"Hey now, I'm plenty into women. I'm not into finding someone to settle down with. Big distinction." Katie set her paperwork on the table.

"I thought you promised your mom you were going to keep yourself open to the idea that someone might actually break through that cold heart of yours." Rhys winked at her to soften the tease.

"Very funny. You're right. I promised my mom and I will try not to be a cold-hearted bitch."

"I never called you a cold-hearted bitch. I just suggested your heart was surrounded with a layer of ice, waiting for someone to come along with a heart-shaped ice pick."

Katie speared a piece of banana from her plate and popped it into her mouth with a smile. "I think you're just trying to win that hundred-dollar bet."

Rhys held her hand against her chest in mock offense. "What? I would never. Although, a hundred dollars would buy me a lot of ice cream." Rhys stood and pointed toward the buffet. "Want me to grab you something?"

Katie indicated the plate of fruit she had grabbed while waiting for Rhys to show up. "I'm good. I don't want to eat something heavy before swinging through the air. I might give the people on the ground an unwelcome surprise."

Rhys walked over to fill her plate with eggs, potatoes, bacon, and toast. She knew she would be engaging in a lot of physical activity kayaking and wanted to have the energy to get through the morning.

When she returned to the table, Katie was reading through the instructions for her date. "It says here Tammy and I have an hour and a half van ride up to Occidental to do our ropes course in the redwoods. That's kinda cool. I actually have a friend who did that a couple of years ago. He said it was amazing. That area is beautiful."

"My ex-girlfriend Vanessa and I used to have breakfast in Occidental occasionally. We loved it up there."

"Are you talking about Howard Station?" Katie asked.

"Yes. That place is awesome. They have the best corned beef hash I've ever had."

Katie nodded in agreement as she placed the paperwork back into her bag. "I agree. I always get the waffles, but I've had the hash and it's amazing. How was breakfast here?"

Rhys popped the last piece of bacon into her mouth and rocked her hand back and forth in a so-so movement. "Pretty good, but it's no Howard Station. We should totally go up there sometime for breakfast." The words were out before Rhys thought about what she was saying. Holding her breath, she saw a flash of fear cloud Katie's face before she smiled and stood.

"Maybe. Should we head for the van and our dates? It's about five minutes before we leave." Rhys quietly exhaled and stood to clear her tray. The lack of response from her was both a relief and disappointment. This girl was going to be a tough nut to crack. "Let's do it. I don't want poor Gretchen to think I stood her up."

"Gretchen does sound like the name of someone who would take offense to you being late for your first date. The Gretchens I've known have always been very earthy, sensitive types."

"Oh God, don't say that. I tend to speak before I think things through on occasion and it has gotten me in trouble before. Fingers crossed this Gretchen is an easy-going one who likes a boyish girl who occasionally makes an ass out of herself."

Katie gently patted Rhys on the shoulder. "That's a tall order, my friend. I'm sure that girl is out there and there's a chance her name might be Gretchen so don't lose hope. I can't wait to hear all about the adventures you and easy-going Gretchen had when we have dinner this evening. Assuming you haven't decided to stay out on your kayaks and live with the hippies. Plenty of Gretchens are hippies, you know."

"Oh, I know, I've met some of those Gretchens in my travels." Rhys's heart warmed as Katie's smile lit up her face. She knew she was heading for a heartbreak, but at that moment, she accepted her fate.

## CHAPTER NINE

Katie waved good-bye to Rhys as they exited the dining hall and headed in different directions. The packet she received that morning contained a sticker with her name, her date's name, and their van number. She felt strange seeing her name listed next to a complete stranger's as if they were already an item. Katie and Tammy. How unfortunate. It sounded like some terrible Barbie beach party guest list.

As she approached the van she saw two couples and a tall redhead very energetically talking to each other.

"You must be Katie. I'm your date, Tammy." Before Katie could offer a proper greeting, Tammy lifted her up in a bear hug and swung her in the air. "You're so little and cute."

When Katie made it back to earth she wasn't sure if she should laugh at the woman who had just treated her like a doll or be offended. "Easy there, I'm a delicate flower." She eased over toward the others, leaving a safe space between them.

"You're funny, too," Tammy said. "We were just talking about who had done a ropes course before."

"Have you?" Katie asked Tammy, but before she could answer, the van driver arrived and asked them to load up. Katie held the door for Tammy as she tried to cram her more than six-foot frame into the back seat.

Once they were settled and the van was underway, Tammy answered Katie's question. "I've done several, including the world's tallest in New York. This will be easy. Have you done one?"

"I've only done one, but I'm pretty comfortable with heights so I shouldn't have a problem," Katie said.

"You'll be fine. Once you get up there just make sure you keep your eyes forward and the rest is a piece of cake. The adrenaline rush is incredible. We're going to have a blast." Tammy put her hand on Katie's shoulder as she made introductions. "Katie, this is Karen and her date, Jennifer, Carmen and her date, Brooke. We all got acquainted while we were waiting by the van."

"Nice to meet you." Katie checked her watch to see how much more time she was going to be locked in the van with the fun bunch.

"What kind of girl are you hoping to find here, Katie?" Carmen asked.

*Oh boy, here we go.* Katie wasn't sure she was ready to answer that question yet so she decided to turn the table. "You first, who are you looking for, Carmen?"

Carmen's smile made it difficult not to grin along with her. "Where do I begin? It took me thirty-five years to come out to my family, followed by five years of struggling to get them to understand why, and now that they have accepted me for who I am, I want nothing more than to find someone I can take home to meet my abuela before she's gone. She won't be around much longer, and I would love to show her I can find love and happiness with a woman."

"That's so sweet, Carmen." Tammy hugged her. "My grandma was always very supportive, but she passed before I found someone to settle down with. She would have been so proud to see me happy."

Carmen smiled and patted Tammy's hand. "I'm sure she would be proud of you for many reasons, Tammy."

Katie turned to the Carmen's date. "What about you, Brooke?"

Brooke blushed as all eyes focused on her. "I come from a small town in Arizona where I'm more of a novelty than an actual person. I'm the only lesbian so finding a date requires a three-hour drive to Phoenix. As you can imagine, it's difficult to maintain a relationship with that kind of distance. So, I picked up my life and moved to the gayest place I could think of, San Francisco. I have a job and a place to live, and this week is my first step at really putting myself out there. I'm going to see how it goes and hope for the best, but mostly I just really needed to be around my people to remind myself that no matter how scary the thought of moving away from my family was, it was worth it to finally be able to live my life."

"That's beautiful, Brooke." Carmen squeezed her shoulder. "Are your parents supportive?"

"They're amazing. I have twin younger brothers and my parents have told us our entire lives that they love us and are proud of us. It was never really a question as to sexuality or our occupations or anything like that. They surrounded us with love and support, and the three of us have never doubted they always would."

"My family situation is like that, too," Katie said. "I don't remember ever being afraid because they never made me feel like I would disappoint them by who I was. They were more concerned about me being a good person who contributed in a positive way to my community. Other than that, no expectations. I completely realize how rare that is and how lucky I am to have the family I do."

"You guys are very lucky," Carmen said. "It took my family a bit, but I think they're doing their best to make up for lost time now so I'm not complaining. I know many people who've never found that support from their family and it just breaks my heart."

They nodded in understanding.

"What about you, Jennifer?" Katie asked.

Jennifer smiled and rubbed her cheeks with her hands as they turned red. "I'm happy to say I'm one of the lucky ones with an awesome family, too. They've always been very supportive, but I'm an introvert so I've had a difficult time putting myself out there to meet people. My parents gifted me this week at the resort to try to force me out of my comfort zone. They're worried I'm going to die alone."

Everyone laughed, but Katie could see Jennifer was only partially joking. "My story isn't far from yours, Jennifer," Katie said. "My family is extremely supportive and wonderful, but they don't believe I can ever be happy without being in a relationship. I tried the relationship thing and it ended in heartache. No, thanks. I'm not saying it's unmanageable for me to ever fall in love again, but at the moment I'm completely content on my own. Unfortunately, my mother and sister are romantics so they believe happiness is a team sport that can't be found without a doubles partner."

"So you aren't looking for a relationship this week?" Tammy asked, looking confused.

"Technically, no. I did promise my mom that I would keep my options open and see what happens so there's that. I'm here for friendships and fun. As for the rest, the jury is still out. I have no expectations I guess."

Tammy smiled, but Katie could tell she was annoyed by her admission. When Katie agreed to go to the resort she hadn't really thought of the fact that she would potentially be robbing another person of a chance to go on a date with someone who was actually looking for love. "I'm sorry if I've taken up a date when you could have maybe found the girl of your dreams. I didn't really think about that part when I agreed to come."

"It's okay," Tammy said with a smile. "I'm never opposed to going on a date with a beautiful woman, even if she isn't one I'll end up spending the rest of my life with. Who knows, maybe you'll be surprised and find that special someone after all."

Katie blushed. "What's your story, Tammy?"

"Well, I recently got out of a long-term relationship and this week is my chance to do a cannonball into the dating pool. I don't want to be alone, and with any luck I'll find some totally hot girl to date who I can parade in front of my ex at our mutual friend Susan's wedding next month." Tammy's innocent open face clouded, and Katie could see she meant business.

"Wow. You aren't messing around," Katie said. "Remind me to stay on your good side, woman. To make up for screwing up one of your chances to find that girl to take I'll make you a deal, if you don't find someone this week I'll totally go with you to Susan's wedding as your fake girlfriend and we'll give your ex a show she won't forget."

"You would do that?" The look on Tammy's face was a combination of jubilation and vengeance. "I just might take you up on that."

Katie turned in her seat to face the other girls. "How about you, Karen? Yours is the only story we haven't heard."

"Oh, I'm just hoping to get laid as much as possible. If I meet someone, awesome. If I come away from the week having had tons of sex, even better. I'm just going with the flow," Karen said.

"I wasn't expecting that one, but I like your style, my friend," Katie said. "I love it when a woman unapologetically owns her sexuality. It sometimes feels like the world is doing its darnedest to shame us for wanting sex, and I call bullshit on that. You just might be my new hero, Karen."

Karen winked at her as they pulled into the parking lot of their destination. "Hopefully, we'll survive this little adventure so I get to actually get laid. I didn't want to say this before, but I'm afraid of heights and tend to vomit when I look down so stand clear."

Despite her initial hesitation, Katie was excited to spend the week getting to know other lesbians. Locked away in her apartment, she'd forgotten how nice it was to be around her people. She felt comfortable in many situations, but there was a sense of belonging she got from being around other lesbians that she didn't get anywhere else. She decided then and there that even though she wasn't looking for a life partner, she could relax a bit and open herself up to finding friends.

For the first time since her mom and Elise gave her the gift of a week at the resort, she felt a calmness come over her. She just might get something out of this week after all.

## Chapter Ten

The moment Rhys arrived in the dining hall that evening she scanned the crowd for Katie. The room was filled with women carrying trays of food, searching for a place to sit. She suspected people would pair off as the week progressed, but for now there seemed to still be a lot of singles. Standing on her tiptoes to get a better view, she felt someone touch her arm.

"Watcha doing?" Katie asked from beside her.

Rhys formed her hands into binoculars, and pretended to search the distance over Katie's head. "I'm looking for my short little blond friend who's supposed to have dinner with me. Have you seen her?"

"I'm not sure your friend would love that you called her short or little, but I suspect she'll let it slide this time."

"Noted. I've seen what happens when someone takes away her cell phone. I don't want to cross that one." Rhys led them both to an empty table near the windows in the back of the room.

Katie smacked her arm. "You better watch it, buddy. I'll have you know I haven't even thought about my cell phone until you so thoughtlessly reminded me just now."

After leaving their stuff on a table to hold it, they stood in line for the buffet style meal. Monday night's theme was Mexican, which was Rhys's favorite. Once she had served herself portions of each dish she headed back to the table to wait for Katie. The large room was full of chatter and excited women bustling about which gave her plenty of people watching for entertainment.

"Is this seat taken?" Katie playfully asked when she returned with her food.

"I'm saving it for my short little friend," Rhys said. "Just kidding. Looks like you're a fan of Mexican food as well."

"I don't trust someone who doesn't like Mexican food," Katie said.

Rhys nodded before tilting her head to take a bite of her taco. "I totally agree. So, how was your date with Tammy today? Was she okay with heights?"

"First of all, Tammy is about six foot two so she's very comfortable with heights. Second, oh my God, that woman is crazy. She was great to hang out with for a bit, but I thought she would surely die at least three times. I guess she's done ropes courses before, but holy shit, she acted like she had absolutely zero fear of falling to her death. Even the safety people were freaking out. They kept saying, 'Now, Tammy. Careful, Tammy. Don't hang off the edge, Tammy,' and running around after her like as mere mortals they would be able to somehow save the Amazonian princess from taking a dive."

Rhys laughed until her sides hurt. "You're going to make me spit up my tacos."

Katie sat back in her chair, and brushed the crumbs from her jeans. There was something so feminine about the way she moved it sent a jolt straight to Rhys's center.

"That's a total waste of good tacos." Katie looked up to find Rhys staring at her.

She did her best to keep her focus on the food and not Katie's lap as she took another bite. "What's a waste?"

"Spitting your tacos. That's a total waste of good tacos. You okay?"

"Yeah, of course." Rhys blushed. She knew Katie had busted her staring. "What's your favorite kind of taco? Soft or crispy?"

Katie hesitated before answering but eventually seemed to accept the change in subject. "It depends on my mood ultimately, but if given the choice between the two I'll take soft corn street tacos any day of the week."

"Yum."

"My parents are both Scandinavian so we didn't grow up eating much spicy food at home, but my siblings and I would ride our bikes into town to buy as many street tacos as we could from our favorite taco truck. Sausalito is a pretty hilly town and we'd eat so many tacos that we'd almost vomit on the way home. Full tummies plus strenuous exercise isn't a good combination."

Rhys gave the taco in her hand a skeptical look. "Ew."

"Too much information?" Katie asked with a wink.

"Little bit, yeah." Rhys popped the rest of her taco in her mouth. "Might I interest you in a soft serve cone and a walk?"

"Perfect." Katie followed Rhys to the line for the soft serve bar. "I've been thinking about that bowl of rainbow sprinkles since I saw them."

"I'm not much of a sprinkles fan."

Katie gave Rhys an appraising look that made her skin tingle. "No, I wouldn't peg you as a sprinkles fan."

"Is that something you're usually good at determining without really knowing a person? Awfully presumptuous, don't you think?"

"There's just something about you that tells me you're a no-nonsense, straight up ice cream kinda person."

"I wouldn't say that. There's all kinds of things you have yet to learn about me. I just might surprise you."

Katie blushed and looked like she was deciding exactly how to respond to that. "You just might be more mysterious than I gave you credit for. I'm glad I have a week to study you. I'm pretty good at figuring out what makes people tick."

Rhys couldn't tell if she was flirting. She seemed kinda flirty, but maybe that was just wishful thinking. Under normal circumstances she would shamelessly flirt back to test the waters, but she had no idea how to proceed with a woman who claimed she wasn't interested but then seemed a little interested.

"Cone or cup?" Rhys asked as they reached the front of the line.

"Cone all the way, man."

"I agree." Rhys pulled out two cones and handed one to Katie. "Why waste a cup when you can just eat the container and not have to throw anything away?"

"Smart and handsome." Katie sighed, spooning sprinkles over her vanilla ice cream. "I can't believe some hussy hasn't snagged you yet."

She was definitely flirting. "Just eat your ice cream, dork." Rhys did her best to keep the smile off her face, but it was a losing battle. Once they both had their cones they exited through the side door and walked into a large courtyard in the center of the property. The evening was warm, but a slight breeze from the ocean helped cool them off.

"Tell me something about yourself," Rhys said as they walked next to each other on the path that would lead them to the beach.

"What do you want to know?" Katie asked. "My life isn't really that exciting."

"What do you do for a living?"

"What do you think I do for a living?"

"Good God, woman. I'm guessing you're an attorney or a therapist because you like to answer questions with more questions."

Katie plopped the last bite of cone into her mouth and wiped her hands on her jeans. "We forgot napkins." She checked her hands for signs of rainbow sprinkle remnants.

"Which is it?" Rhys asked. "Lawyer or therapist?"

"Wrong on both accounts although I see your reasoning. I've always been kinda private, and answering with a question is a bad habit. I'm a greeting card artist. Bet you didn't expect that one."

"Really? I never would have guessed that. I don't think I ever even knew that was a job someone would have, but now that I know I think it's awesome. I never thought about who designed cards. I've never been good at remembering to buy them, but when I do I like to take my time and pick out the perfect one. I wonder if I've ever given someone a card you've created." Rhys mimicked her head exploding which made Katie laugh again. Katie had a great laugh.

"It's a good job. I do some cartooning and some sketching. Sometimes I can't believe I can make a living doing something

I'm passionate about. I'm very fortunate." Katie took Rhys's hand and pulled her toward a spot between two dunes where they could watch the waves crash against the shore while still being sheltered from the wind. "What kind of name is Rhys? I've of course heard it before, but it isn't common. What's the story behind you ending up with such a cool name?"

Rhys sat next to her in the sand. "Nobody's ever called my name cool before. I've gotten plenty of Reese's Pieces and Rhys Crease which I never understood but never thought it's cool."

"Rhys Crease?" Katie asked.

"Right? Kids are so stupid sometimes. Anyway, to answer your question I'm Welsh and my first ancestor to come to this country was named Watkin Rhys. It's tradition for the oldest child of each generation to be named either Watkin or Rhys as part of their name. My father is Brandon Watkin. I'm Rhys Gwyndolyn after my mother, Gwyn."

"Wow, that's quite a name and quite a history. So you must be the oldest of your generation. Does that name come with great responsibility or is it just a name?" Katie picked up a stick and smoothed the sand in front of where they sat.

Rhys sat forward so she could watch what was happening. "We're woodworkers and the business will eventually go to my sister and me. Well, me, but I'll share the responsibility with her."

"That sounds like a lot of pressure. Are you scared to have that on your shoulders some day?" Katie used the stick to draw waves crashing against rocks in her sandy canvas.

"I'm actually not as scared as I thought I would be. My dad's in great health so I don't expect it will be anytime soon which might be why I'm so calm about it, but also we're a well-oiled machine at this point. When the time comes, I'll have my part of the business and my sister, Max, will have her part. We're very close and I trust her with my life so I know she'll always do what's right for the business and her family. She's my best friend." Rhys pulled a few strands of grass from a hill of sand and added it to Katie's impromptu artwork.

"That's beautiful. I can't believe you made something recognizable with a stick in the sand."

Katie smiled and leaned back to look at the entire drawing. "It's okay for the tools I had." Taking a deep breath, she closed her eyes. Rhys took that opportunity to really look at her. Even in the low light she could clearly see how beautiful Katie was. She ached to run her fingers through her shoulder length hair and kiss a line from the spot right behind her ear to her delicate collarbone.

Closing her eyes before she did something stupid like moan out loud, Rhys leaned back in the sand and laced her fingers behind her head to stop the impulse to touch her. How long could she keep this game up? Under normal circumstances, if Rhys was this strongly drawn to someone who didn't return the attraction, she would distance herself. Gain some perspective. The problem was she couldn't imagine distancing herself from Katie. Especially when they would be in such close contact this week. Rhys would just have to stay strong and keep her hands to herself when this was very likely the only chance she'd ever have to spend time with her. Next week they would go their separate ways and there was no guarantee that Katie wouldn't be out of her life forever. She hoped that wouldn't be the case, but Rhys knew it was a distinct possibility. She'd just have to enjoy the time they had and be content with that. Easy peasy. She'd done harder things in her life. Surely she had. She was sure if given time she could think of lots of examples of times when she wanted someone this much and had to—

"Want to head back? Your short little blond friend is getting cold." Katie's voice startled Rhys from her thoughts, causing her to sit up abruptly.

"I'm sorry." Katie stood and reached a hand down to help her to her feet. "I didn't mean to scare you."

Rhys brushed the sand from her pants and shook her head. "You didn't, I was just thinking."

"Anything you want to talk about?" Katie asked. Rhys's mind raced to come up with something to say as they slowly walked back toward the resort.

"No, it's nothing. Sorry Tammy didn't end up convincing you love was worth the trouble." As they approached the resort, the sound of laughing and chatter began to drown out the relaxing rhythm of the waves behind them.

"She was nice enough, but first of all we looked insane next to each other since she was a foot taller than me, and second, there just wasn't a spark between us so even if she hadn't made me feel Lilliputian it wouldn't have made a difference. Besides, I'm not built for love, remember?" Katie playfully punched Rhys on the shoulder once for each of the last words to drive her point home.

"I had no idea the problem was that you weren't actually built for love. That's an entirely different issue from you just not wanting to fall for someone. I've never actually heard of someone not being built for love. I don't think it's possible."

"It's possible, my friend, I'm living proof."

"I thought you were supposed to leave yourself open to the possibility. That's going to be difficult if you're literally not constructed in a way that would allow for the receiving of love."

"Smartass." Katie rolled her eyes in mock irritation.

As they approached their rooms, Rhys wasn't ready for the night to end. She crossed all the fingers she had buried in her pockets and hoped she would be able to spend just a little more time with the object of her attraction. "Here we are, my lady, I have escorted you to your room. Are you ready to turn in or should we do another loop around the gardens?"

"I think this is it for me. Thanks for the chat. I had a great time. Should we do it again tomorrow?" Katie pulled the key card from her back pocket and stuck it in the slot on her door to unlock it. "Wait. How was your date? I totally forgot to ask. Will you and Gretchen be purchasing tandem kayaks in the future?"

Rhys unlocked her own door. "Let's just say Gretchen will most likely be purchasing kayaks with her best friend, Cynthia, whom she hasn't figured out she's in love with yet but the rest of the world would know after spending ten minutes with her."

"I'm sorry, that's a bummer," Katie said.

"Well, one down, five dates to go. Last Resort hasn't failed me yet, but we're off to a slow start." Rhys winked as she opened her door and leaned against the doorjamb. "It's been really nice getting to know you, Katie. I'm glad you came even if you'll be breaking hearts all over this resort with your love sucks attitude."

"Hey." Katie feigned shock as she clutched her chest. "I'm very up front with everyone when we meet, and who knows, maybe Princess Charming will sweep me off my reluctant feet."

Rhys couldn't help the hopeful feeling that she would be that Princess Charming. Katie was giving her mixed signals in the worst way, but she couldn't bring herself to be angry about it. The only thing she felt in the moment was hope.

"Night, Katie."

"Night, weirdo. I'll see you at breakfast. Remember, no peeking inside your envelope. I like to see the look on your face when you find out who your date will be. It reminds me of watching a kid open their presents Christmas morning."

Rhys flipped Katie the bird. "You're a jerk. I like surprises, what can I say?"

With a final wave, Katie stepped into her room and shut the door. Rhys heard her slide the locks and turn on her television. She wasn't expecting the depth of the feeling of loss as she turned to walk into her own empty room.

## Chapter Eleven

The following morning Rhys and Katie met in the dining hall for breakfast again. After a quick bite to eat they opened their envelopes and found that Katie would be going to a local farmers market with a woman named Brooklyn, and Rhys was scheduled to do a whale watching tour with Scarlett.

"I hope she's Scarlett Johansson. She's always been on my list of top five potential future wives."

Katie rolled her eyes. "I can't wait to hear who the other four are. I wouldn't have pegged you for a ScarJo fan."

"What can I say, I'm a sucker for blondes." Rhys didn't realize the implications of her statement until a blush spread across Katie's face. Gathering her things from the table, she held her breath waiting to see if she would say anything.

"I'll keep that in mind. Maybe I can convince you to have dinner with your favorite blonde if Scarlett ends up not living up to your expectations."

Rhys liked the flirty tone of her response but tried to play it off as casually as she could. "I don't know about *favorite* blonde since ScarJo and I have had a thing for years, but I suppose if you and Brooklyn aren't picking out china patterns this evening we could have dinner together. Same place, same time?"

"It's a date. Don't get eaten by the whales today, Jonah. See you in a bit." Katie squeezed her arm. Rhys watched Katie walk away until she lost sight of her in the crowd of women rushing off to their designated places. As she placed the name tag on her shirt with both her and Scarlett's name and bus number written in bold pen, she wished she was spending the day with Katie. Their easy conversation the night before had played over and over in her head since they parted ways and she found each moment without her laced with the anticipation of the next they would share. It was maddening.

"You must be Scarlett." Rhys approached a slightly taller woman waiting next to the bus.

"Hello, Rhys." They shook hands and then Rhys introduced herself to the other two couples in their group. "Have any of you been whale watching before?"

The other women shook their heads as they all climbed into the bus. Rhys and Scarlett were the last to board, delegated to the back seat since all other seats were taken. Once they were settled, Rhys took a moment to get a read on her date for the day. Scarlett was very fair with blond hair, blue eyes, and delicate features. She was pretty in an understated kind of way.

"How was your date yesterday, Scarlett? Did you make a connection?" Rhys asked in an attempt to break the ice.

"She was nice. I'm not very comfortable talking about her with you. We should focus on the date we're on and not worry about the one that came before."

Rhys felt scolded and noticed the other women giving her apologetic looks as she met their eyes. Obviously, Scarlett had made an impression on them before Rhys had arrived at the bus. Great.

Throwing caution to the wind, she decided to not let her date suck the fun from the van and directed her question toward the others. "Okay, best and worst thing that happened on your dates yesterday. I'll go first. My date's name was Gretchen and we went kayaking. She was lovely. I would say the best part was being on the water and being outside and the worst was the sack lunch they gave us. The bologna was green and the only vegetarian option my poor date had was an apple. I felt terrible for her. I gave her my apple, but I know it couldn't have been a very satisfying meal after the workout we had in the kayaks. Now your turn, Vanessa," Rhys said, reading the name tag from the girl in front of her.

"My date's name was Emily and we went for a bike ride. The best part for me was also being outside and the worst was when Emily fell off the bike and blamed me even though I was nowhere near her. It was a bit of a shock and the day went downhill from there."

Vanessa's date, Frankie, stuck out her bottom lip in sympathy. "I'm sorry, Vanessa. That sucks. I promise not to blame you if I fall out of the boat." Everyone laughed, especially Vanessa as Frankie continued. "My date's name was Moonbeam, I shit you not." Rhys heard a disapproving noise come from Scarlett at Frankie's minor curse word. "None of you will be surprised to find out that Moonbeam lives on a commune with her entire family in Mendocino County and is looking for someone to move back there with her to be a part of their colony. I believe it's a free love situation so if any of you are into that kind of scene, I suggest you find Moonbeam."

Everyone laughed except for Scarlett who sullenly stared out the window. Rhys shook her head as she craned her neck to read the name tag of one of the two women in the front seat. "How about you, Janine?"

Janine seemed a little embarrassed as she looked toward her current date with an apologetic smile. "I hope this doesn't make you feel weird, Carmen, but I had a wonderful time with my date yesterday. We went to Armstrong redwood grove and had a lovely time hiking and getting to know each other. I'm actually going to ask to be paired with her again. We didn't get back in time last night to make our request before they had already assigned today's dates."

Carmen smiled and patted Janine's hand. "Totally fine. I actually had a really great time with my date, Brooke, yesterday at the ropes course and would love to see her again. It didn't even cross my mind that we could request to be put together. I have no idea why I didn't think of it. Let's enjoy the day together for what it is, a chance to make a new friend."

"Awe, that's sweet," Rhys said. "Hey, you wouldn't happen to have been on the ropes course with a woman named Katie were you?"

"Yes," Carmen said. "What a sweetheart. Poor girl spent the entire day trying to keep her date alive."

"I heard Tammy was a handful," Rhys said.

"Super nice, but my God, that woman should have been a stunt double. She walked around that course like she was walking to the mailbox on the corner not balancing on a string one hundred and fifty feet above ground. Crazy woman. She was a lot of fun, though."

As the van pulled up to the dock where the whale watching boat was moored, Rhys waited for the others to exit the van before following her date out the door. The wind was brisk as they walked through the crowd of tourists toward their boat. When they stepped on board the others paired off to find seats and left Rhys with Scarlett.

"Sorry I don't seem to be who you were hoping to spend your time with. I promise to do my best to make the day as good as possible. I'm actually a pretty nice person if you give me a chance," Rhys said. She couldn't imagine what they'd answered in the questionnaire to make it match her with Scarlett.

She gingerly sat in a single chair which forced Rhys to sit across from her rather than next to her. She wasn't exactly eager to sit next to her either.

"I'm sorry," Scarlett finally said as the boat began to pull away from the dock. "I was raised in a very strict home and wasn't prepared for the secular onslaught I've been forced to witness since arriving at the resort."

"Secular onslaught? What did you think you would find at a lesbian hookup resort? I'm not sure you knew what you were signing up for." Rhys didn't know what to say to her that wouldn't offend her even more than she already was. How in the world did she get matched with this person? "Did something happen yesterday that upset you? If you need to talk, I'm happy to listen." Rhys smiled to put her at ease.

"I'm fine. Nothing major happened. My date was very respectful yesterday and didn't do anything to offend me, but the girls in our group were talking about things that aren't appropriate. I told them as much and they thought I was trying to be funny. I was extremely embarrassed and uncomfortable so I just kept my mouth shut. My date, Francine, was very kind and did her best to insulate me from the riffraff, but once they realized I was uncomfortable they decided it would be fun to tease the virgin."

"Virgin," Rhys exclaimed in shock before immediately regretting her reaction. "I'm so sorry. I'm an idiot. Please continue."

Scarlett looked at the other passengers as they gathered at the rail to watch the dolphins play alongside the boat. Without looking at Rhys, she continued. "It isn't like being a virgin is the craziest thing in the world. Lots of people wait for marriage. It doesn't mean there's something wrong with me."

"Not at all. I'm sorry if my reaction made you feel like I thought there was something wrong. I admire that you stand by something you believe in. You'll make some lucky woman very happy someday. Do you mind if I ask how your church is regarding your homosexuality?"

Scarlett's cheeks turned red and she adjusted her position in the hard chair. "They're fine. I belong to a very open and accepting church. I don't know if I'm a lesbian or not since I've never really felt an attraction to a man or a woman, but I prefer the company of women so I assume I am."

"It's none of my business, but have you ever sought the advice of a doctor regarding your lack of interest in others? I've heard of women with similar issues who were able to live a balanced life with a therapist and doctor's help." Rhys felt for her. Her libido had always been a bit hyperactive, which has its own challenges, but to never feel attraction for someone else must feel lonely.

"It doesn't bother me. I don't want to take medications because I don't think there's anything wrong with not being interested in someone sexually. Why is that so difficult to understand? I want companionship but don't understand why it has to be so tied up in sexual feelings." Rhys could see Scarlett was getting upset and wished she knew the right thing to say to comfort her without making her uncomfortable.

"Would you like my opinion? It's okay to say no," Rhys said. When Scarlett gave her a silent nod she leaned forward so they wouldn't be overheard by the others. "I have a friend who is asexual. I'm no therapist, but I suspect that might be you as well. My friend is a great guy, full of love and funny as hell, but he's just never really felt an attraction for anyone. He's actually had sex with both men and women testing to make sure he just didn't know what he was missing, but even though he may have enjoyed aspects of the interactions, he never had sexual feelings for his partners. It was more about satisfying a physical itch of his own rather than sharing something with someone else. He joined a support group in the city and eventually found someone to share his life with who is also asexual. They're actually very happy together and one of the coolest couples I know. They're wonderful parents to two little girls they adopted and lead lives full of love. He told me there are many asexual Christians in his support group. Maybe you'll find someone who will make you happy and understand where you're coming from."

Scarlett stared at her until she started to feel uncomfortable at the scrutiny. "I'm sorry if I overstepped. I promise you I was only trying to help." Rhys sat back in her seat and watched the crowd at the rail.

"No, I'm sorry. I didn't mean to make you uncomfortable. I've never had anyone actually listen to me and respect my feelings in that way. My friends at church have always said God would send me the right person when I was ready, but no one has ever mentioned asexuality. I don't think I even really know what that is, but the story of your friend makes me think I should have signed up for that group instead of trying to force myself to find someone at this resort. I don't know how I'm going to make it through the rest of these dates. I'm miserable and it's only day two." Scarlett started to tear up as Rhys knelt beside her chair and delicately rested her hand on her back.

"It'll be okay. If it will make you more comfortable, I'll go with you to the main office when we get back to the resort and we'll see if we can get you a refund for the rest of the week. Did you drive your own car, or would you need to call someone to get you?"

"I drove my Prius. I didn't want to bother anyone to drop me off." Scarlett wiped her eyes.

"Let's enjoy the beautiful scenery. Maybe we'll get lucky and see a whale."

Scarlett smiled at Rhys's attempt to lighten the mood and stood to walk to the rail. Rhys never expected to play therapist on her second date, but she did sign up for a week with lesbians so you just never knew what was going to happen.

## CHAPTER TWELVE

"Thanks for the great day, B." Katie gave her date a hug. "I still can't believe someone turned in your wallet. When you realized it was gone I thought for sure it was picked right out of your pocket."

"They'd need pretty nimble fingers to get it out of these tight jeans without me noticing. Besides, they wouldn't need to when I'm so distracted by baked goods I just leave it on a table in a crowded farmers market. I can't believe it was turned in either, but I'm certainly glad there are still good people around." Brooklyn walked with Katie through the front doors of the resort. "Want to have dinner together? I wouldn't mind spending more time with you."

Katie felt a flash of panic as she thought of an excuse to end her time with her date. Brooklyn was a lovely woman but was obviously interested in much more than Katie was able to give even though Katie had been quite clear about what she was willing to offer. Before she was forced to make up a reason, she saw Rhys walk out of the front office and give a blond woman a hug. The sudden twinge of jealousy at seeing the interaction left Katie a little confused, but she brushed it off as relief that she had found an excuse to part ways with Brooklyn.

"I'm so sorry, I have a standing dinner date with my friend Rhys all week. I'm going to have to pass, but I had a great time and I'm sure I'll see you around." Katie gave her a hug she hoped didn't seem like too much of a brush-off and waved as she walked toward Rhys.

"What's up, buttercup?" she asked as they reached each other outside the dining hall.

"Was that your date?" Rhys raised her chin, indicating the woman still watching Katie as she walked away.

"Yep. That was Brooklyn. She was very sweet and I could totally see being friends with her, but she definitely wants more than I'm willing to offer. What's with you and the blonde in the office? Did you get in trouble?"

Rhys playfully smacked Katie's arm as she searched the room for a place to sit. "You can't get in trouble if you never get caught. Let's sit over there." Katie was led to a table close to the soft serve machine. "I figured we'd end up here anyways so we might as well sit near it."

"You're such a smarty pants."

Once they had deposited their things at the table, they both stood in line for food. Tuesday appeared to be Italian, which was Katie's favorite so she piled her plate with everything she could find.

"You aren't messing around," Rhys said when they sat down.

"Italian is a very serious food."

"There's no way you're going to get all that food into that teeny tiny body."

"What is it with you and tiny jokes? I'm five foot two. I'm not exactly Thumbelina." As soon as Katie saw the look of joy on Rhys's face she realized her mistake in possibly inadvertently giving herself a terrible nickname.

"Oh my God, you are absolutely Thumbelina. It's taking all my will not to break into the song from the Danny Kaye movie, *Hans Christian Anderson*. Know what I mean?" she asked.

"Of course I know what you mean. I'm Scandinavian, remember? I had the movie memorized by the time I was old enough to talk."

Rhys started to quietly hum the tune Hans sings to the little girl in the movie while moving her thumbs like they were dancing. Katie tried not to laugh but couldn't help herself as Rhys attracted stares from those around her. "You're a nut, Rhys Gwyndolyn."

"Whoa. I usually only hear my middle name when I'm in trouble. Maybe I shouldn't have shared that little tidbit with you."

"Your secret is safe with me, but I can't promise I won't use it to fight back if you start calling me Thumbelina." Katie used her bread to wipe the last bits of marinara from her plate. "Boom. How's that for a tiny little body? And now I'm ready for my soft serve and sprinkles. You're going to have to roll me out of here for our walk of course." Rhys stood.

"I'll get the cones, you get our stuff. We should drop it off in our rooms before our walk so we don't have to carry it. We need to remember napkins this time."

"Good thinking. You're coming up with all the good ideas tonight." Katie picked up their stuff from the table. "Don't cheap out on my sprinkles, woman. I want to see it rain sprinkles all over that thing."

"Yes, my liege." Rhys scooped the rainbow colored bits of candy over Katie's ice cream and handed it to her. "Ready?"

They wound their way through the dining hall and stopped by their rooms to drop off their bags and grab a blanket to sit on. The sun was sinking toward horizon as they walked down the path to the beach.

"How was your date today?" Katie asked as she finished off her cone.

"It was…interesting," Rhys said.

"Interesting doesn't sound exciting. You went whale watching with Scarlett, right?"

As they approached the same spot between the dunes where they had talked the night before, Rhys laid out the blanket she brought from her room and sat on one side, leaving room for Katie on the other. "In theory, but I spent the time consoling my date instead of watching whales." Rhys leaned back on her elbows as Katie turned to face her. She couldn't help but notice the strong woman laid out before her. She'd looked at Rhys's body many times at this point, but the prone position she was in pulled her shirt just tight enough across her chest to give Katie a view of her perfectly athletic torso and breasts.

"This should be an interesting story," Katie said, clearing her throat. She willed herself to look into Rhys's eyes and away from her chest. Her heart sank as a knowing smile flashed across Rhys's face. The last thing she needed was her one true friend here thinking she was interested in something more than friendship. That wasn't on the table, no matter how tempted Katie was to touch her boobs. That being said, she'd been up front with Rhys from the beginning so as long as Rhys knew not to expect more, there wouldn't be anything wrong with a little touching, right?

"It's a sad story actually. Scarlett is a very religious person and it sounds like she might also be asexual. I think she's struggled with guilt over not being attracted to anyone and confused her lack of attraction as something being broken inside. I've seen it before. It's sad to feel like something is wrong and no one understands you." Rhys lay down on the blanket and put her arms behind her head.

Katie lay next to her, resting her head on Rhys's folded arm. "Is this okay?"

"Of course."

"I feel bad for Scarlett. Why were you in the front office with her? Is she okay?" Katie reveled in the warmth of Rhys's body as they both stared up at the stars.

"She's fine. I told her about a friend who is also asexual and recommended she find a support group in San Francisco with people who will understand what she's going through. She was miserable and didn't want to stay at the resort any longer so I went to the office with her to ask for a refund for the remaining days."

"Did they give it to her?" Katie rolled onto her side facing Rhys and slipped an arm over her middle while she rested her head on her shoulder. Rhys wrapped her arm around her and pulled her closer. Katie felt guilty for accepting the affection from someone when she knew it wouldn't lead to anything more, but she couldn't remember feeling this content in a very long time and didn't have the strength to end the contact.

"They did. They were a little resistant at first until I reminded them that forcing her to stay and date people she doesn't want to date would only lead to frustration for not only her but her future dates. In the end they were actually cool about it."

Katie soaked up the warmth from Rhys's body and felt herself relax into her solid chest. "You're so warm you may never get rid of me."

"I'm okay with that."

Katie was afraid to look up at Rhys so she buried her face even farther into her broad shoulders. "Tell me a story about little Rhys and it has to be embarrassing." She felt Rhys shake with a laugh which made her smile.

"Embarrassing, huh? Only if you promise to do the same. One embarrassing story for another."

"Deal."

Rhys rested her chin on top of Katie's head and pulled her closer. "Are you warm enough?"

Katie sighed and gave Rhys's middle a squeeze. "I am. Now stop stalling, woman. I need a story and make it a good one." Katie closed her eyes and luxuriated in the way their bodies fit perfectly together. She'd always been a very tactile person and had spent hours cuddling with friends, but there was something about Rhys's broad shoulders and strong frame that made her feel safe.

"Man, you're a tough crowd," Rhys said. "Okay, let me think for a minute. My entire life is one embarrassing moment after another."

"I find that hard to believe. You seem like a cool cucumber."

"I've got you fooled. They must have put something in those sprinkles you put on your ice cream."

"They are magic. Now, no more stalling, entertain me."

"Wow. Okay. No judgments, right?"

"No judgments." Katie noticed Rhys's shirt had pulled up, exposing the smooth flesh of her stomach, and she fought the urge to slip her hand under the hem of the fabric. She had no idea why she felt such a strong need to stop herself. She'd been with several women since Amber and she'd never hesitated to get physical with them. She was up front with them on what she wanted and they had willingly agreed to keep things casual. Who's to say Rhys wouldn't be equally interested in something casual? Katie knew that wasn't what Rhys wanted.

"I can't believe I'm going to tell you this story."

Katie gave Rhys's middle a pat for encouragement. "Come on. You're working this up so much, it better be good."

"I'm not promising it's good but it's definitely embarrassing."

"Perfect. Out with it."

"There was a time, many years ago, when my little sister stole my girlfriend."

"Max stole you're girlfriend? That's shitty but not embarrassing," Katie said.

"Well, Max was six."

Katie burst into laughter while Rhys covered her face. "Holy crap, Rhys. I'm going to need all the details."

"The little vixen's name is Anna Jones and she's the daughter of our father's second cousin, Brenda."

"Wait, Anna's your cousin and she was your girlfriend?"

"No, well, technically, yes but a distant cousin, and since I was eight, Max was six, and she was seven, the relation part didn't really mean anything at the time. I was madly in love with her, though. We used to swim in the pool at her house pretty much every day during the summer. When someone in San Francisco has a private pool, you take advantage of that shit."

Katie nodded in agreement. "That is a rare find."

"They had an awesome tornado slide that spit you out into the pool, and Max and I used to dare each other to slide down in ways I hope my children never attempt. It's a miracle we aren't both dead. Anyway, I decided that since we liked each other so much we should probably be girlfriends, which would inevitably lead to marriage. I explained my logic to Anna and she agreed."

"That tracks," Katie said.

"Eight-year-old logic is pretty flimsy. So we were girlfriends but we knew enough about relationships to know our parents wouldn't understand how serious we were. We decided to keep it all on the down low, holding hands out of their eyesight and stealing little kisses under the tornado slide."

"I bet you were freaking adorable when you were a kid."

Rhys smiled at the compliment which sent tingles down Katie's spine. She really had a great smile.

"In the meantime, Max was watching my budding relationship with Anna and decided she'd like her to be her girlfriend, too."

Katie laughed when Rhys rolled her eyes. "I think I see where this is going," Katie said.

"Yep," Rhys answered. "So, one day when I had to go to the dentist, Max had a little talk with Anna and told her it only made sense for them to be girlfriends, too, since Max and I shared everything and all. She agreed and just like that, they were dating."

"I can't believe she was so easily convinced to cheat on her one true love."

Rhys gave Katie a sad puppy dog face.

"Poor baby," Katie said.

"Yeah, poor me," Rhys frowned. "So my girlfriend and Max were having a grand old time holding hands and making future plans when they found themselves under the tornado slide. Innocent little Max had no idea this was the kissing spot so she was shocked when Anna pulled her face toward hers and laid one on her. Her first kiss."

Katie laughed until tears fell from their eyes.

"That was the point where I came home from the dentist and found Max kissing my girlfriend under the tornado slide."

"That animal," Katie added with amusement. "What did you do?" she asked, wiping tears from her eyes.

"I decked Max right in the mouth."

"You what?" Katie asked, sitting up to look into her face. "You punched your baby sister?"

"Well, yeah, she kissed my girlfriend. I don't regret it one bit."

Katie collapsed on the blanket laughing. "I had no idea you were so quick to resort to violence."

"I've matured a lot since then. Now I'm more of a lover than a fighter."

Katie smiled. "I bet."

"Now you. It's your turn."

"Me?" Katie yawned as she racked her brain for a story that could compete with the one Rhys had told. "I can't think of anything right now. I'm exhausted."

"Nope. I told you a totally embarrassing story, now you have to share something. That was the deal."

"Yeah, yeah. Okay. There's a chance I might have peed my pants one time because I didn't want to interrupt a girl I had a crush on when she was telling me a story."

"What?" Rhys wasn't sure she had actually heard her correctly. "You peed yourself so you didn't interrupt her?"

"Yes." Katie shrugged. "In my defense I was only twelve and she was telling me about this total asshole she had a crush on that made fun of her lunch box."

"You might be the sweetest person I've ever met."

Katie blushed at the compliment.

"That's not enough, though," Rhys said.

"What are you talking about? That's totally embarrassing."

Rhys shook her head. "It might have been embarrassing, but come on, I gave you a big story with kissing and fist fights and all kinds of excitement. Yours just involved you being so sweet you peed yourself. I'm going to need something more than that."

"Geez. I had no idea you were this demanding," Katie said.

"I'm literally getting older as I wait…"

"Wow, okay, let me think." Katie thought of several embarrassing moments in her life but knew Rhys wouldn't be satisfied unless it was truly embarrassing.

"Story."

"Okay, here goes. The summer after I graduated high school I thought maybe I should have sex with a boy just to make sure I wasn't wrong about the whole lesbian thing."

"I wouldn't have pegged you as someone who was into guys." Rhys looked apologetic when Katie gave her a stern look.

"Do you want to hear my story?"

"Yes, sorry."

Katie gave her a wink and continued. "My brother's friend John Harrison had always been very flirty with me and he seemed like a nice guy who would treat me with respect so I asked him if he would be my first. He was a little hesitant, which I have to admit, hurt my feelings. I thought maybe it was because he was friends with my brother and was afraid of upsetting him, but I worried it was also because he thought I was hideous."

"We know that wasn't the case," Rhys interjected with a smile. "Thanks." Katie beamed at her. Compliments from Rhys seemed to hit her right in the heart. "A couple days after I had asked him he called and told me his parents were out of town for the weekend and wanted to know if I wanted to come over and hang out. I stole condoms from my brother's room, put on the sluttiest thing I owned, and drove to his house. He answered the door dressed in slacks and a tie like a forty-year-old man on his way to a job interview." Katie could feel Rhys laugh.

"I take it John hadn't done this before either?" Rhys asked.

Katie traced the design on Rhys's shirt with her finger. "No, I was definitely going to be his first, which was a little surprising since he'd been on the football team in high school and those guys pretty much had girls lined up willing to do all the things. John always seemed different though. Gentler somehow. It's probably why I chose him in the first place. He was really cute, but it's not like I'd ever felt any attraction to him. Anyway, he made us a very nice dinner and then we went to his room to watch a movie. We sat on his bed and as the time ticked by I started to wonder if anything was actually going to happen. I mean we were watching *Wild Orchid*, and the people in the movie were getting way more action than me."

Rhys laughed hysterically. "My parents would have died if they knew I watched that movie at my cousin Dylan's house in the ninth grade."

"I hope my kids never watch something like that and if they do I never want to know about it."

"You want kids?" Rhys asked.

"Of course. I would love kids someday. I just hope they're the super sweet and innocent kind that do everything they're supposed to and never create an awkward situation where I'm having to explain something I had hoped to never have to explain."

"Mm-hm," Rhys said. "You might should stick with dogs. I suspect little Katies are going to be pretty mischievous."

"Hey." Katie poked Rhys in the side. "I was a good kid. For the most part."

"Speaking of innocent Katie, back to your story. You're on the bed watching a dirty movie and nothing has happened so far."

"Right. So we're watching the movie and I realize if anything is going to happen, I'm going to have to get the ball rolling so I slid on top of John and straddled his hips."

"Holy shit. You were already an old pro," Rhys said.

"I was tired of waiting for him, and at that point I only had an hour and a half before my curfew."

"I get it, carry on."

"Okay, so I straddle his hips and start to unbutton his shirt. He looked at me like I was going to devour him whole, so that was a little discouraging, but I soldiered on. I leaned down and pulled a nipple into my mouth, giving it a gentle suck."

Rhys cleared her throat and shifted her body.

"You okay?" Katie asked, looking up.

"Yeah, I'm good, go ahead."

Katie could hear Rhys's breathing get faster. She knew the story was affecting her in ways she hadn't expected, and the thought that she could excite Rhys in that way made her smile.

"Now is the embarrassing part. I was doing my best to get things heated up, so I pulled off my shirt and bra and placed his hand on my breast. He immediately burst into tears. I quickly pulled on a shirt and did my best to comfort him, but he was so embarrassed at that point he just cried. When he finally calmed down, he told me he was gay." Katie looked up into sad eyes. "I felt terrible for him and so embarrassed that I'd just sexually harassed the poor boy."

"Oh, sweetie, you didn't sexually harass him. He was aware of what was happening, and I assume he didn't try to put a stop to it before he started crying?"

"No." Katie sighed. "I noticed hesitation, but I never realized what he was going through. I felt horrible but it brought us closer. We're still friends to this day. He's married to a park ranger and they've adopted three kids."

"I love happy endings." Rhys's grin was contagious and Katie couldn't help smiling back.

"You're a good egg, Rhys. I think it's a good thing we met. I'm not sure how I would get through this week without you."

Rhys turned toward her and smiled leaving their faces only inches apart. "No matter what else happens this week, it was worth every penny to have found you, my tiny little friend."

The heat of a flush swept up from Katie's heart and warmed her cheeks as she gazed into the most beautiful brown eyes she'd ever seen. The steady sound of the waves was soon drowned out with the rapid beating of her heart. She was sure Rhys could hear it like the beat of a drum, steadily thumping faster and faster as they edged closer and closer.

Katie felt the slightest whisper of softness as their lips touched before she abruptly sat up, realizing she was dangerously close to going down a road she knew she would regret. She really liked Rhys, and the last thing she wanted to do was make things awkward between them.

The abrupt distance left a look of disappointment on Rhys's face before she quickly recovered and stood to help Katie to her feet. "It's getting late. You ready to head back to get some shut-eye? Who knows what adventures tomorrow will bring?"

They folded their blanket and walked the short distance back to their rooms in silence. As they said good night, Rhys lingered at her door as if there was something she wanted to say but ultimately turned toward her room.

"Two down and four to go," Katie said. Rhys unlocked her door. "Maybe tomorrow you'll meet the girl of your dreams."

"Maybe. Night Katie." She stepped into her room and closed the door behind her, leaving Katie feeling more alone than she could ever remember feeling before.

"Goodnight, Rhys."

## Chapter Thirteen

Rhys checked the time on the alarm clock once more before burying her face in the pillow and releasing a muffled scream. Why did she insist on torturing herself by falling for unavailable women? She knew a therapist would say she was self-sabotaging herself for some reason, but why? Why would she do that? She wanted nothing more than to settle down with a nice girl and start a family. Why was that so difficult? She was starting to think there wasn't one available woman in Northern California who wanted the same things she did. She knew that was ridiculous, but thus far she hadn't found any indication that it wasn't true.

She closed her eyes and concentrated on relaxing her body, starting with her feet. After a minute she wiggled her toes to make sure they felt relaxed. Was it considered relaxing them if you moved them? Shouldn't you keep them completely still if the goal was for them to relax? She wondered what Katie would say about that and then smacked herself on the forehead for thinking of the woman she couldn't keep out of her thoughts. She wondered if Katie had gone to bed or if she was still awake, maybe reading a book or watching a show. Rhys decided she would probably hear sound through the wall if she was watching a show so she discounted that idea.

Rhys sat up and rubbed her eyes before checking the time again. It was ten o'clock. She'd thought she might get to bed early so she would be rested for whatever tomorrow had in store for her, but she felt wide awake. Part of her wanted to go next door to see if Katie was still awake. Maybe she'd want to play a card game or watch a show with her. At the thought of watching a show with Katie, Rhys pictured them snuggled together under the covers, Rhys with her back against the headboard and Katie snuggled into her side. She thought of the way Katie felt in her arms on the beach, and then she was right back to the feelings she'd been trying to get rid of since she'd left Katie that night.

Why would Katie snuggle up to her when she knew she didn't want the same things? Rhys couldn't decide if she should be angry with Katie or if she was making something out of nothing. Katie had told her she didn't want a relationship and it wasn't like snuggling together meant anything other than what it seemed. A lot of friends snuggled together, and it was nothing more than that. She wasn't sure how to process their near kiss, but she would have to deal with that later. For now, she was going to try to enjoy her time at the resort and enjoy whatever Katie was able to offer.

With that problem resolved, Rhys lay back down and closed her eyes. She tried the relaxing exercise once again, and this time she refused to move her feet, even though she felt a slight itch on one of them. "God dammit." She sat up and swung her legs over the side of the bed. The clock on her nightstand said it was ten thirty which meant the resort's club would be in full swing. Maybe being around other people and music would force her to think of something other than Katie.

With a sigh, Rhys stood and flipped on the light. She hadn't packed for anything like going to a club, but she settled on her black jeans and the black sweater Max convinced her to bring. She pulled them on and ran fingers through her hair before grabbing her room key and heading toward the club.

There were more people out and about than she expected. She waved to a couple she recognized before reaching the ballroom they'd set up as Club Bump. The thump of the music she felt when she pulled the door open was a welcome distraction. After ordering a whiskey sour at the bar, she surveyed the crowd looking for someone she might recognize. Just when she thought she was out of luck, she heard someone call her name and turned to see Carmen waving her to a table with two blond women. As she got closer, she realized one of them was Katie.

"Hey, guys." She sat in the available chair which happened to be next to Katie. "Hey, Katie."

"I thought you were sleeping." Katie leaned close to Rhys so she could be heard over the music.

"I tried. I couldn't settle down." Rhys smiled. "I thought you were sleeping, too. I almost stopped by to see if you were awake but didn't hear any sounds coming from your room so I thought you were already asleep."

"I almost was, but Brooke stopped by and asked me to come with her to the club so she could see if Carmen was here. I think there's something happening with them."

Rhys looked toward the couple in question as Carmen whispered something in the ear of the woman she assumed was Brooke that caused her to giggle like a school girl. "I think you're right."

"Hi, I'm Rhys and you must be Brooke. I've heard wonderful things about you."

Brooke blushed and turned to Carmen, giving her a sweet kiss on the cheek. "It's nice to meet you, Rhys. I've heard a few things about you, too. This one hasn't stopped talking about you all night."

Rhys turned to Katie who blushed and looked like she wanted to crawl under the table and hide. "I was just—" Katie started, but Rhys held out a hand and pulled her to her feet.

"Dance with me?" Rhys wasn't much of a dancer, but when Katie nodded her agreement she hoped she was good enough to pass as one as they threaded their way through the crush of people and onto the dance floor. The song wasn't anything Rhys recognized, but she did her best not make a complete fool of herself as she followed the beat and tried not to trip on her own feet. Katie was quite a good dancer, and soon Rhys realized she was barely moving because she was so focused on watching her.

Before she could be too embarrassed, the music changed to something slow, and Rhys held out a hand inviting Katie to come closer. "Mind if I lead?"

Katie leaned back so she could look into Rhys's eyes and smiled. "I assumed that's what you would want."

"What do you want?" Rhys gently rocked them back and forth to the rhythm of the music.

"Sometimes I'm not sure." Katie buried her face in Rhys's shoulder. "Can we just enjoy this for now?"

Rhys pulled her closer and allowed their bodies to meld together. "Sure." Katie's body felt so perfect against her own. The idea of her only having this woman for a week made her sick to her stomach. What kind of cruel joke was it that she would find someone so perfect and not be able to take it further than a one-week cuddle fest?

When the music changed again to something fast, Rhys guided Katie back to their table where their friends had ordered fondue.

"You guys want to share this with us?" Carmen asked, dipping an apple in the bowl of hot cheese.

"That looks awesome." Rhys picked up a long fork and stabbed a chunk of bread to dip. "Let me get the next round." She flagged a waitress over and everyone ordered another drink. The fondue was good and reminded Rhys of celebrating her parents' wedding anniversary every year at a local fondue restaurant. They would all go to dinner together as a family, and then Rhys and Max would be dropped off with their aunt and uncle for an overnight while their parents would celebrate the rest of the night on their own. Rhys had always thought they were doing something innocent like bowling when she was a kid and would beg her parents to include them. She thought they refused because Max was sometimes a handful and resented her for ruining it for both of them. Once she was old enough to understand what it was they were actually doing, she was mortified that she had been such a thorn in their side when they only asked for one night alone together a year.

"What are you smiling about?" Katie asked. Rhys speared an apple, dipped it into the cheese, and offered it to Katie who gratefully took it. "Thanks."

"You're welcome. I was just thinking of having fondue with my family when I was a kid. I don't know why I don't have it more."

Katie patted Rhys's flat stomach which sent a jolt of pleasure to her core. "Looks like you burn enough calories to reward yourself with fondue now and again."

Rhys smiled and rubbed her stomach where Katie's hand had been. Every part of her wanted to suggest they go out for fondue together when they got home, but she wasn't sure how Katie would feel about the invitation. It sounded an awful lot like a date. She had said she was open to finding friends, and fondue could be friendly, couldn't it? Rhys thought of her favorite fondue restaurant that was built in an old kiln that created the bricks that were instrumental in rebuilding San Francisco after the 1906 earthquake. Some of the tables were built into the exposed-brick tunnels that were once the ovens used to prepare the bricks. They called the area lovers lane and the romantic setting was somewhere she had dreamed of taking someone special someday.

She shook her head to dispel the image of her and Katie sitting close while they enjoyed a meal there. Rhys stood and waved good-bye to her friends. "I'm going to head back to my room. You kids have a great evening." Before Katie was able to respond, Rhys was through the crowd and out into the cool air of the evening. The chill helped clear her mind as she walked toward her room.

"Rhys," she heard Katie call from behind her. She had hoped to sneak away without a problem so she could go back to her room and wallow in her sadness, but apparently, she was destined to be tortured. The mature part of her mind told her to let it go. Katie didn't owe her a damn thing and she had been very clear about what she was willing to give. Rhys understood that and could deal with that, but the part of their relationship that was so obviously pulling them closer was getting too hard to ignore and that irritated her to no end.

"What's up, Katie?" Rhys asked, continuing her walk back to her room once Katie was by her side. "Did you have a good time?"

Katie looked at her quizzically as she struggled to keep up with Rhys's longer stride. "What's up with you? Is everything okay?"

Rhys looked at her and shook her head, disgusted with her own behavior. She pushed out a deep breath and smiled. "Yeah, I'm sorry. I'm tired and this week has been a bit of an emotional roller coaster." Katie nodded without saying a word.

"It's my thing though. Don't get a sad face. I didn't mean to bring you down."

Katie looked up at her as if she wanted to say something but wasn't sure what to say.

"Here we are," Rhys said when they reached their rooms. "You have a great night, Katie. Thanks for hanging out with me."

"Night, Rhys. Sweet dreams." Katie gave her a sad smile before going into her room.

## CHAPTER FOURTEEN

Katie leaned back against her door and sighed. What was she getting herself into? She wasn't supposed to be having these feelings for someone, especially someone she just met. How was she going to be able to keep her hands to herself for the next week when all she wanted to do was march over to Rhys's room right now and remove every piece of clothing between them.

The frustrating part was that if this was a normal situation she would probably just see where their attraction led, confident she'd be able to stop things before they got too far down the road by distancing herself from the other woman. Surely this fire would burn out once they were able to scratch that itch a time or two.

This wasn't a normal situation. Avoiding Rhys for the rest of the week would be impossible and awkward. Rhys didn't seem like a casual sex kinda girl, and the thought of derailing her chances of finding someone else wasn't an option for Katie. She wouldn't do that to her.

Katie toed off her shoes and walked into the bathroom to start her nightly routine. She pulled on her pajamas and began removing her makeup. Even though she didn't wear much, it was always refreshing to scrub her face clean before bed.

She'd just turned on her electric toothbrush when she heard a quiet knock on her door. "Fuck." Fear shot through her as she looked at her disheveled appearance in the mirror. The person at the door was very likely Rhys, and she wasn't exactly looking her cutest at that moment.

"Hello?" she called as she scrambled around the room looking for something else she could throw on that would not completely embarrass her. "Shit, my hair." The headband she used to keep her hair off her face so she could wash it was still on her head, pushing the blond strands straight up toward the ceiling.

"Katie?" The whispered voice through the door sounded much higher than Rhys's deeper tone.

"Yes." Katie answered as she walked closer and peered through the peephole in the door. "Is that you, Brooke?"

"Yeah, it's Brooke. Can I come in?"

Katie pulled open the door and stood back to allow Brooke into her room. "Hey, is everything okay?"

"Yeah, it's okay, I'm okay...kinda."

She looked frazzled as Katie led her over to the club chairs in the corner of the room. "What's going on?" Katie did a quick scan to make sure she didn't seem injured.

"I'm so sorry to bother you this late. You look like you're ready for bed."

Katie swiped the headband from her forehead and finger combed her hair down as much as possible. "No, I was getting ready, but I'm not going to sleep anytime soon. What can I help you with?"

"God, Katie, I'm freaking out. I don't even know where to start."

Katie reached out to take Brooke's hand in hers, hoping the contact would comfort her. "Just start at the beginning. Take all the time you need."

"I think I'm falling in love with Carmen." Brooke smiled at the mention of Carmen's name, even though she was the one mentioning it. "Correction, I know I'm falling in love with Carmen. Hard."

Now that she realized nothing terrible had happened, Katie smiled and squeezed Brooke's hand. "Yeah, I kinda thought that might be the case by the way you guys were looking at each other at the club. Did something happen after we left that caused you to panic or is it just the overwhelming feelings of love blowing your mind."

Brooke sat back in her chair. She covered her face with her hands, but Katie could see the blush on her cheeks where they peeked out between her fingers. "Yes," Brooke said. "All of the above."

"We can work through this together. First, what happened when Rhys and I left?" Katie stood and walked to the small fridge in the front of the room. "Beer?"

"Yes, please."

Katie pulled out two bottles of Negra Modelo and popped the caps off. She handed one to Brooke and tapped their bottles before sitting back in her chair. "Okay, what happened?"

Brooke took a hearty sip of her beer and kicked off her shoes, obviously planning to stay awhile. "When you guys left Carmen asked me to dance."

"Is she a good dancer? I imagine she'd be a really good dancer."

"She's a fantastic dancer."

Katie's mind drifted back to her dance with Rhys. The memory of the warmth of her body as she guided Katie across the floor sent goose bumps down her arms and hardened her nipples to painful points. She cleared her throat and took another sip of her beer, leaning forward to conceal her body's reaction. "Then what happened?"

"Then we went back to our table and talked a little more. She's so smart, Katie. Like super smart. She's also kind, and handsome, and so interesting. I know you don't know her well, but she's done so much in her life. Much more than I have."

"She sounds amazing."

Brooke blushed. "She is. She's really amazing. I don't want to make it sound like she brags about that stuff. She doesn't. Things just naturally come up in conversation. She's actually quite humble. I think she knows that I haven't done as much and she doesn't make me feel bad about it or like she thinks any less of me. She's already talking about us going on adventures together and sharing all these things with me as if we're already a couple."

This was very likely where Brooke's panic was coming from. "And how do you feel about the idea of being in a relationship?" Katie was doing her best to lead Brooke to the point without making her feel pressured to give answers to questions she wasn't ready to think about.

"I feel...I feel..." Brooke was obviously struggling to put words to the feelings that were swirling around her.

"Scared?" Katie suggested.

"No, not scared really. I trust her. I don't think she's going to intentionally hurt me."

"Unsure?"

"No, I'm confident Carmen and I could make each other happy."

"Okay." Katie took another sip of her beer and studied Brooke's face. Searching for what to say that would help Brooke describe what she was feeling. "Is it too good to be true?"

"Yes. That's it. It's too good to be true. Carmen is too good to be true. The fact that we met so quickly in the week is too good to be true. The idea that I waited my entire life and moved away from my home and my family hoping to find someone and I'm not even here a year and boom, there she is. Like it's the easiest thing in the world. She's just…there. And she likes me, too. I'm no expert on this stuff, but I get the feeling that she's really into me and I'm so into her and it's all just so much." Brooke drained the last of her bottle and dropped her head into her hands. "What am I going to do, Katie? Am I being an idiot and setting myself up for disappointment? Are these feelings too good to be true?"

Katie stood and pulled two more beers from the fridge for them. Brooke accepted hers and patiently waited for her reaction. Katie had no idea what to say. She felt in a way she was struggling with the same feelings with Rhys. She was adamant with her family that she wasn't interested in falling for someone. There was no possible way she was going to actually find a woman at this resort that she would have honest feelings for. Not possible. And then she met Rhys. Rhys with her kind heart and quick wit. Rhys with this depth and intelligence that made Katie hang on her every word. Rhys was too good to be true, and Katie was sure that if she wasn't so crazy attracted to her and in this ridiculous resort, she would be able to gain perspective and realize that this was all just a fantasy. She knew that wasn't what Brooke wanted to hear though, and she honestly didn't believe Brooke and Carmen's situation was exactly the same. They both wanted to find a partner. They were both normal people who didn't carry the scars and baggage that Katie carried. Maybe they were different.

"I think if you don't allow yourself to believe it's possible that you and Carmen are the real thing and what you have isn't too good to be true, you'll always wonder if you denied yourself your one true chance at something real."

Brooke grinned and leaned back in the chair. "Yeah, I think you're right. I owe it to us both to see where this thing between us goes. Thanks for listening."

"You bet. I'm really happy for you, Brooke." Katie really was happy for them both. She hadn't known either of them long but liked them both a great deal. She'd seen the way they looked at each other at the club that night, and it was obvious how gone they were for each other.

"What about you and Rhys?"

The unexpected question pulled Katie from her thoughts. "What about us? We're just great friends."

"Uh-huh, you looked like you were really great friends when you were dancing. Carmen and I both felt the heat between you from the other side of the room. Don't play coy with me."

The idea that Brooke saw something between them and she thought Katie was just denying it irritated her. "You figured us out. We're hiding our torrid love affair from you guys." Katie stood and gathered their empty beer bottles hoping the cleanup effort would be a hint that it was late and she should leave. She had no idea why she was so upset about the idea that someone might think she and Rhys had anything other than a friendship. She was feeling it herself so why wouldn't the people around them pick up on that energy?

When Brooke didn't make a move to leave, Katie pulled two bottles of water from the fridge and sat back down. "Nothing can happen between us. I'm not going to deny that there's sexual tension happening, but that's it. How could there not be? If the situation were different and she and I could have our fun and then go our separate ways without being forced to spend the next week awkwardly avoiding each other, I won't deny that something might happen. As it stands, we're trapped in this fishbowl, and the last thing I want is to ruin the friendship she and I have found with each other."

Brooke smiled and silently sipped her water.

"What?" Katie was getting more and more irritated with Brooke by the minute.

"Is that truly what you think? You think there's just this sexual tension between you because you're both hot for each other and the sex would obviously be off the charts?"

"Pretty sure that's not at all what I said. I admit there's something between us. We're drawn to each other, but that doesn't mean we should jump in bed. I value our friendship more than that and I'm not willing to risk losing that because I'm so attracted to her. It's just not worth it."

The conversation was turning into much more than Katie was ready for. This was supposed to be about Brooke and Carmen, not Rhys and her. What did Brooke expect her to do? Knock on Rhys's door in the middle of the night and seduce her? What then? What would happen when they woke up tomorrow morning in each other's arms after what she was sure would have been a night full of mind-blowing sex and then off they would go on their dates for the day, like nothing had happened. Like they hadn't just crossed a line that they never should have crossed. Then tomorrow evening, things would be awkward and they wouldn't have their normal banter and snuggle on the beach that Katie had quickly learned to look forward to. If she were honest with herself, it was the part of the day she looked forward to the most. She'd found herself checking her watch when she and Brooklyn were at the farmers market, mentally counting the time until she would see Rhys again. And that was the problem. That was reason enough to not dive headfirst into a situation they would risk losing everything over. Sex wasn't worth that. She could get sex from anywhere. Well, not anywhere, but there were plenty of other people who would be willing to have a no strings attached romp with her that wouldn't cost her a friend she'd quickly learned to care a great deal for.

"Would you like to know what I think?" Brooke asked.

Katie sighed and walked toward the door. "I'm pretty tired. You mind if we call it a night?"

Brooke paused at the door and wrapped her arms around Katie. The unexpected embrace caught her off guard, but she eventually relaxed into it and soaked up the friendly affection she desperately needed at that moment.

"Thanks for listing to me and for the advice, Katie. I really appreciate your friendship and I want you to know that if you decide you're ready to talk. I'm more than happy to listen."

They pulled away from each other, and Katie silently nodded. She wasn't ready to voice the feelings she had swirling around inside her heart, but it was nice to know when she was, she had someone to turn to.

"I'm sorry I—"

"Don't apologize, Katie," Brooke interrupted as she opened the door. "You'll talk about it when you're ready. Until then, don't forget why you're here. You may not be here to find love, but you shouldn't deny yourself the chance to have fun. You're at a beautiful resort, for goodness sake. Stop worrying about what might happen and enjoy what's right in front of you."

Brooke kissed Katie's cheek before turning to walk out the door.

"Night, Brooke," Katie said as she stepped out to watch her disappear down the path toward her own room.

When she turned back, she looked toward Rhys's door. She allowed herself a moment to imagine knocking and Rhys answering in a T-shirt and cute boxers. Would she invite her in? Katie stepped toward the door and lifted her hand, ready to knock. She could get an answer to all these questions right now. It would be so easy to do. Katie rested her forehead on the door and quietly pressed her open hand against the cool surface. What the hell was wrong with her? This was insane. These feelings were insane, and they were starting to freak Katie out. She had to get a grip and remember her actions had consequences. She needed to think things through before she screwed up something worth so much more than sex. Katie turned, and walked into her room. The sun would be up soon and she needed to at least try to get a little sleep before she had to face another day and another date with someone she knew would never measure up to the one person she wanted to spend her time with.

## Chapter Fifteen

Wednesday morning came sooner than Katie wanted. Bleary eyed and exhausted, she applied more makeup than usual in an attempt to cover the signs of fatigue. When she arrived a few minutes late to the dining hall for breakfast, she worried she might have missed Rhys but found her at a table near the yogurt bar talking to a raven-haired woman.

"Hey," Katie said when she sat down.

"Hey, Katie, this is Brandy. We both like pecans in our yogurt." Rhys and Brandy seemed like old friends sharing an inside joke.

Katie pushed down her irritation and painted on a smile. "Hey, Brandy, I prefer almonds, but I'll take pecans in a pinch." Rhys and Brandy laughed again, but Katie only offered a forced smile. She knew it was ridiculous to be irritated with Brandy, but she'd learned to look forward to the time she and Rhys shared alone in the morning. Katie realized she had no reason to expect Rhys to feel the same, but she was still disappointed.

"I'll be back. I'm going to grab some yogurt for myself." Katie walked to the yogurt bar and took her time layering fruit, nuts, granola, and yogurt into her parfait dish, intentionally leaving out pecans. When she returned to the table, Rhys was alone. "Where did Brandy go?"

"She went back to her friends. You okay? You seem…"

Katie sighed and dipped her spoon into her yogurt. "I'm fine."

"Okay." Rhys didn't seem convinced. "I just…you just seem…"

"Tired?"

Rhys smiled apologetically and pushed a mug of coffee toward Katie. "Yeah, tired. Here, drink this."

"Thanks. Brooke stopped by last night for a chat and we were up pretty late. I didn't get much sleep."

"Is she okay?" Rhys seemed genuinely concerned which tugged at Katie's heart and helped pull her out of her funk. Being grumpy with Rhys wasn't going to make Katie feel any better and wasn't fair to her. Katie's confusion over her feelings wasn't Rhys's fault. Not really a coffee drinker, Katie grimaced when she took a sip of the warm liquid in Rhys's mug. "God, there's no sugar in here at all."

"Yeah, sorry, I drink it with cream and no sugar. I probably should have mentioned that."

Katie took another sip and pushed the mug back to Rhys. "It's okay. I just wasn't expecting it. Mind passing me my envelope? Let's see what's in store for us today." Katie tore her envelope open and read the paper inside. "Looks like I'm going hiking in Armstrong Redwoods State Reserve with a woman named Amelia. I love it up there. It was one of my father's favorite places to hike so I've spent many a Saturday exploring the trails. I never get tired of it."

Rhys smiled at Katie's enthusiasm. "I love it up there, too. As you can imagine, woodworkers love to be around trees. I always thought I would buy a little place on the Russian River near Armstrong someday and be surrounded by redwoods."

"That sounds like heaven," Katie said. "Would you leave the city to live up there?"

"I couldn't really ever leave San Francisco so it would be more of a weekend house. Even though it's only a little over an hour away, I wouldn't want to be that far from my family. I would be miserable with a commute like that."

"Me, too. I couldn't leave the city, but I might buy a little cabin next to yours on the river tucked away in a redwood grove. We can lay out on a blanket and look at the sun stream through the branches." Katie realized she had closed her eyes as she daydreamed of their house on the river and sat up straight before she made even more of a fool of herself. "Who did you get and where are you going?" she asked.

Rhys stared at Katie for a moment before looking at the paper in her hand. "It looks like I'm going to the Legion of Honor with Sofia to look at art."

"Oh, man." Katie looked at Rhys's paper. "You're so lucky. I love the Legion. I could spend hours just walking from room to room, studying every stroke."

Rhys smiled as she began packing up her bag. "I'm sure it's not as exciting for me as it is for a true artist like yourself, but I'm very happy with my destination today. Same time, same place for dinner?"

Katie finished her yogurt and picked up her bag to follow Rhys out the door. "Same time, same place. Have fun and good luck today." She slapped her name tag on her shirt and scanned the lines for her assigned transportation.

"Same to you, bye." Rhys climbed into a waiting van.

Katie walked down the line of vehicles until she finally found the one she was looking for and climbed in. There were four women already seated so Katie sat on the last empty bench at the front. When her date finally joined them, Katie's heart jumped at the beautiful redhead with "Amelia & Katie" emblazoned on her name tag. Willing her heart rate to slow, Katie moved over to make room on the bench seat.

"You must be Amelia."

"That's what they say." Amelia shook Katie's hand and gave her a heart stopping smile. Before she could ask another question, Amelia was tapped on the shoulder by the woman sitting behind her. They had obviously met earlier in the week as they excitedly chatted about mutual friends who had hooked up the night before.

Katie took the opportunity to relax, and enjoy the scenery. Her thoughts immediately drifted to Rhys, and she wondered how her date was going. Being an artist herself, the Legion of Honor Fine Art Museum was an obvious favorite of Katie's. She stared out the window and imagined being there with Rhys. They'd share opinions on their favorite pieces and discover parts of the museum they had somehow missed on previous trips. She couldn't remember ever feeling as comfortable as quickly with anyone else as she did with

Rhys. She had a way of putting her at ease that was addictive. It was hard to believe they'd only known each other a few days and after a few more they would most likely be out of each other's lives forever. They could always be friends after the week of course. It wasn't out of the question, but something about the idea of bringing Rhys into her real world scared the crap out of her. Katie had plenty of friends she loved dearly, but something about the way Rhys made her feel set off internal alarms. She wasn't sure if she was ready to invite those feelings into her real life, away from the safety and anonymity of the fantasy world the resort created.

When the van approached the ranger station at the entrance to the park, Katie checked her shoelaces and picked up her backpack in preparation for getting out. After a quick head count they were given sack lunches with instructions about where and when to meet later that day. Katie and Amelia checked their gear one more time before setting off for the trailhead.

"What kind of trail are we looking for?" Amelia asked as they checked the map.

"I'm fine with whatever you're comfortable with. I will say I wouldn't mind being able to chat, so probably not something terribly strenuous where we'll feel too out of breath to enjoy each other's company. How about this moderate two-point-three-mile hike with a gradual five-hundred-foot climb to the Armstrong Tree?" Katie ran her finger along their route indicated on the map as Amelia watched.

"That sounds perfect. You have beautiful hands by the way. Strong but also delicate. If I were to guess I would say you're an artist of some sort." Amelia studied Katie's hand before threading their fingers together and starting down the trail. "Do you mind holding hands?"

"Um, sure, and you're right about the artist thing. I'm a greeting card artist by profession, but I work with all types of mediums. How about you, what do you do?" Katie wasn't sure how to react to the hand holding, but she had to admit it felt nice to touch someone. Holding hands didn't mean they were getting married and having babies. Schoolkids held hands. Grannies held hands on occasion. Of course the feelings holding Amelia's hand stirred in Katie were very different from schoolkid or Grannie feelings. She stared down at their joined hands and for a moment wished she was holding Rhys's hand.

"I was transferred to the Bay Area eighteen months ago with IKEA. I'm an interior designer who sets up the display rooms."

"That sounds like a neat job," Katie said.

"It's not bad. I love interior design and used to have my own business, but a friend turned me on to this job and I couldn't pass up the benefits it offered. At the time, I was married to a woman who was terminally ill and health care was a big concern." As the trail narrowed they stopped holding hands and walked single file.

"I'm so sorry, Amelia. I can't imagine losing a wife like that. My father died a couple of years ago and it was the most difficult thing I've ever gone through."

Amelia gave Katie a sad smile as the trail widened and they once again walked side by side. "Thanks. It was the most difficult thing I've ever gone through, too, but Casey was brave until the very end. She never gave up hope and somehow kept a positive attitude even when I was a complete mess."

"She sounds like a very special woman."

Amelia smiled and nodded. "She was the best. I was in a rut for a couple years, but when this transfer came up, I hoped it would help me move on if I had a change of scenery. It was difficult to leave my family and friends, but it's been just what I needed to try to put my life back together. I feel like I'm in a really great space now."

"I'm so glad you were able to find some peace." Katie wasn't sure what else to say so she squeezed Amelia's hand as they walked silently through the forest of gigantic trees and enjoyed the quiet beauty of their surroundings. Katie appreciated that Amelia didn't feel the need to fill the silences with chatter. The ability to just be with someone and share a silent moment was hard to find.

As they approached a relatively open place in the trail, they decided to stop for a lunch break. A small side trail led them away from the main path and offered a little privacy to relax and eat. They found a perfect spot at the foot of a redwood where Amelia spread out a small blanket she'd packed in her backpack and invited Katie to sit with her.

"You thought of everything. I'm lucky when my socks match," Katie said.

Amelia pulled off her shoes, socks, and T-shirt leaving her only in shorts and a sports bra. "You don't mind, do you? I need to cool off. The trail is deceivingly strenuous with that climb." Katie blushed as Amelia lay back on the blanket and folded her hands behind her head. "Why don't you join me?"

Katie had never been embarrassed of her body, but pulling her shirt off and exposing herself next to Amelia wasn't going to happen. She settled on just her socks and shoes.

"Where did you come from before you moved here?" Katie balled up her backpack to place under her head like a pillow.

"Texas. I grew up in West Texas but escaped to Austin when I left for college." Amelia closed her eyes as she soaked in the little bits of sun that streamed through a break in the trees to the forest floor. She was absolutely stunning and Katie could feel her head spin a bit as she took the opportunity to really look at Amelia. This was exactly what she needed. What better way to get her mind off Rhys than lying on a blanket in the middle of a forest with a totally hot woman? If anything was going to get her mind off Rhys, Amelia was it. So why was she thinking of Rhys? Dammit.

"Where are you from?"

Katie heard the question and knew she should have an answer, but the soft light dancing across exposed, sun-kissed skin short-circuited her brain temporarily. "I'm so sorry, what did you ask me?" Amelia caught her appraisal and smiled.

"I asked where you were from. Did you grow up in the Bay Area?" Amelia turned on her side and scooted a little closer, tracing a finger along Katie's bicep as she waited for an answer.

"Um, I'm from Sausalito, just north of the bridge. I live in San Francisco now." Katie took a deep breath in an attempt to get her hormones under control. The lazy trail Amelia's elegant finger traced felt like fire as Katie tried to remind herself to continue breathing. Under normal circumstances, Katie had no doubt she'd have been thrilled about the direction things were going, but at the moment she only felt frozen with indecision. Her body said full speed ahead, but her heart told her this wasn't the person she wanted to be doing these things with. What the hell was wrong with her?

"It must have been nice growing up around all this beauty," Amelia said, sliding her hand under the material covering Katie's stomach. Katie sucked in a breath as warm fingers lazily drew circles against her skin.

"It was nice," Katie said. "Really nice." She watched as Amelia's hand crept higher toward her breasts.

"Is this okay?" Amelia nuzzled into her neck leaving little kisses along the way. "I've been thinking about touching you since I saw you, and now that you're next to me you're impossible to resist. If you're uncomfortable I'll stop, but I really hope you don't want me to."

Katie couldn't deny her attraction to Amelia. She wouldn't even try. She couldn't deny that the way Amelia was touching her was turning her on physically, but it didn't feel right. It felt good but it also felt dirty and wrong. It wasn't as enjoyable as it should be and that left Katie feeling sick to her stomach. She knew she had to stop this before it went any further.

"Amelia—" Before Katie was able to respond, Amelia delicately nipped her bottom lip before drawing her in for a kiss. "I want you to stop." Katie pulled back and saw confusion in Amelia's eyes.

"I'm sor—"

"Is that you, Amelia?" Katie startled when she heard a voice and footsteps coming toward them from the main trail.

"It's me. One second, Emily. We'll gather our stuff and be right there." Amelia gave Katie an apologetic smile. "I'm so sorry, Katie. Do you mind if we hike with my friends a little?" Amelia asked.

"Totally fine." Katie quickly straightened her clothes and donned her socks and shoes. A flood of relief blanketed her as she thought about the awkwardness that might have happened had they not been interrupted. What was wrong with her? She felt like she'd almost betrayed Rhys. Someone she wasn't even in a relationship with.

Once everything was packed up, they found their way back to the main trail where Amelia's friends were waiting. Katie tried not to read too much into her sudden hesitation to make out. She was in an incredibly odd situation and the idea that she wouldn't want to make out on a trail where anyone could have seen them was not such a strange thing. That's all it really was. The Rhys thing was confusing, but Katie told herself it was only because they'd been spending so much time together. Nothing more. Not willing to pick apart her logic, she pushed thoughts of Rhys out of her head and decided to focus on the trees for the rest of the day. Trees seemed like a much safer bet.

## Chapter Sixteen

Hey, Katie Bear," Rhys said when she found her already sitting at a table in the dining hall that evening. "How was the date with Amelia?"

"It was pretty good. How was your date with Sofia at the Legion of Honor?"

"It was great." Rhys reached out her hand to pull Katie toward the buffet line. "They had an excellent exhibit on Rodin. Sofia wasn't into sculpture as much as I was, but she really enjoyed the photography collection. She works at a gallery in the South Bay so it was interesting to hear her talk about different aspects of the photos that I never would have noticed."

"I didn't realize you were so into sculpture."

Rhys gave her a confused look as she filled her plate with fried rice and broccoli beef. "Haven't I told you what I do for a living?"

"You told me you work for your family's woodworking business. I assumed that meant you were a carpenter."

With their plates full, Rhys led them back to their table. "Well, I am a carpenter and a good portion of the business is mostly cabinetry and fine woodworking, but my specialty is sculpture. My dad and sister run the cabinetry side which frees me up to focus on my art." Rhys blushed when she realized how passionate she'd gotten talking about her job. "Sorry, I'm a dork."

"No, that's amazing. I had no idea you were artistic. I wish they hadn't taken your phone away so you could show me some of your work."

"Hey, before I forget, I told Brandy we'd go to karaoke tonight after dinner. How's your singing voice?"

Katie set down her fork and leaned back in her chair. "Brandy, the yogurt and pecan girl from breakfast? Why would you do that?"

"Why would I do what?" Rhys was completely confused about why Katie suddenly seemed so upset.

"Why would you commit me to something without even asking?"

"I…" Rhys's mind conjured up a million possible responses, but she knew none of them would make the situation better.

"I'm not your girlfriend, Rhys. You can't just make decisions for me without asking. Even if I was your girlfriend, I'm not your property."

"Katie, I—"

Katie wiped her mouth with her napkin and stood to leave. "I think I'm going to call it a night. You—"

Rhys felt her world start to spin out of control. She knew she'd messed up and Katie had every right to be upset. She had to really think hard about what to say next. There was no doubt in her mind that it could make or break the relationship they'd only just started to build.

"I…I'm sorry. You're right. That was a total dick move. Forgive me?"

Katie hadn't sat back down but she also hadn't walked away so Rhys took that as a win.

"Come on, let's get our ice cream and take a walk," Katie said.

They were quiet as they walked side by side toward what had become their spot on the beach between the dunes. Once they were settled in, Rhys finally broke the silence that had fallen between them.

"I'm really sorry, Katie. I wasn't thinking."

Katie blew out a breath and gave Rhys a sad smile. "I'm sorry my reaction was so dramatic. You didn't deserve that. My ex was really controlling, and I don't think I've completely let the feelings of resentment about it go."

"I get that. I had no right to assume—"

"Hey, apology accepted. I know you weren't trying to upset me. It's my own issue and it's something I'm going to have to work through."

Rhys reached over and squeezed Katie's knee affectionately. "Thanks."

Katie stuffed the last of her ice cream cone into her mouth and brushed off her hands. "We shouldn't be having these things every night. I'm going to have to buy a new wardrobe when I leave."

Rhys smiled at her attempt to break the ice and decided just to let the uncomfortable moment they had pass for now. "Tell me more about your hike today?"

Katie shifted uncomfortably and stared at her hand as she drew her finger through the sand.

"It was nice. I love being up there and Amelia was very interesting. She's an interior designer who lost her wife to cancer a few years ago."

"That's terrible, poor Amelia."

"We didn't talk about it much. It's difficult to know what to say when someone goes through a traumatic thing like that. Everyone handles it differently." As if by instinct, Katie touched a silver compass pendant that hung from her necklace.

"That's beautiful."

Katie smiled and finally looked at Rhys for the first time since they'd sat down. Rhys watched affection and sadness cloud her blue eyes as she held the pendant out where she could see it. "My dad gave it to me." Katie kissed the pendant before tucking it back into her shirt. "We used to sail together, just the two of us, and when I left for college he gave it to me so I could always navigate my way home."

"He sounds like a great dad." Rhys cautiously scooted a little closer to her.

"He was the best. He was my best friend."

Rhys didn't miss that she was speaking of him in the past tense. "I'm so sorry if I brought up a difficult subject."

"Not at all. We lost him a few years ago. You'd think I wouldn't be such a baby about it still, but sometimes it just hits me that he's gone and I can't stop the tears from coming." Katie gave her a brave smile as Rhys wiped a tear from her cheek.

"Loving someone and being sad that they're gone doesn't make you a baby. It makes you a compassionate human."

"I know. I just don't talk about this stuff very much. It's hard."

Fighting every instinct she had to wrap her in a hug, Rhys tentatively reached out and squeezed Katie's hand where it rested in the sand. "I'm sorry for your loss."

"Sorry I'm such a sad sack. I didn't mean to bring the mood down."

"No worries. I'm glad you told me about him." They laid back on the sand and stared up at the stars. "I like getting to know you, and what happened to your dad is part of your story. I have both of my parents, but I worry about my dad all the time. He doesn't always take care of himself like he should and like you and your dad, he's my best friend."

"Is your mom around?" Katie asked.

"Yes and no. She's awesome, but she's a professional violinist who travels a lot with symphonies. Not that she wasn't ever around, but she's never been a part of our lives as much as our dad. She's always been a bit of an outsider by her own choice."

"Not my mom," Katie said. "She's all up in our business. I love her dearly, but the woman drives me to madness sometimes."

"Oh yeah, she's the blackmailer, right?"

"That's her." Katie scooted closer and snuggled into Rhys's side. "She writes romance novels and thinks everyone should have the great love affair she had with my father and the couples in her books have."

"You don't believe that's possible?" Rhys asked as she rubbed her hand up and down Katie's arm to keep her warm.

"I do believe it's possible and that's the problem. My mom and dad had the most beautiful love story ever told. They were meant to be together, and now he's gone and she's alone and she'll never have that again."

Rhys propped herself up on her elbow and looked at Katie in confusion. "I'm sorry but that's crazy. Are you telling me you don't want to let anyone close because you're afraid you'll lose them like your mom lost your dad?" Rhys didn't know why the idea of Katie denying herself love to protect herself from ever feeling pain frustrated her so much. She knew lots of people who had the same philosophy, but the idea of this woman, this wonderful, beautiful, perfect woman shutting herself off to love just so she didn't potentially get hurt some day really pissed her off.

"Jesus, Rhys, what are you pissed about? It has nothing to do with you."

"I'm not pissed." Hearing the frustration in her voice, Rhys took a deep breath and tried again. "I'm not pissed. I'm just sad."

"Okay, I'll bite, why would you be sad?"

Rhys knew there was nothing she could say that wouldn't cause Katie to pull back from her so she tucked her true feelings away and did her best to bullshit her way out of the corner she'd painted herself in. "I'm just sad that a great woman like you will never allow someone to love her. It's a shame."

"Yeah, well, I tried allowing someone in and it didn't turn out so well."

Rhys resumed her position on the blanket and pulled Katie back into her side. "You certainly don't have to talk about something you don't want to talk about, but…want to talk about it?"

Katie draped an arm over Rhys's middle and rested her head on her shoulder. "Ugh, I hate this story."

"Like I said, you don't have to share anything you don't want to talk about." Rhys's heart broke when Katie silently wiped a tear from her cheek. "You okay, sweetie?"

Katie tucked her head under Rhys's chin and let out a sigh. "I'm okay. I feel bad for laying all my baggage on you this evening. You're going to avoid me like the plague tomorrow."

"Not even close. Lay it on me."

The sand shifted as Katie sat up. She turned so she was facing Rhys and pulled her hand into her lap. "Do you mind if I hold your hand? I need to borrow some strength if I'm going to bare my soul."

"Always." Rhys squeezed Katie's hand before entwining their fingers.

"Okay, here goes." Katie cleared her throat before telling Rhys about her father's suicide and the note he left each of them and how none of them had found a way to move past it. Rhys listened and held Katie's hand through the entire story. When Katie was done, she slumped back in the sand next to Rhys and cried into her shoulder while Rhys wrapped her arms around her and rocked her back and forth.

"Let it out, sweetie. I got you." Rhys felt her own tears tickle her cheek as she comforted Katie.

When the emotions seemed to be slowing down, Rhys pulled a clean handkerchief from her pocket and gently dabbed the wetness from Katie's cheeks. "There."

Katie took the white cloth from her hand and studied it. "You keep a hanky in your pocket? How old-fashioned of you."

Rhys tried to take the handkerchief back. "Make fun of my hanky and you don't get to use it."

Katie tried to hold it out of Rhys's reach, but her arms weren't long enough. Rhys stretched over the top of her and plucked the hanky from her hand.

"That's not..." Katie started but her words trailed off when she looked up into Rhys's eyes as she hovered above her. "Fair," she finished.

Before she could convince herself it wasn't a good idea, Rhys leaned down and gently kissed Katie's lips. "I'm so—" Katie threaded her fingers into the hair on the back of Rhys's head and pulled her down for a deeper kiss. Rhys was dizzy as her mind tried to process what was happening. How could this be happening? Should she stop? Could she stop? Katie tasted sweet like the ice cream, and Rhys was pretty sure she'd never been kissed like this before.

When they finally pulled back to catch their breath, Katie covered her face with her hands. "Fuck."

"I'm sorry, Katie." Rhys's heart sank.

"No, stop, it's fine. It was...wonderful. I just..."

"You aren't looking for a relationship."

"Exactly."

Rhys sighed and fell back onto the sand next to Katie. "What if I said I could deal with that?"

"What are you talking about?" Katie sat up facing Rhys.

Rhys sat up next to her. "What if I told you I understand what you can and can't offer me and I'm willing to have these few remaining days with you, no strings attached, no pressure, and at the end of the week we'll go our separate ways."

Katie cupped Rhys's jaw with her hand and leaned in for one final peck on the lips. "I would say that sounds amazing, but I can't ask you to do that. You deserve so much more than I'm emotionally capable of giving you right now."

"I don't need—"

"You do." Katie stopped her before she could argue her case. "I don't want to screw up the friendship we've found. I can't get through this week without you, and if we have sex that's only going to muddy the friendship waters. I don't want to risk that."

"What if we just did the kissing part?"

Katie pulled Rhys's hand up to place a kiss on her palm. "You're hard to resist, but I think this is the right thing to do. Your date tomorrow might be the girl of your dreams and then it'll be super awkward between us. I don't want that. You don't want that."

Rhys stood and held out a hand to help Katie to her feet. "Want to head back? It's getting chilly." Katie studied her for a minute before taking the offered hand and standing.

"Are we okay?" Katie asked.

The cool breeze from the ocean whipped Katie's hair into her face. Rhys brushed a blond lock out of Katie's eyes and tucked it behind her ear. "We're okay. I understand what you're saying, even if I don't like it."

"Friends?"

Rhys did her best to hide her disappointment and stuck out her arm for Katie to wrap around for the walk back to the rooms. "Friends."

## Chapter Seventeen

The next morning as Rhys walked to the dining hall to meet Katie for their regular breakfast date, she decided it was time to move on and allow herself to be open to the idea of finding someone else before her time at the resort was over. She realized the night before that she had held out hope she would be able to charm Katie into giving her a chance. She needed to get past that if they were going to be able to remain friends.

When she entered the room, she found Katie sitting at their normal table with a bowl of oatmeal. She had worried the kiss they shared the night before might have scared her away so she was relieved to see things seemed to be back to normal.

"Hey, Katie Bear," she said.

"Why 'Katie Bear'?" Katie asked with a chuckle.

"Because you're cute and snuggly but a little grumpy in the mornings like a bear." Rhys smiled as she dropped her envelope on the table and turned toward the breakfast buffet. "I'll be right back."

Once Rhys returned with her own bowl of oatmeal, they pulled out their envelopes and tore them open. Katie was the first to read the enclosed card. Rhys was startled when she heard a gasp and looked up to see Katie's face was white as a ghost. "What?"

"Read your card," Katie said.

Rhys pulled out her own card to read who her date for the day would be. "Oh." She read the name Katie with Chinatown as their location. Maybe it was a different Katie. There were lots of Katies in the world, but she could tell by the look on her face that it wasn't a different one.

"You know what? I can just go to the front office and tell them we'll need different dates today. We should have clued them in to our rule that we're off limits to each other." Rhys stood to go to the office, but Katie stopped her. "It's fine. I'm sorry. The idea of spending the day with you is really exciting. I just feel terrible you're wasting one of your dates on me."

"Not to get all Nicholas Sparks on you, but any time spent with you isn't wasted time. I'm not going to try to pretend I wouldn't jump at the chance to be more than friends, but you have been very clear what your boundaries are and I respect them. This is going to be an awesome day hanging out with the coolest girl I know." Rhys painted on the brightest smile she could while inside her heart was breaking.

She swallowed past the lump in her throat when Katie fixed the name tag to her shirt that read "Katie & Rhys." She was going to have to snap out of this lovesick sad puppy thing if she was going to convince Katie she truly was satisfied with only a friendship.

The other couples were already seated when Katie and Rhys arrived at the van, leaving them the back seat to crawl onto. The trip to Chinatown wouldn't take long so they didn't bother getting too settled. Things felt awkward between them, and Rhys hoped once they were out of the van and left to their own devices she would be able to cheer Katie up. As they drove across the Golden Gate Bridge toward San Francisco, they listened to the others chatting. Rhys felt the slight pressure of Katie's leg against hers as they sat side by side. The urge to reach over and slip her hand behind Katie's neck and run her fingers through her hair was almost overwhelming. This was going to be such a long day.

Once they were dropped off and told where and when to meet the van, they pulled out the tour map they were given. "Have you done the Chinatown tour before?" Katie asked as they both looked at the stops on the map.

"Like a billion times. It's one we like to take guests on when they visit. How about you?"

"Us, too." Katie folded up the map and stuck it in her pocket. "Want to just walk around and see what kind of trouble we can get into?"

"Let's do it."

Katie held Rhys's hand so they didn't lose each other in the crowd of people. Rhys was never big on being in crowds, but something about the hustle and bustle of Chinatown had always been fun. It reminded her of an amusement park with all its bright colors and interesting shops. Rhys pulled Katie to a stop so they could peruse the knickknacks at a store so full of things it spilled out onto the sidewalk.

"How do you feel about stuff?"

"What kind of stuff?" Katie asked.

"Toys and knickknacks and stuff, stuff."

"Like this?" Katie held up a tiny stuffed monkey with a grin on his little face. "He kinda reminds me of you actually. Look how happy he is."

"Oh, crap." Rhys held her breath from what she knew was coming next.

"Monkey, that's it. If you get to call me Katie Bear, I get to call you Monkey. It's cute." She put the stuffed monkey to Rhys's cheek as if it was kissing her.

"I think this one might be more appropriate." Rhys picked up a stuffed panther and held it next to her face for comparison.

Katie looked thoughtful before shaking her head. "Nope. Definitely the monkey."

With a sigh, Rhys placed the stuffed panther back on the pile and picked up a stuffed rhino. "This one. It's big and strong—"

"And stubborn. That's tempting because you're super stubborn, but no, the monkey is better."

"How do you know rhinos are stubborn? I've never heard that before, and besides, I'm not stubborn."

"Everyone knows rhinos are stubborn and you, my friend, are super stubborn so don't be so stubborn and just accept that you're the monkey."

Rhys mumbled under her breath and handed the man behind the counter two dollars for the stuffed monkey. "At least now you have a souvenir to remember me by."

"I won't need the monkey for that. I could never forget you." The comment was lighthearted, but they both grew quiet as they continued down the street. Rhys knew she was going to have to put some distance between them after their date if she was going to preserve her heart, but the thought of wasting what little time they had left together, not actually being together, made her chest tight.

They weaved their way through the crowd and Katie once again took Rhys's hand so they wouldn't be separated by the bodies pressing into them. "Let's get some food and head to Portsmouth Square so we can talk." The feel of the delicate little hand in hers felt so natural. Rhys threaded their fingers together as she pulled Katie toward a place where they could get something to go.

Once they had their lunch they made their way back through the crowd toward the park where they would find relative calm. Rhys led them to a shady spot under a tree where they picked through the assortment of items they ordered. "There's so much, I don't even know where to start." Rhys took her first bite of spicy sweet goodness.

"It's all so freaking good." Katie dipped her chopsticks into the container Rhys was holding.

Rhys couldn't help but smile at the comfort they felt with each other. "So, can I ask you a question?"

Katie looked a little weary but nodded her head. "Go ahead."

"Have you ever been in a relationship, like a long-term, romantic relationship, other than Amber?" Rhys set her food down and scooted back to lean against the tree as she waited for the answer. As the moments passed and Katie hadn't looked up from her food, Rhys began to think she wasn't going to get an answer, but she finally sighed and set the container of fried rice on the ground and wiped her mouth with a napkin. Rhys's instinct was to tell Katie she didn't have to answer because she didn't want to make her feel uncomfortable, but her curiosity won out. She wanted to know if there was a reason Katie was so against love other than the failed relationship with Amber or if she'd just decided it was a bad idea from that one bad experience.

"No, I haven't been in a long-term romantic relationship other than Amber."

"How long were you guys together?" Rhys picked up the container of broccoli beef and took a bite, doing her best to seem as casual about the conversation as she could.

"We were together four and half years until one day I came home early from a work trip to find her fucking my best friend since childhood in our bed."

"Oh, Katie." Rhys had no idea what else to say. "I'm so sorry."

"Yeah, well, it is what it is, I guess. I should have known better. It's not like I hadn't seen the signs things weren't good. After my dad killed himself I was so focused on my family that I didn't give her as much attention as I should have. We argued about it all the time, but we were all so lost we wanted nothing more than to be with each other. I needed my family and they needed me."

"Of course. That makes perfect sense, and if what's her name didn't understand that, she was a bitch."

"Amber, her name is Amber."

"Amber's a bitch."

That got a small smile from Katie. "She was a bitch. I usually feel like I need to stick up for her because she wasn't completely wrong. I've never been good at balancing my introversion with caring for someone else. I'm just not built that way. Relationships take so much more work than I'm willing to deal with. Besides, my family is a huge part of my life and I refuse to get into another situation where someone makes me choose between my relationship and my family."

They both startled at the defining sound of tiles being shuffled on a mah-jongg table near them. Rhys watched the men set up the tiles for a minute before looking back at Katie. "Why do you think you have to choose between your family and a relationship? Wouldn't a long-term girlfriend be included into your family?"

Katie picked at the container of moo shu pork with her chopsticks. "I would love that, but it's just never been my reality.

Amber was my only long-term relationship, but I had other relationships before her and women just don't seem to be interested in being involved with a family that isn't their own."

"What kind of family time are we talking about? Is this like a constant hanging out with them type of thing?"

"Right after my dad died, it was. I was lost and confused and heartbroken. So were they. I felt like I needed to be near them to keep myself tethered to the earth."

"And now?" Rhys asked.

"Now we get together for Sunday lunch every week, and I might talk to them on the phone once or twice at the most. I'm actually a very independent person and they can be a little meddlesome if I'm not careful. Especially my sister, Elise."

"That sounds totally reasonable and normal. I live in an apartment above our family warehouse. I don't see them every day, and it's often my cousins who are sent to gather things from the warehouse since my dad and Max are always at the worksite, but I do see them often."

"Has that ever caused an issue with someone you dated?"

Rhys shook her head. "Only the time a girl I was seeing decided she wanted to invite my cousin David into our bed."

"What?" Katie covered her mouth in shock.

"Yeah, it was pretty awkward. Poor David had no idea what was happening until he showed up at my apartment after she had texted him from my phone, as if it was me. We were totally having sex and he walked right in thinking I'd asked him to come over to help me move a piece of furniture. I freaked out and started yelling at him to get out, but Cassie jumped up, naked mind you, and invited him into bed with us."

"Yuck."

"Right? I was completely mortified and so was David. Needless to say, that was the end of my relationship with Cassie, and it took months for things to be normal with David. He wasn't mad, but it was just so awkward."

Katie shook her head. "That's terrible."

"It was horrible. You done with the food?" Rhys asked as she gathered up their containers.

"Yep, let me help."

They threw away their garbage and found a quiet spot on the grass that gave them a little sun, but not so much it would be uncomfortable. Rhys stretched out on the lawn and threaded her fingers behind her head. She had expected Katie to cuddle up to her like she had the other times, but she kept her distance.

"Hey."

"Yeah," Katie answered.

"Have you ever snuggled with a monkey?"

That made Katie smile. "I have, but it's not fair of me to keep snuggling with you and then putting on the brakes when things start to escalate."

"Come on, I'm a big girl. Snuggle with me as a friend. I promise not to try anything funny."

Katie snorted and stretched out next to her in the grass, resting her head on Rhys's arm.

"You're the best snuggler ever," Katie said.

Rhys smiled and bopped her on the nose with her finger. "Yep." They both giggled and the tension between them seemed to ease.

"I love a sunny day in the city," Rhys said as she inhaled a lungful of air and slowly blew it out. She could feel her muscles start to relax as the warmth from the sun bathed her in comfort. "I could get used to this."

"Me, too." Katie said, snuggling closer into Rhys's side.

The feel of Katie next to her sent Rhys's heart into overdrive. She knew she needed to talk about something that would hopefully distract her from the feel of Katie's body pressed against her own. "Tell me about your family."

"What do you want to know?" Katie played with the string hanging from Rhys's hoodie which caused Rhys's nipples to harden.

Rhys cleared her throat and took a deep breath to calm her libido. *Focus, Rhys.* "Everything. Tell me about your siblings."

"Okay, there's my older sister, Elise, and my twin brother, Andy."

"You and your brother are twins? That's awesome. Are you guys cosmically connected? Can you tell what he's feeling right now? Are you close?"

Katie put her hand on Rhys's arm as if to calm her rapid-fire questions. "Yes, Andy is my twin. We're nothing alike although I do feel extremely close to him. We've always been two members of the same team which was sometimes difficult for Elise. She's only a year older and I'm probably more like her, personality wise, but I would agree that Andy and I are cosmically connected," she said.

"Are you and Elise close?" Rhys asked. She felt bad she was grilling her, but she was curious and Katie didn't seem to mind.

"We're very close. Elise is married to a man named Jeff who is a great guy, but evidently has been burying himself in work and neglecting his family. They have three kids who are all my absolute loves, but they're also little heathens. Actually, the oldest one, Garret, is a sweetheart. He's eleven. The twins, Maddie and Mason, are five and they are going to send Elise to an early grave. I feel bad for her because I think a lot of their acting out is trying to get their dad's attention, but he's not the one who has to deal with it. Elise was a GAP model when she was in college and the head cheerleader before that. She's stunningly beautiful, but I can see that life is starting to take a toll on her and it breaks my heart."

"I hope I don't sound like a total creeper, but stunning beauty must run in the family," Rhys said.

Katie smacked her on the shoulder. "You're a charming little monkey, aren't you?"

"I was wondering when the monkey thing was going to come back into play," Rhys said, rolling her eyes in mock frustration. "Let's go for a walk. We have about an hour before our ride is back."

"Sounds good." Katie accepted the offered hand as Rhys helped her to her feet.

They walked in the opposite direction of Chinatown, away from the crowds of people.

"Tell me about your family. What's Max like?" Katie asked.

"She's a couple of years younger than me and we couldn't be more different, but we've always gotten along really well. She and my dad run the cabinet side of the business, and when Dad retires Max will take that part over completely. She's super talented. My dad has always been a great teacher, but Max also has a gift for fine woodworking that can't be taught. She's in high demand in the city. I'm really proud of her, if you couldn't tell." Rhys blushed when she realized she was gushing.

"It sounds like you have every reason to be proud of her. My brother is an incredible guy but a bit of a drifter. He was blessed with great looks and charm for days, but he's always been restless. He models and supports himself, but I don't know if he'll ever settle down and get a real job. He was married a few years ago, and when it didn't work out he became a wild child. He's settled down some, but he's still living like he's twenty-two." Without realizing what she was doing, Rhys took Katie's hand as they walked side by side.

"Let's double back so we can meet the van. It should be there soon." As they walked the busy streets, Rhys wondered if she was going to be able to make it the rest of the week pretending she wasn't falling head over heals for Katie. The more time they spent together, the harder it was to deny how she felt.

"Katie…" Rhys started but stopped when she lost the confidence to say how she felt.

"Yeah?"

"Nothing. There's the others. The van should be here any minute." Rhys felt deflated that she'd lost the nerve to be honest about her feelings. If she couldn't even take this one risk, maybe she should just put some distance between them and try to move on. She was quickly heading dangerously close to completely torturing herself and that just wasn't her style. She swallowed past the lump in her throat and decided she'd have to start tonight.

## Chapter Eighteen

When they arrived back at the resort, Katie walked toward the dining hall expecting Rhys would follow, but when she realized she was alone she turned to find her standing in one spot with a confused look on her face. "What's up? Aren't you ready for dinner?"

"Would you be terribly upset if I skipped dinner tonight?" Rhys asked.

"Not at all, are you feeling okay?" Dinner and their walks on the beach had been the highlight of her days all week so Katie did her best to hide her disappointment that Rhys might not be up for it tonight.

"I'm okay," she said. "I think I just need a little alone time if you don't mind. I think the activities of the week are starting to catch up to me."

Katie knew Rhys was hiding something but didn't want to pressure her so instead she stood on her tiptoes and gave her a kiss on her cheek and a big hug. "Thanks for an awesome day. It was perfect."

"Back at you." Rhys touched the freshly kissed cheek with the tips of her fingers. "I'll see you for breakfast?"

"Sounds great." Katie walked toward the dining hall. Once inside she saw Carmen and Brooke sitting together and waved at them. They waved her over and gave her a hearty hug before insisting she sit and have dinner with them.

"What's going on, Katie? Where's your girl?" Brooke asked.

"What girl?"

"She means Rhys. You guys usually have dinner together every night. Is she okay?" Carmen asked.

Katie studied her hand for a minute, thinking about how good it felt earlier when it was cradled in Rhys's. "She's fine I think," she finally said. "We were matched together today for a date in Chinatown, and when we came back she said she was going to her room to rest."

She saw Brooke give Carmen a knowing look as they stood. "Let's go see what's on the buffet tonight. I'm starving." Katie stood and walked with them to the line. Once their plates were full, they sat back down and began to eat.

"How was your date today?" Brooke asked. "Did you guys have a good time?"

Katie swallowed the bite in her mouth and thought about their day together. She couldn't think of a day when she'd been as content since before her father died. Rhys was fun and easy to talk to and made Katie feel safe.

"We had a great time," she said.

"I'm sure you did." Carmen smirked from behind her glass of iced tea.

"She's my friend, dorks. We're just friends. We agreed to use today as an opportunity to hang out but not expect things to come of it that aren't possible."

"Why aren't they possible?" Carmen asked as she pushed her empty plate away. "Don't shoot the messenger, but seeing you together it's pretty clear how you feel about each other. You're like a couple of lovesick teenagers."

Katie's first instinct was to deny their attraction, but she knew it would be no use. Rhys did make her feel like a lovesick teenager, and it was clear the feelings were mutual. Allowing them to go down that road would only ruin the friendship they'd found, and Katie wasn't willing to risk losing Rhys when things inevitably went south if they were more. She knew nothing she said to her friends would make them understand so she didn't even try. The important part was that Rhys said she understood. As long as they were on the same page, it didn't really matter if others understood.

"You guys are saps. Not everyone can ride off into the sunset together like you two apparently will." They blushed and smiled at each other as Katie gathered her things and stood. "I'm going to catch you later. I need to drop stuff off at my room and then I might take a walk. See you tomorrow?"

Carmen stood and gave Katie a quick hug. "For what it's worth, I hope you don't shut yourself off to the possibility of love so long you miss a good chance at finding it. Sometimes it's worth the potential heartache."

"That's what I keep hearing." Katie waved good-bye and turned to walk to her room. She knew Carmen was right of course. Denying yourself love wasn't any way to live, but once you'd built a wall around your heart it wasn't so easy to break. Katie was feeling things she knew could lead her further down that road, but while part of her wanted to dive right into the scary waters, another part wanted to run the other direction as fast as she could.

As she approached her room, she was more than a little tempted to say "fuck it," knock on Rhys's door, and spend the remainder of the night showing her exactly how she felt about her. Deep down she knew it would be a mistake on so many levels, and the last thing she wanted to do was give Rhys reason to hope for more than she was ready to give.

Once she was safely in her room, she dropped her things on the floor and collapsed into bed with a heavy heart. She could hear Rhys's TV next door and realized she was watching one of her own favorite shows, *Parks and Recreation*. Katie couldn't help but smile when she heard Rhys laughing at the ridiculousness happening on the TV and felt even lonelier as she wished they were watching it together. "Jesus, Katie, stop being such a sap." With a sigh of resignation, she removed her clothes and climbed beneath the covers.

When she closed her eyes she couldn't help but think of Rhys at the park that day as they stretched out on the grass and later when they held hands as they walked together before the van picked them up. In those moments she wasn't thinking about the future or worrying about what could possibly happen someday. She was only thinking about how good she felt resting her head against Rhys's shoulder and how adored she felt as they walked hand in hand. Maybe if she could allow herself to live in the moment more and not agonize over what could happen in the future she would be able to open herself up to the feelings and all the scary stuff that came with them? Maybe. She knew she wasn't there yet, but it was only Thursday. Katie vowed to talk to Rhys at their after-dinner walk the next night about how she was feeling. She realized in that moment she wanted to try with Rhys more than she had ever wanted to try with anyone since Amber. Maybe even more than with Amber. Her relationship with Amber had been fun at times and they'd loved each other, sure, but Amber never made Katie feel the way Rhys made her feel.

Katie knew she not only owed Rhys a talk, but she owed it to herself. With that settled, she allowed herself to drift off to thoughts of Rhys she'd never let herself imagine. Thoughts of a possible future that both scared and excited her. For the first time in years, that fear didn't make her want to run away.

## CHAPTER NINETEEN

Friday morning, Rhys woke with a throbbing headache. When they returned from their date the day before she had to get as far away from Katie as she could so she went to her room and felt sorry for herself. Wallowing in her sadness and frustration didn't seem to make her feel any better so she decided to turn on her favorite show and watch episode after episode until she fell asleep. Katie had been funny and charming on their date and made Rhys feel like she needed nothing else in the world than to spend one more moment with her. As they rode in the van on the way back from Chinatown, she felt like she was being torn apart.

With the light of the morning came the sobering reality that she was facing another round of seeing Katie and not being able to share how she felt for fear of scaring her away. The last thing she wanted to do was upset Katie, but she knew she had to do something to push herself through these last two days. No matter how right she knew she and Katie could be together, she couldn't make her love her. She had to move on.

Two more dates, and then Sunday they would head home and she would try to put this week and Katie out of her mind. She could at least try. She climbed into the shower to do her best to wash off the smell of sadness. Whoever her date was today, it wasn't their fault she had fallen for someone so completely unavailable. She couldn't even be upset with Katie. She had been honest with her from the start, and even though she sometimes seemed like the ice was beginning to thaw, she was true to her word and would always remind her there would never be anything beyond this week.

Rhys had come to the resort to find someone to spend her life with and had let herself fall for the one girl who didn't want the same thing. She wasn't surprised. She had a gift for making things harder than they had to be, and this week was just the latest in a long line of women she fell for who couldn't give her as much as she was willing to give. She had two more chances to find love this week and she wasn't going to waste them.

Once she was dressed, she jogged to the dining hall to grab a bagel and meet Katie for their scheduled morning joint envelope opening. "Hey, Katie." Rhys walked over to their normal table with a bagel in her hand. "Sorry I'm late."

"No problem." Katie pushed her plate of food away and turned to her. "Did you sleep okay last night?"

"Good. Yeah. Just fine. Ready to open our envelopes?" Rhys hated to seem short with her so she smiled to soften her words. She ripped into her envelope, then read the card indicating who her date for the day would be. "I'm going to the Marin Headlands with Addison. Nice. I love hiking around up there."

"Me, too." Katie opened her envelope. "Looks like Aubrey and I are getting massages. That's a bummer."

"You don't like massages?" Rhys asked.

"They're okay. I enjoy them when I'm with friends or family or someone I trust, but I don't know how I feel about being naked around someone I don't really know."

"You don't usually know the masseuse do you?" Rhys asked as she attached her name tag to her shirt and started walking toward the vans while still nibbling on her bagel.

"No, but that's different. They seem more like doctors and not someone I'm on a date with."

Rhys stopped and turned to look Katie in the eyes. "If you're not comfortable you should talk to the office and tell them you want a different date. You shouldn't do something you aren't comfortable with."

"I'll be fine," Katie said. They walked toward the vans again. "Thanks for your concern though. I appreciate you caring about how I feel."

Rhys stopped and turned to face Katie once again. "Always." She gave her a quick kiss on her forehead before waving good-bye and climbing into her van. As she walked to the back and sat in the last seat, she looked out the window to find Katie still standing next to the van with a smile on her face. Rhys wasn't sure how to interpret that but knew it would be foolish to read too much into it.

"Is this seat taken?" a dark haired woman asked as she indicated the seat next to Rhys.

"Nope." Rhys scooted down the bench to make room for the new arrival. "You must be Addison, I'm Rhys." As they buckled in and shook hands, Rhys was taken by the piercing blue eyes that stared back at her through long black lashes. Addison was beautiful, and she was rapidly feeling like a complete dork as she stared at her without being able to put words together to say anything.

"Nice to meet you, Rhys. Have you been to the Marin Headlands before?" she asked.

Rhys tried not to stare at the hint of cleavage that peeked out above a red-and-white plaid shirt unbuttoned just enough to expose the tank top underneath. "Marin, yes, Headlands before." The words were correct, but she knew as they tumbled from her mouth they weren't in the correct order.

Addison touched Rhys's arm. "I think we're going to have a great time today. You're adorable."

As the van pulled away from the resort for the short trip to the Headlands, Rhys smiled because she wasn't sure what else to do. She had to get control of her hormones before she made an even bigger fool of herself than she already had. If there was any hope of distracting her mind from thoughts of Katie, she hoped Addison would be it.

"Are you from the Bay Area?" Rhys asked as she tried to focus more on Addison's face and less on her boobs.

"I live in Petaluma so more North Bay, but technically, yes. How about you?"

"Born and raised in the City. I've never lived anywhere else, but I've spent lots of time in Sonoma County and I've had many dinners at Old Chicago Pizza in downtown Petaluma. I love that place." Now that conversation was starting to flow, Rhys felt more settled and thought she just might make it through the day without completely embarrassing herself.

"I love that place, too. We usually go there before we see a show at the Mystic Theater."

"We used to see an all-girl AC/DC cover band at the Mystic called AC/DShe who were awesome." The van pulled off the freeway and wound down the road to a parking lot.

"I've seen them like three times there. They haven't been around for a few years, but that lead guitar chick was so hot. One time she pulled me up on stage and ground her ass against me a little as she played. I thought I was going to pass out," Addison said.

"I think I'm going to pass out just picturing it."

Once the van parked, they disembarked and looked at the trail map posted at the junction of several paths. "Do you have a trail preference?" Addison asked as they studied their options.

"Not really, but what do you think about doing the lagoon trail around the Rodeo Lagoon and down to the coastal trail to the beach?" Rhys traced her proposed route on the map with her finger.

"Perfect," Addison said. "I like the idea of ending up on the beach and having some time to hang out and watch the waves. Do you come out here often? I've been several times, but it's so close to you in the city it's much more convenient."

"I don't get out as much as I would like. I love nothing more than being outside, but living in the city I tend to pretty much stay in one place. I live above my workshop so other than an occasional trip to the store, I don't leave much. Sometimes I need to get away from the hustle and bustle and I'll ride my bike up the coast to Bodega Bay or Jenner. The ocean calms me like nothing else so I gravitate to it when I need to clear my head." Now that they were out of the van Rhys was able to see Addison better and noticed that although she was about the same height as Katie, she seemed different in every other way. Where Katie was blond and compact, Addison was dark and delicate. The contrast was good. Rhys needed to get her mind off of her troubles, and spending the day with someone who seemed nothing like the object of her affection was the best way to do that.

"When you say bike do you mean motorcycle or bicycle?" Addison asked.

"A nineteen sixty-seven Triumph Bonneville named Bonnie. She's my pride and joy, but I probably spend as much time fixing her as I do riding her."

"Lucky her." Addison winked and Rhys felt her cheeks flush.

She cleared her throat and decided to go for it more than she usually would. "You should go for a ride with me sometime. Do you like to ride?"

"I love it, but I'm too chicken to get a bike of my own. I'd love to ride with you though. Anytime."

Rhys smiled at her as she started to sweat more from the flirting than the physical exertion of hiking. When she pulled her long-sleeved shirt off, she noticed Addison checking her out. She smiled and pulled the bottom of her shirt back down after it crawled up in her effort to pull the outer layer off. "Let's sit on this bench for a sec so I can put my shirt in my backpack if you don't mind."

"I don't mind. I wouldn't mind pulling out my water bottle and a snack anyway."

They sat on the bench as they each had a granola bar and water. "What do you do for a living in Petaluma?"

"My family owns a dairy farm that will eventually be mine someday. We're just a small family farm, but a few years ago my parents started making artisan cheese which has become the main purpose of our dairy at this point. We still sell milk to stores, but the cheese has become much more profitable. We sell to local retailers and a bunch of restaurants all over California." Addison stood and stretched while Rhys finished the last couple bites of her bar.

"That's so cool," Rhys said. "I hope I don't embarrass you by saying this, but it's totally hot that you're a farmer."

Addison linked her arm through Rhys's as they started back down the trail. "Not embarrassed at all, but I'm afraid it might not be as romantic as you think and I might not look as hot as you're imagining when I'm covered in dirt and cow shit. I spend a lot of my time looking a mess."

"Well, the Farmer Addison I'm picturing in my head is crazy hot and doesn't smell anything like cow shit. Let me have my fantasy, woman."

As they approached the end of the loop and started down the coastal trail, Addison squeezed Rhys's arm and slid her hand down to thread their fingers together. Rhys felt a jolt of excitement followed by a feeling of guilt as if she was cheating or something. She wasn't though. Katie had made it very clear she didn't want Rhys. She was going to have to get over it and just enjoy what Addison was willing to share with her.

"Let's stop here on the beach and have our sack lunches."

Rhys realized her mind had drifted off thinking about Katie, and she worried she may have been neglecting Addison. She had to do a better job of clearing her mind of Katie and being in the present with Addison.

"What do you do for a living?" Addison asked as they pulled out their packed lunches.

"I come from a family of woodworkers. I'll inherit the business someday, but for now I mostly only carve wood sculptures."

"That sounds awesome. I had no idea you were an artist. I would love to see your work someday."

Rhys took a bite of her sandwich and leaned back on her elbow in the sand. Addison scooted around and pulled Rhys's head into her lap as she lazily ran her fingers through her hair.

"That feels amazing." Rhys closed her eyes and luxuriated in the feeling of nails on her scalp. "Maybe I'll pick you up on my bike and take you to see the pieces of mine on display in Sonoma County. There's maybe four or five up there that I can think of right now. And you can show me how to milk a cow."

Addison picked up Rhys's hand where it rested on her stomach. She brought it to her mouth and planted delicate kisses all over her palm. "I suspect these strong hands are good at doing all sorts of things."

Rhys felt a flood of wetness between her legs and stood before things escalated any further. "Ready to head back?" She gathered their things and helped Addison to her feet.

"Sure," Addison said. "I hope I didn't make you uncomfortable. I can be forward sometimes, but I would never want to upset you."

"No, no, no." Rhys took her hand again as they walked. "I just wasn't expecting it and I'm wound a little tight right now. Totally not your fault. Sorry I'm such a dork."

Addison seemed to relax a little at Rhys's reassurance. "You're not a dork. I'm having a great time hanging out with you. I wish you had been my first date of the week and not almost my last."

Rhys struggled with her mixed emotions when she thought about how different her week would have been had she sat next to Addison that first evening instead of Katie. Would that have been better? Even though the thought of finding someone at the start who was funny and attractive and obviously interested in something more than a weeklong friendship was appealing, she wouldn't have wanted to miss out on the time she spent with Katie. She was with Addison now though and owed it to herself to see where this led.

"Do you want to ask the office if they'll put us together for our date tomorrow, too?" Rhys asked.

"I'd love that. At least we'll have a couple of days to hang out together before we have to go. Want to have dinner together tonight?"

This was the big test. She didn't want to abandon Katie when Rhys knew she would be expecting her, but she also didn't want to make her feel bad that she had found someone else to hang out with. What did it matter though? Maybe this would be a perfect opportunity to prove to Katie that she wasn't just pining over her and was moving on with her life. She would probably be happy to know Rhys found someone else and wouldn't be following Katie around like a lost puppy anymore.

"I would love to have dinner with you except I have a set dinner date with my friend Katie every night. Would you mind if she tagged along? I know it's not terribly romantic, but I hate to ditch her at the last minute and leave her to have dinner alone. I did that last night and I would hate to do it two times in a row."

"Are you and this girl dating?" Addison asked.

"Nope. Katie is super cool and I love hanging out with her, but we're just friends." Rhys pulled Addison against her side.

"Sounds cool then. I can't wait to meet her."

As they boarded the van for the trip back Rhys hoped she wasn't making a colossal mistake by getting Katie and Addison together. With any luck, Katie would appreciate the fact that Rhys had a new person to focus her attraction on, leaving their relationship exactly where she wanted it as just friends.

## CHAPTER TWENTY

Have you guys seen Rhys?" Katie asked Carmen and Brooke as they stood in the line for dinner.

"I saw her heading toward the office earlier but haven't seen her come in the dining hall yet," Carmen said.

Just as Katie finished loading her plate with a hamburger and fries, she saw Rhys enter through the side door and look around. She waved her hand to catch her attention, then turned to Brooke and said, "Found her. You guys have a great night." As they walked toward each other she noticed a beautiful dark-haired woman trailing behind with a finger looped in Rhys's belt. What the hell?

"Hey, Katie," Rhys said when they met in the middle of the room. "Addison is going to have dinner with us tonight. Do you mind?"

Of course she minded. Katie held her breath as she struggled to hide her shock. With herculean effort, she plastered a smile on her face and held out her hand to greet the interloper. "Hi, Addison, it's a pleasure to meet you. I'm Katie."

Addison returned her handshake with one hand as she wrapped her arm possessively around Rhys with the other. "It's great to meet you, too."

She wanted to smack this woman already. Who did she think she was putting her hands all over Rhys when she'd only known her for half a day? They must have had *some* date. A thousand pictures of Rhys and Addison kissing, Rhys and Addison laughing, Rhys and Addison making love flashed through her mind as her blood pressure began to rise.

"You go ahead and find a table and we'll be right there once we get our food." Rhys took her floozy by the hand and headed toward the food line. What the hell had happened? Katie had just seen Rhys a few hours ago and she hadn't known this woman existed. How could just a few hours in the Marin Headlands lead to them already touching each other and having dinner together even though Katie was the one who had dinner with Rhys? That was their special time together.

"You okay, sweetie?" Carmen asked as she and Brooke approached Katie who was still standing in the middle of the dining hall holding her tray of food. "Who was the woman with Rhys?"

"Her name is Addison, and apparently, she was Rhys's date today in the Marin Headlands," Katie said with a snarl.

"She's smoking hot," Carmen said. Both Katie and Brooke gave her looks that could kill. "Sorry, Katie."

Carmen turned toward Brooke and kissed her on the lips. "She's nowhere near as hot as you, my sexy little beast." They kissed again and pulled Katie with them toward their table. "Come sit with us," Carmen said. "They'll find you when they're done, and by the look on your face you're going to need backup."

Once Rhys and Addison had their food, they found Katie. "Hey, guys," Rhys said as they sat. "This is my friend Addison. Addison, this is Carmen and Brooke. They were matched day one and have been inseparable ever since."

"How sweet." Addison took Rhys's hand and kissed it. "I was just telling Rhys I wished we could have met on day one. I feel like I've wasted an entire week I could have been getting to know her. I guess I'm lucky they eventually got it right, even if it took them until Thursday."

Katie pushed back the urge to vomit as Addison gushed over Rhys. Half a day and she was already talking like they were soul mates. Katie looked at Rhys, but she wouldn't meet her eyes.

"Well, tomorrow you'll have one more chance to meet Ms. Right before the end of the week. Who knows who that will be?" Katie pushed her plate of barely touched food away.

"Actually, we talked to the front office when we got back from the Headlands and asked to be matched again for tomorrow's date." Rhys gave Katie an apologetic look.

Addison happily stuffed fries in her fucking gorgeous face as she smiled and informed everyone they would be going wine tasting the next day.

"How was your date today, Katie?" Rhys asked.

Katie had a terrible time with Aubrey that day and still felt gross just thinking about it. Aubrey tried to get frisky with her as they soaked in the mineral pools at the spa and acted offended when she was turned down at every attempt.

"It was okay. If you guys don't mind, I'm actually going to head to my room to wash all the oils and stuff off and get to bed early." Katie stood and walked away without looking back.

Once she was out the door and clear of the stuffy room, she sat on a bench, dropped her face in her hands, and began to cry. What did she expect? Of course someone else was going to find Rhys. Someone who was sexier and could offer her something Katie had very clearly told her she couldn't provide. It was extremely selfish for Katie to feel any kind of jealousy or anger at Rhys for moving on. She deserved more than Katie could give, and Addison was obviously more than willing to provide that for her.

"Hey." Rhys sat on the bench next to her. "You okay?"

Katie wasn't ready to admit the source of her sadness so she blamed it on the first thing that came to mind. "I'm sorry. That date today really threw me for a loop. Nothing terrible happened, but I just wasn't expecting Aubrey to be quite so aggressive with her attentions."

Katie could see Rhys puff up a bit and felt bad for blowing her emotions about the date up more than she was actually feeling. She was very creeped out about what happened, but she knew the root of her emotions at the moment had more to do with Rhys finding a beautiful woman who would love her than the asshole she went on a date with that day.

"Do you want me to talk to her?" Rhys looked around as if the woman in question was standing near them.

Katie smiled at her protectiveness but placed her hand on her arm to calm her. "I'm okay, really. She was a creep, but I'll never have to see her again so I'm totally fine."

"If you're sure." Rhys wrapped her arm around Katie.

"Addison seems super nice." Katie felt Rhys stiffen at the mention of Addison's name.

"She's very nice. Sorry I brought her to dinner without being able to give you much warning. Life without a cell phone is a pain in the butt sometimes."

Katie smiled as she felt her emotions slide back into their little bottle where she could control them better. "It's no problem. I'm glad you guys had a nice day. I think I'm going to go get that shower and hit the hay."

"Why don't you come hang out with us? We might play some darts or something."

The idea of forcing herself to play nice with Addison while watching her put her hands all over Rhys gave Katie a headache. "That's okay. I really think I'm just going to head to my room. Thanks for the offer though."

Rhys stood and held out a hand to help Katie to her feet. When they were both up, Rhys wrapped her in a hug and kissed the top of her head. "I hope your date tomorrow is better than the one today. If you need me to kick Aubrey's ass, the offer is still on the table."

"Thanks"

"Hey, Katie," Rhys said when she started to walk towards her room.

Katie stopped and turned to face her. "Yeah"

Rhys hesitated then shook her head. "Nothing, have a great night."

"You, too. See you tomorrow." Katie turned and continued down the path to her room, doing her best to hold the tears back that threatened to fall.

## CHAPTER TWENTY-ONE

The next morning, Katie stayed in bed longer than she should and had to rush to get to the dining hall to meet Rhys for breakfast. She wasn't sure why they were still meeting since Rhys already knew who and where her date would be that day, but since they hadn't talked about not meeting, she decided to go just in case.

As she entered the room, she saw Rhys and Addison sitting together chatting over breakfast, and the sight was a punch to the gut. Rhys was laughing at something Addison said.

Forcing a smile, Katie sat at the table with the two lovebirds. "Good morning, sorry I'm late." Not missing the look of irritation that flashed across Addison's face, Katie turned to Rhys. "I guess I'm the only one who needs to open a date envelope this morning. I'm ready to get this week over with."

Knowing the card was going to have some name other than Rhys sent a pang of sadness to Katie's heart. She could have been the one in Rhys's arms. They could have been going on a date, and instead she had to watch Addison drape herself all over her.

Katie pulled the card from the envelope and read her fate aloud. "Her name is Jennifer and we're going to Safari West."

"Safari West is awesome. Have you ever been?" Addison asked as she leaned over Rhys to spear a potato from her plate and pop it into her mouth.

Irritated by the forwardness of the woman, Katie gritted her teeth and took a deep breath before answering. "I haven't, but I've heard it's great."

"You're going to have a great time. I've been a few times. We even spent the night in the Safari tents once or twice. Will you come up on your bike and take me for an overnight in the tent sometime, baby?" Addison asked before brushing Rhys's bangs from her eyes and kissing her on the lips.

Rhys looked a little conflicted about what to say as she smiled apologetically at Katie and nodded at Addison before stuffing a forkful of pancakes in her mouth.

"What bike?" Katie asked, turning her attention to Rhys. "I didn't know you had a motorcycle."

Addison purred a little as she looked at Rhys like she would devour her. "I bet she looks crazy hot with her legs wrapped around that beast."

Katie had hit her Addison limit. She couldn't sit and watch this woman fuck Rhys with her eyes any longer. "Well, I'm out. You guys enjoy your day. Will I see you at the beach party tonight?"

"Yeah, of course, I'll see you there." Rhys stood to give Katie a hug good-bye, but with an awkward wave, Katie walked around the table and out the side door to the relative safety of the outside world. The crisp morning air helped to clear her mind as she looked for her van. She wouldn't miss this part of the resort for sure. The anxiety of not knowing what her date would be like was exhausting, and even though she understood some people would thrive in that type of situation, she felt like she might never date again.

Once she found the correct vehicle, she boarded and chose the middle bench seat. As she settled in, her date arrived and sat next to her. "Hi, I'm Jennifer," she said as she buckled herself in.

"Nice to meet you, I'm Katie."

Jennifer introduced herself to the other passengers and they all began chatting with each other while Katie looked out the window.

"I'm sorry, Katie," Jennifer said after a few minutes. "I'm talking to everyone other than you." Jennifer was an attractive woman. Katie guessed her to be in her late thirties with short brown hair and beautiful green eyes. Her smile lit up her face, and Katie wished she was in a different space where she could be more open to getting to know her instead of only feeling like crawling into bed and crying.

"No problem. I'm probably not the best company today anyways. I'm sorry you got matched with a dud on your last date," Katie said.

Jennifer picked up Katie's hand from the seat and held it between her own. "I know we've only just met, but do you want to talk to me about what put that frown on your face?"

Glancing around at the other passengers, Katie realized everyone else was engaged in their own conversations. "I'm not sure where to start. The simple truth is I'm a stubborn idiot who has probably let someone really special slip away while I was being a big chicken. I figured it out too late, and now she's found someone else."

"Ouch. I've been there," Jennifer said.

Katie couldn't believe she was spilling her guts to a stranger, but without her normal support group of friends and family, she was desperate to talk to someone and Jennifer seemed willing to listen. "What did you end up doing? I'm going to need you to give me a miracle broken heart fix if you don't mind."

"No pressure there," Jennifer said. "Unfortunately, my story doesn't have a happy ending which is why I'm here. They aren't kidding when they call it Last Resort."

"Since you're on a date with me on the last day I assume you didn't find anyone on the other dates?" Katie asked although she felt a little bad being so forward.

"I met several really nice women, and some of them I would absolutely date if my heart didn't belong to someone else. It's been a year since my girl left me, so my friends pressured me into coming here and diving back into the dating pool, but I'm just not there yet. They had good intentions, but I'm not ready and I'm not sure when I will be. I suppose that's dramatic and I will find someone, but the way I feel right now says it isn't looking good. So the truth is, you've been matched up with the dud today, not me."

Katie knew she should reassure her and tell her there would be someone else, but she just didn't have the energy. She was feeling just as hopeless herself. "Do you mind if I ask what happened to the evil woman who stole your heart?"

"As much as I would love to paint her with that brush, it would be completely unjustified. I'm the guilty party in this scenario, and it's a mistake I'll regret for the rest of my life."

"I'm sorry." Katie squeezed her arm.

"Thanks. It's my own damn fault. I blew it and now I'm just trying to live the best life I can. Now let's hear your story. What did you do and how are we going to fix this?"

"Well, the short version is I'm afraid of putting myself out there and failing. I'm afraid of getting my heart broken again so I stuff it away in a little corner and don't let anyone have access to the parts that really matter. My family forced me to come here this week, and I swore I wasn't going to let myself get caught up in the moment and do something I was only going to regret. So I didn't. I met a girl who makes me happy. Like truly, happy. She makes me feel like I don't really care what happens around me because as long as I'm with her, the world is just as it should be. She makes me laugh. She makes me want to pull out my old shriveled up heart and wrap it up in a bow and give it to her, no matter what happens after that." Katie's heart raced as her feelings for Rhys came flooding to the surface and tears threatened to spill from her eyes.

"She sounds great," Jennifer said. "Do you know how she feels about you?"

"I do." Katie's cheeks warmed from embarrassment. "She's much better at being a normal human and has made it clear that she feels the same way."

"That's good. Have you told her how you feel?" Jennifer asked.

Katie dropped her face into her hands as Jennifer rubbed her back in support. "I can't believe how stupid I am. I think it's been obvious how I feel, but I've told her over and over that a relationship isn't possible. I bet her one hundred dollars the day we arrived at the resort that I wouldn't fall in love, for Christ's sake. Who does that? What's wrong with me?"

"Someone who is afraid of getting hurt," Jennifer said. "That's who does that. Why don't you just tell her tonight at the beach party? It's going to be your last chance before you have to go back home. Not to sound like the voice of doom, but you'll regret it if you don't."

"I know you're right, but there's one more problem." Katie wiped her eyes. "I waited just long enough for her to give up and find someone else. I'm sure they'll be at the party tonight, and the last thing I want to do is cause a scene and possibly cause an issue for Rhys with Addison. She seems to really like this girl even though Addison acts like a horny teenager when they're together. I would say I don't get what Rhys sees in her, but the girl is super fucking hot. Like model hot. Way hotter than I can compete with."

"Do you really think Rhys would pick this woman over you because you think she is hotter than you? From what you've said of Rhys, I find that hard to believe. Besides, you're smoking hot yourself," Jennifer said.

"I don't. I know she wouldn't choose someone only by their looks, but when one girl has done nothing but prove to you how broken she is and the other is all in and looks like she should be selling lingerie, it's difficult to believe she would choose the chicken."

"I hear what you're saying, but I think you need to let her make that call. If she's the person you think she is, she deserves to know how you feel."

Katie sighed and leaned her head back against the seat. "That's the other problem. I don't even know how I feel. I've never felt like this before, and I think I know, but what if I'm wrong? What if I put myself out there and I was totally wrong?"

"First of all, welcome to the world of love. It always feels like standing on the edge of this cliff at first where you want to dive into the water, but the idea of jumping from that high scares the shit out of you. It sucks and it's wonderful all wrapped up into one scary bundle."

"You make it sound so appealing."

"It can be, and when it's right, it's the greatest thing you'll ever do. My opinion is that you need to go to this party tonight and try to get her alone to spill your guts. This is your chance. If it doesn't work, then it's not like you would have had her anyway, but if it does, it has the makings of a very happy life."

"Thanks, Jen, I really appreciate the chat." The van pulled into the parking lot of their destination.

"Anytime. Thank you for listening to my sad story."

"Will I see you at the party tonight?"

Jennifer pulled her shoe up to tie a lace that had come undone. "I think I'm going to skip the party tonight. I'm not really in that space right now."

"Are you sure I can't convince you to go?" Katie asked.

She smiled and kissed Katie on the cheek. "I'm sure, but I'll be with you in spirit. If you need to talk after, my room is 817. I'll be awake watching the *Ice Road Truckers* marathon so I'll be up pretty late."

"*Ice Road Truckers* has sucked me in more than once. It seems like such a silly show, but I can't resist the drama."

"Right? I love it." Jennifer waved at the women from the back seat to exit the van before them. "You're going to be okay, Katie. You need to trust that Rhys is the woman you think she is and take that first step. It's grand gesture time for you."

Katie felt more scared than she had before talking to Jennifer, but she did feel like she had a plan which helped her tremendously. Now she just had to put that plan into action.

## Chapter Twenty-two

R hys had finished cleaning herself in the shower several minutes before, but as she let the water rush over her head she hoped it would wash away the heartache she felt. She and Addison had spent a wonderful day wine tasting in Sonoma County before coming back to the resort for a quick bite to eat. She looked for Katie at dinner, but she was nowhere to be found. It was just as well. Addison acted like a different person when Katie was around, and Rhys wasn't eager to deal with that.

She suspected the possessiveness was because she picked up on the feelings Rhys had for Katie, but there was really no need. Rhys had no chance of Katie being brave enough to admit she felt the same so there was no reason to pee a circle around her when she was around.

Addison was a great girl, but Rhys couldn't see things lasting with her. Even if her heart didn't already belong to Katie, she didn't want a relationship with someone she couldn't see every day. Addison would never move away from her farm, and Rhys could never leave her family business so even though they were enjoying these last couple of days at the resort together she knew they would need to have a talk about expectations before they left for the party.

When she finally turned off the water, she heard a knock at the door. "Just a minute," she called as she slipped on a pair of boxers and an undershirt she found lying on the bathroom floor. It was a bit tighter than she liked to wear in public, but it would have to do for now.

"Who is it?" she asked as she padded across the carpet to the door.

"It's me, baby. Are you ready to go? You've been showering forever, and people are already gathering on the beach," Addison said.

Why Addison so quickly started calling her baby, she'd never understand. They'd only just met and had never even really talked about anything other than the idea they might hang out a few times after the week was over. Between the possessive behavior and the rush to establish themselves as a couple, Rhys was more and more confident that she needed to step back from Addison before things went much further. She liked Addison and could see them being friends, but it was becoming clear that unless Rhys pumped the brakes, Addison was going to be sending out wedding invitations by the time they left the resort.

Rhys opened the door so Addison could enter and was a little frightened to see the predatory look in her eyes. "Fuck, baby, maybe we should just skip the beach and have our own private party in your room. You look hot."

"Easy there, tiger," Rhys said, slowly backing away. "I promised Carmen and Brooke we would meet up with them. Let me throw some clothes on and we'll head out."

Addison stalked her across the room and slipped her hands into Rhys's boxers. "Can I just get a quick snack before we go?" She began to remove the final barrier between her and her goal.

The sudden warmth of Addison's hands as they slid against Rhys's bare skin made her jump. She gripped Addison's wrists to pull her hands from her shorts, then scrambled into the bathroom with her clean clothes and locked the door behind her. Rhys sat on the edge of the bathtub and tried to think of what to do. She liked Addison and didn't want to hurt her, but she was so not in the same space that Addison was. Even if Rhys didn't have feelings for Katie, Addison would be freaking her out right now.

"Why do you keep avoiding me, Rhys? Why won't you let me touch you?" Addison asked through the door.

Rhys sighed. This wasn't going to be easy. How in the world had she gotten herself in this situation in two days? Two days. She'd had women move quickly before, but this was insane. Rhys thought back on all of her interactions with Addison and tried to pinpoint something she might have done or said that would have given her the idea that she was ready for the U-Haul after only knowing each other for a few short hours. This was one of those situations where she knew she should just be direct with Addison and tell her to back the hell off, but the thought of hurting her feelings bummed her out. She was entirely too nice, and she knew that was exactly how she got herself in this jam.

When Rhys walked into the room, she found Addison sitting on the edge of the bed. She sat next to her and blew out a breath. "We need to talk."

"That would be nice." The frustration in Addison's voice was evident.

"I'm not trying to avoid you. I feel like we had a really great couple of days and I like you a lot, but things just aren't going to work between us."

Addison stood so quickly the movement almost toppled Rhys off the bed. "What are you talking about? Things are so good between us."

"Can I ask you a question?"

"What?"

Addison was angry, and Rhys did her best to keep her tone even to help calm the situation. "Would you ever consider living in San Francisco? Truthfully."

"Why are you asking me that? You know my father is grooming me to take over the farm."

"Exactly. And I'm taking over my family business." Rhys was silent to let the reality of their situation sink in.

"You wouldn't even consider a long-distance relationship?"

"I would if there was a possibility that it would eventually not be a long-distance relationship."

Addison sat back on the bed next to Rhys. "Okay. Can I ask you a question?"

"Sure."

"Does this have anything to do with Katie?"

Rhys rolled her eyes, frustrated that Addison would bring Katie into this. She couldn't deny that she had feelings for Katie, but a relationship with her wasn't ever going to happen so it was none of Addison's concern. "This isn't about Katie, this is about us and whether a relationship is something we could realistically have. It isn't. I really like you, Addison, but the reality of our situation is that we both have huge family responsibilities that make it impossible for us to ever be more than friends."

Addison was silent as Rhys pulled on her shoes. "You okay?"

"I'm fine."

The disappointed look on Addison's face tugged at Rhys's heart. "I'm really sorry, Addison. I'm not trying to be a dick here. I think you're a great woman and someone is going to be lucky to have you someday." Rhys slid closer to her and wrapped an arm around her shoulders. "And then you guys can have ten little farmer babies who will grow up and take over the family farm."

That brought a smile to Addison's face and she visibly relaxed, resting her head on Rhys's shoulder. "That would be really nice."

"See? I'm sorry you didn't find that person this week and I'm sorry she wasn't me."

Addison kissed Rhys's cheek. "Me, too."

"Are you ready to go hang out with our friends one last time?"

"You mean your friends," Addison said. "They don't like me, and I'm sure it has everything to do with Katie."

"Katie?" Rhys stood and checked her hair in the mirror once more before picking up her room key and walking toward the door. "Why would they not like you because of Katie?"

"Because she's in love with you. They're just being good friends. I don't blame them or anything, but it's hard to be around them when she's around. Will she be there tonight?"

Rhys stood by the door and waited for Addison to join her. "I'm not sure if she will or not, but she's not in love with me. Katie isn't interested in love, and even if she did feel anything, she wouldn't allow herself to act on it."

"You're blind, my friend."

"I don't want to get into it. It doesn't matter. If someone is rude to you, I'll take care of it. Let's go have a good time and enjoy our last night here before we have to rejoin the real world. Ready?" Rhys ushered Addison out of the room before any more talk about Katie could happen.

Addison took Rhys's hand as they walked down the trail toward the massive bonfire raging on the beach. Rhys grabbed a beer for herself and a hard apple cider for Addison before they wove their way through the crowd until they found Carmen and Brooke talking to some other friends.

"Hey, guys," Rhys said before giving them each a hug. "How long have you been out here?"

"We just came out a few minutes ago. Tammy and Cassandra were telling us they heard there's supposed to be a big storm tomorrow so we might try to get out of here pretty early to beat the rain."

"Really? That sucks. I have my bike so I'm going to have to try to beat it so I don't end up blown off the bridge."

"It can get dangerous across there, so you be careful, my friend." Carmen tapped her bottle against Rhys's and they all sat down in the sand to chat. "Where did you say you lived, Addison? On a farm or something?"

"Yeah, Petaluma on my family's dairy farm," Addison said.

Rhys listened as the others asked Addison questions about the farm. She did her best to focus on the conversation but couldn't stop herself from watching for any sign of Katie. What was she going to do about Katie? She knew it was probably a fool's errand, but they should talk before the night was over. Rhys didn't want to regret not telling Katie how she felt before they went their separate ways. It would be up to Katie where things went from there.

"Would you mind getting me another one?" Addison asked.

"Hmm?" The question pulled Rhys from her thoughts. "What was that?"

"Would you mind?" Addison waved her empty bottle in front of Rhys.

"Sure." Rhys quickly downed the last of her beer and excused herself to go to the drink table. She knew she should pace herself so she didn't do something stupid, but the slight buzz she was already getting helped distract her from her emotions.

"Hey, stranger."

Rhys popped the top off another beer and turned to find Katie next to her. The light of the bonfire flickered across her face, and Rhys felt her skin tingle with goose bumps.

"Hey," Rhys said as they shared an awkward hug. "How was your final date?"

"It was…not at all what I expected," Katie answered.

"That's cryptic."

Katie grabbed a bottle of whiskey to share with the group. "Jennifer and I had a really good talk. It was nice. She's a great gal."

"That sounds—" Rhys was cut off when Addison called her to come back to the group. "Come on, everyone's over there. You hanging with us?"

"Sure," Katie said. "Hey, do you think I can steal you away for a chat later? In private?"

"Rhys?" Addison called again.

"Sorry," Rhys said. "Absolutely. I wanted to talk to you, too."

"Perfect." Katie smiled as they walked toward their group, and it warmed Rhys's heart to know that smile was for her.

"Look who I found at the table with all the alcohol." Rhys laughed when they approached and everyone hugged Katie. "And we come bearing gifts."

"Whiskey?" Tammy took the bottle from Katie and opened it so they could all share. "Let's find a place to sit and start our own fire."

Once they'd gathered wood, lighter fluid, and matches, they found a secluded place between the dunes to start a fire away from the crowd. It reminded Rhys of the time she and Katie had spent between the dunes during their stay at the resort, and it made her sad that they'd never have a chance to spend that kind of time together again.

As they passed the bottle of whiskey around, they talked about the highs and lows of the week at the resort. Before long, someone pulled out a couple of joints and they began to pass them around as well. The more Rhys drank and smoked, the funnier everyone's stories became. When the bottle was finally empty, Tammy suggested they play a game of truth or dare. Rhys decided that was the perfect time to excuse themselves so she and Katie could talk, but as she opened her mouth to speak, Katie surprised her by agreeing to play the game. Curious, she decided to wait to see how it played out.

Cassandra was the first to spin the bottle which landed on Katie. "Katie," Cassandra slurred. "Truth or dare?"

Katie rubbed her chin as if she was in deep thought. "Dare."

"Ohh...brave one, aren't you?" Cassandra rubbed her hands like she was planning something truly evil. "Okay, I dare you to flash us your boobs."

"Seriously?" Katie asked. "I'm going to need another drink first." Carmen immediately handed Katie her beer, and everyone laughed when Brooke smacked her on the arm. Katie took two big sips before handing it back. Rhys watched intently as Katie slipped her arms into her shirt and removed her bra before pulling it out through a shirtsleeve and tossing it onto the fire. The entire sequence of events left Rhys slack-jawed as everyone cheered Katie on.

Rhys could feel Addison watching her intently so she did her best to seem casual about the whole ordeal. With her bra out of the way, Katie took a deep breath and pulled the hem of her shirt up to expose her breasts for a few seconds before slamming it back down.

Everyone around the fire went wild except for Rhys and Addison who hadn't taken her eyes off of Rhys the entire time. Rhys cleared her throat and took another drag from the joint she was handed before passing it to Addison, hoping it would distract her.

Once the laughter died down, Katie took the bottle and spun it in the sand. Rhys closed her eyes and pleaded with the whiskey bottle gods to not let it land on her. The entire situation was awkward enough already. When she heard the crowd yell Tammy's name, she let out the breath she'd been holding.

"Truth or dare, Tammy?" Katie asked.

"Truth," Tammy said immediately. "I don't trust that evil look in your eye so there's no way I'm saying dare."

Katie leaned toward Cassandra when Cassandra pulled her closer to whisper in her ear. Katie nodded when Cassandra pulled back. "Tammy, are you going to have sex with Cassandra tonight?"

Cassandra laughed as a grin spread across Tammy's face. "All signs point to yes."

Katie passed the bottle to Tammy so she could spin. It landed on Carmen who looked at Brooke then answered, "Truth."

Tammy thought for a moment before asking her question. "How soon after you met did you and Brooke have sex?"

"That's not fair." Carmen blushed. "You already know the answer to that one because you caught us in the act."

"Well, this just got interesting," Addison said. "Do tell and remember, you have to be honest."

"It was on our first date on the first day. Brooke and I really hit it off," Carmen began.

"That's an understatement," Brooke chimed in.

With a wink toward Brooke, Carmen continued. "Anyways, after we did the ropes course everyone was eating their lunches, and Brooke and I snuck back to the van and had sex."

"Which is where I caught them when I went to get a bottle of water," Tammy said.

"Wait," Katie piped up. "This was all going on while I was eating my sandwich and I had no idea? Please tell me you didn't do it on my seat."

Carmen assured Katie it was their own seat.

"I can't believe I'm only just hearing about this," Katie said to Brooke who sheepishly shrugged.

"Your turn to spin, Carmen," Tammy said.

"Can you toss me the bottle? I'm not sure I'm in any shape to stand right now," she said as the others laughed.

Rhys watched the bottle as it spun around in the sand, finally landing on her.

"Rhys," everyone said in unison. Fuck, she thought as she saw the evil glint in Carmen's eyes. Afraid she would ask her something about Katie if she asked for truth, she chose dare. The seconds felt like minutes as Carmen thought about what to dare her. Finally, she silently mouthed "sorry" to Rhys before saying, "Rhys, I dare you to kiss Katie on the lips."

The group fell silent. Addison sat up straight and looked at Rhys as if waiting to see what she would do. Everything seemed to move in slow motion as Katie stood and walked toward her. She ignored the warning bells going off in her head and got up to meet Katie halfway. They looked at each other for a moment before Katie placed her hand behind Rhys's neck and pulled her down for a kiss. It was meant to be a quick kiss. Carmen had only said they had to kiss each other on the lips, but at that first touch, the rest of the world fell away. Rhys was lost in the feel of Katie's body pressed against hers, of their mouths—

"Rhys?" Addison's voice cut through Rhys's cloud of lust. "What the fuck, Rhys? What are you doing?" The interruption pulled them out of the moment and back to the beach, surrounded by their group of stunned silent friends.

"Oh fuck." Rhys pulled away from a dazed Katie. She turned to see Addison storm off into the dunes. "Um, fuck, I'm sorry, guys. I have to…" Realizing she was an incredible asshole, she ran after her, leaving her friends behind.

When she finally caught up to her, Addison was crouched in the dunes crying. "I'm so sorry," Rhys said, kneeling beside her. "I'm a massive asshole."

"Fuck you, Rhys," she said. "I knew this was about Katie."

"It's honestly not about Katie. Not only about Katie, at least."

Addison rolled her eyes. "Why didn't I trust my instincts and realize this would happen? I knew you were in love with each other. I knew it. I tried to convince myself it was only her, but I saw how you looked at her. It drove me mad because I really liked you."

"I'm so sorry, Addison," Rhys said. "You definitely deserved better and there's no doubt I'm a huge dick. I shouldn't have let things get that far just now and I'm truly sorry."

Addison wiped her eyes with her shirtsleeve and released a breath. "I'm just embarrassed."

"I know. I have no reasonable excuse. I'm drunk and high and this has been an incredibly confusing week emotionally, but that's no excuse."

"Why weren't you just honest with me from the beginning?" Rhys knew she was right and didn't have a good answer as to why she wasn't up front with her from the start. "Because I'm chicken. I was afraid to admit to not only you but to myself about how much I'd fallen for Katie. I know saying this is only hurting you and I'm sorry for that, but I want to be honest."

"Now you want to be honest?" Addison said. Rhys could tell she was partially teasing her. "How do you know she doesn't feel the same way?"

"She's told me repeatedly that she isn't interested in love. My heart doesn't want to believe her, but my head can't pretend she wasn't more than clear about her feelings." She leaned back against the dune. She was starting to sober up as the events of the evening flashed through her mind, leaving her sick to her stomach.

"I know you say she's told you she doesn't love you, but I've seen how she looks at you, and that wasn't the kiss of someone who isn't in love. You can't convince me otherwise. Look, you're still an asshole, but for some crazy reason, I still like you. You've broken me of the spell I was under about you, but I would like to remain friends. I might need a few weeks to get the picture of that kiss out of my head, but I'll get over it." Addison playfully punched Rhys's arm.

"I get it," Rhys said. "I really am sorry about everything. I'm normally a really nice person who would never dream of breaking a girl's heart. That's just not usually me. I've never felt like I do for Katie and she has me all tied up in knots."

"You just met her. How do you know you love her?"

"I've known her twice as long as I've known you. Please don't be mad at me for asking, but why are you so upset about a relationship with someone you only met a couple of days ago?"

"Touché," Addison said. "My excuse is that I was hurt very badly by someone I trusted. I've closed myself off, and when I met you something just clicked. I felt something I hadn't felt in a long time, and I think I may have gotten carried away. Living on a dairy farm is a lonely life."

"For what it's worth, you deserve someone who can give you all that and more."

"What about you? What is it about Katie that has you all tied up in knots so quickly?"

"That's a good question," Rhys said as the events of the last week flashed in her mind. "It's not something I can explain. It's like I've been waiting for her to come into my life, and now that she's here, she doesn't want me."

"She wants you, Rhys. She's just not ready to admit it," Addison said with a sad smile. "You don't think it would be worth talking to her one more time?"

"I don't know. Maybe."

"I can't believe I'm giving you advice on your love life."

Rhys smiled. "We're friends, right?"

"Don't get too cocky. You still have a lot to make up for, buster."

"I agree," Rhys said. "And I promise to do my best to make amends. We better get back to the party. I suspect everyone is wondering what the hell happened."

"I think Carmen knew exactly what was going to happen." Addison stood and helped her to her feet. "You need to talk to Katie. If you don't, you'll regret it and I'll have to listen to you blather about it over coffee sometime in the future. If you don't mind, I think I'm going to just head to my room."

"No, I'm sorry, Addison. I hate that I've ruined your night."

Addison smiled and kissed Rhys on the cheek. "You didn't. I'm actually pretty tired and not looking forward to facing all those people again. I've made my dramatic exit so I'll just leave it at that."

"I'm sorry." Rhys felt terrible for upsetting Addison so much.

"Don't be. Talk to her, Rhys. She needs to hear you say it."

"I will." Rhys hugged Addison and watched her turn to walk back up toward the resort. "Hey, Addy." When Addison turned back toward Rhys, she blew her a kiss. "Thanks, friend."

Addison caught it and placed her fingers on her lips. "Drive safe going home tomorrow."

"You, too." When Addison was out of sight, Rhys walked back to where her friends were. The crowd had thinned around the main bonfire as others broke out into smaller groups on the beach. Rhys noticed Katie was gone. "Where did Katie go?" she asked Carmen.

"She said she wanted to go for a walk and headed back toward the rooms."

Brooke gave Rhys a quick hug and pushed her toward the trail to the resort. "Go get her," she said.

"Thanks." Rhys jogged away. She had no idea what she was going to say when she found Katie, and if the way her mind was spinning was any indication, it would probably be embarrassing, but at that point she didn't care. She had to get it off her chest, and Katie would either fall into her arms or break her heart. There really wasn't any in-between.

The first place she decided to check was her room. She knocked gently and called her name, but when there was no answer she knocked harder.

The person in the room next to her pointed toward another part of the campus. "She's not there. I saw her crying and walking that direction."

"Do you have any idea where she went?" Rhys asked.

"I don't but she was pretty upset. What did you do to her?"

Rhys sighed as she thought about the question. "If you see her will you tell her I'm looking for her? I'll be in my room."

"Sure, Rhys, see you around if I miss you tomorrow."

"Thanks, Janet, good luck with your new shop," Rhys said as Janet slipped back into her room. She had no idea what she should do. She thought about walking around looking for Katie but was afraid it would be silly to leave her room since surely she would come back there eventually.

As the hours passed, Rhys kept getting up to quietly knock on Katie's door, but she never heard a sound. She started to really worry when the sun began to come up, and she was just about to head to the office to see if they would help her search for her when she saw Casandra, bags in hand, going to check out.

"Hey, Casandra. Did you see Katie after the party? I'm getting really worried. She never came back to her room last night."

"Oh yeah, I think she went to Jennifer's room. She was pretty upset after that kiss. Maybe she's there?"

All the blood drained from Rhys's face and she felt like she was going to be sick. "Jennifer?"

"Yeah, she was Katie's date yesterday morning at Safari West. There's nothing between them, but I know Katie enjoyed talking to her so they probably spent the night trying to figure out what happened with that kiss," Casandra said. "Totally hot, by the way."

"Thanks," Rhys said, not sure how else to respond.

"See ya around, Rhys. Keep in touch." Casandra waved as she walked away.

Jennifer? Talking all night? Rhys knew Casandra was probably right and they were very likely only talking, but she wasn't sure if she should stay or go. Would Katie even want to see her if she was so upset that she spent the night in someone else's room?

Rhys decided to get herself packed up and ready to go and she would talk to Katie when she returned to her room. She had to at least try to explain herself before leaving it to Katie to decide what the next step would be.

A couple of hours later, the clouds started to move in as the promised storm arrived. Rhys didn't want to have to ride her bike back over the Golden Gate Bridge in a storm so she decided she couldn't wait any longer. Not sure what else to do, she pulled out a paper and pen and poured her heart out. When she was done, she folded the letter and slipped it under Katie's door. She walked around the main area once more before she had to check out of the resort. She'd done what she could and now all she could do was wait.

## Chapter Twenty-three

"Wake up, sleepyhead."

Katie opened her eyes to find Jennifer sitting next to her in bed, and the events of the evening before came rushing back. Ugh. "Oh my God, Jen. I can't believe I fell asleep."

"No problem. I'm glad I could be here for you. Are you feeling better?"

Katie slipped her legs off the side of the bed. "No." She'd poured her heart out to Jennifer the night before, and the light of the morning only brought more questions than answers. She needed to get dressed and find Rhys. She didn't want to leave without at least telling her how she felt. It would be up to her to decide what happened next between them.

"What time is it?"

Jennifer checked her watch. "Ten o'clock."

"Ten? It's barely light outside. Shit, shit, shit, my sister is picking me up at ten thirty. Fuck." Katie picked up her jacket from the back of a chair and started for the door.

"A huge storm blew in this morning so it's pretty dark and menacing outside."

Katie gave Jennifer a big hug. "Thank you so much for taking care of me last night. I was a mess. I hate that I have to run off like this, but let's be sure to get together for coffee in a week or so. I would really love to keep in touch."

"Me, too, and think about what I said. Don't cut your nose off to spite your face."

"I will. Thanks again, Jen." Katie shut the door and walked as fast as her barely awake legs would take her back toward her room. When she approached their building, the sky opened up and the rain began to pour. The thought occurred to her that she might not like what she found once she arrived. Even though it would break her heart to find Addison there, Katie knew she had to take that chance.

By the time she reached Rhys's door she was soaked to the bone. She brushed her hair back from her face but knew there was no way to help her already bedraggled appearance. *Here goes nothing.* Before she could talk herself out of it, she pushed the embarrassment aside and knocked. When there was no answer she knocked again, louder this time. "Rhys?" she yelled through the door. "Are you in there?"

"She's gone, sweetie," a voice said from a couple of doors down.

"Hey, Janet, what do you mean she's gone?"

"She was knocking on your door last night looking for you and then again this morning, but Casandra told her you were in Jennifer's room so she packed up and left. Something about the storm."

"Fuck." Katie tried to hold back the tears that threatened to fall. "Thanks, Janet. Maybe I'll see you around?"

"If you ever find yourself in Fresno, make sure you look me up. I own Janet's Reptile Shop on Shaw Avenue." Janet gave one final wave and rolled her suitcase toward the office.

"See ya, Janet." Katie quickly unlocked her door and stepped into her room. As she stood there dripping on the carpet, she tried to decide what her next move was. How was she supposed to find her? Why the hell didn't they exchange phone numbers before now? She knew the answer to that, but now that she actually decided maybe this was inevitable, she wished she'd gotten it just in case. As she bent down to take her shoes off she realized she'd been standing, and dripping, on a folded piece of paper on the floor. As she carefully brushed the dirt smudge from her shoe off the back, she pulled the wet paper apart to read what was inside.

"Shit." She wanted to cry when she realized who the letter was from. Most of the words were visible, but the rain had smeared some of them.

*Dear Katie,*

*I'm so sorry I wasn't able to say good-bye in p<smudge>. I'm on my bike and was afraid to ride it back over the bridge in this storm. Know that I would have given <smudge> see you once more. First let me tell you how happy I am we met. I can't believe it's only been a week since they took your cell phone and you thought you were going to die. Lol. I know this sounds insane, but the moment I saw you sitting at that table on day one I knew you were the girl for me. This crazy feeling came over me that I was finally home. I remember thinking to myself "There she is" as if I'd been searching for you my ent<smudge>ife and finally found you. It's like there's some force pushing us toward each other and it's impossible for us to resist.*

*We may have only met a week ago and have so much to learn about each other, but I know my feelings are true. You've been very clear since day one that you don't w<smudge> give your heart away. I totally get it. You're afraid of the pain that comes when you lose someone who is your world, but listen to me when I tell you that for me it's too late. I've fallen. I'm there and I know deep in my soul that we belong together. I'm here holding out my hand, and you just have to reach out and grab it. We may not have forever, but I promise to make every day we do have the best days I can.*

*I love you, Katie. I'm pouring my heart out and leaving it to you to decide what happens next.*

*Your loving and devoted monkey, Rhys G<smudge>dolyn Mo<smudge> (415)5<smudge>613*

"Fuck." Katie quickly threw things into her suitcase. Elise would arrive to pick her up any moment and she had no time to lament the fact that of all things smudged, the phone number had to be one.

She couldn't stop the tears from flowing down her face. Why had she been such a colossal idiot? Rhys was quite possibly the best thing that ever happened to her and she had fucked things up at every turn. Katie knew she had to fix this.

Once she'd stuffed the last of her things into her bag, she gave her room a once-over making sure she didn't miss anything before running to the front desk to check out. She knew she looked like a mess since she hadn't showered in twenty-four hours and had been at a bonfire on the beach, drunk and slept in her clothes since then.

"Thank you so much for staying with us, Katie." The woman behind the desk printed out a receipt and handed her the envelope with her phone. "Did you find love?"

The question seemed strange and she felt weird answering, but she wanted to be honest. "I think love may have found me." The woman behind the counter gave her a confused smile as Katie rushed from the office into the torrential rain, dragging her belongings behind her.

## CHAPTER TWENTY-FOUR

R ain soaked Rhys from head to toe on her drive home. Between the gusting wind and downpour, she wasn't sure she was going to make it at times. Once she was safely inside her garage, she peeled away her sodden outerwear and boots, grabbed her soaking wet duffel bag of clothes, and padded up the stairs to her loft leaving wet sock prints in her wake. The heater to her living space hadn't been on while she was away, and the chill of the room cut through to her bones.

She turned on the shower to let the water heat up and cranked up the thermostat before shedding the remainder of her clothes on the bathroom floor. The warmth made her skin tingle as the water beat against her chilled body. She closed her eyes as her mind drifted to thoughts of Katie. The drive had been so dangerous she wouldn't allow herself to go there before, but now that she was safe at home she felt the heartache once again. Her tears started to fall as she slid down the tile wall of the shower and curled into a ball on the floor as the room filled with steam.

She wondered if Katie had gotten her letter and if she had, what next? Her instinct was to scour the internet for a way to reach her, but she knew that would be a mistake and a little bit creepy. Rhys would be easy enough to find with the things she shared with her, and it was up to Katie to make the next move.

When she noticed her skin start to shrivel up like a prune, Rhys got out of the warm embrace of her shower and dressed in the most comfortable pajamas she could find. She wasn't going to start working until the next day, but she had a week's worth of emails and voice messages to catch up on before then. As she sifted through the Viagra ads and desperate pleas to help a poor Nigerian prince transfer millions to her bank account, she listened to her various voice mails.

Her eye doctor called to remind her she had an appointment the following week. Her cousin wanted to know what she should get their aunt for her birthday. The third voice mail was from the panicked director of the Eagle Lake Nature Center in Juneau, Alaska. Rhys had shipped the two large eagle sculptures for them before she left, and he was calling to say one fell off the truck as they were unloading it, breaking a wing from the majestic bird. The man was distraught and begged Rhys to let them fly her to Alaska as soon as possible to repair it in time for their grand opening.

Rhys knew the repair would be tricky but possible, and she thought the distraction of a trip might help keep her from obsessing over Katie. Without allowing herself to over-analyze her decision to go, she pulled out her phone and texted Max to ask if she could stop by. She lived in another part of the huge building that housed their family business, so while Rhys waited for her to arrive, she called the director back and told him she would be on the first available flight out.

A few minutes later, she'd booked a flight for that evening and emptied her bag of dirty clothes from the previous week so she could start packing warmer ones for her trip to Alaska. "Rhys?" Max called from the workshop floor a few minutes later.

"I'm up here," Rhys called back.

"Hey, how was last week? Did you bring back a wife?" she asked as she plopped herself on Rhys's bed and sent the neat stacks of clothes toppling to the floor.

"Watch it, jerk-off," Rhys said. "It was good, and no, no wife. It seems that's more difficult than you would think."

"Tell me about it," Max said as she watched her refold the clothes that fell on the floor. "Did you meet anyone you even thought might have potential?"

"That's a difficult question to answer." Rhys scoffed as she forcibly stuffed her clothes into the bag.

"Wait, aren't you supposed to be unpacking, not packing?"

"Oh yeah, I have to fly to Alaska tonight. Can you drop me off at the airport? One of the eagle sculptures I did fell off the truck and a wing broke off so they're flying me up for an emergency repair before their grand opening."

"Yikes," Max said. "That's a bummer. Those were incredible."

"I'll have to see the damage to know for sure, but I think I'll be able to repair it without it being too noticeable." Rhys zipped up her bag and headed to the computer to print out her plane tickets. "Want to take me to lunch before my plane leaves? I got a four o'clock flight out of SFO on Alaska Airlines. That gives us a couple of hours before I need to be at the airport."

"Sounds great. Then you can tell me about this difficult woman you met at the resort," Max said. "My car's out front."

Rhys picked up her bag and turned off her electronics as they walked to the car. "I never said she was difficult. She's actually funny, beautiful, smart, and a talented artist, but she's hesitant to let her guard down long enough to allow herself to love someone."

"Sounds like you had an interesting week." Max pulled out of the drive and headed toward their favorite brew pub.

"You could say that," Rhys said. Over the next two hours, she told Max the story of everything that happened the previous week including a general idea of what the letter she wrote Katie said. Max listened quietly, injecting questions periodically to get a full picture of the situation. When Rhys was done with her tale, she drank the last of her pint of beer and dropped her face into her hands. "What do you think? Am I doing the right thing by giving her space or am I stupid to not try to contact her?"

Max wrapped an arm around her and pulled her in for a hug. "I know it's taking every bit of willpower you have, but you really need to let her come to you. You've told her how you feel and it's up to her to decide what to do next. Except for that whole weird Addison thing at the end of the week, it seems like you've done all you can do. She'll come around, and if she doesn't, do you really want to chase after this girl forever? You deserve better than that, no matter how awesome she is."

"I know you're right. I want to try to control the situation because it's difficult to sit back and do nothing, but chasing after her will only lead to more frustration. This trip to Alaska is probably for the best. That will give her a little time to process things, and who knows, maybe I'll hear from her." Rhys knew the possibility of a message from Katie would be on her mind the entire time she was gone.

"That's the spirit." Max paid the bill and walked to the car. "It's the whole thing about setting the bird free and if it comes back, it liked you and wanted to be your bird, but if it doesn't then it was someone else's bird anyways."

"Wow, Max, have you ever thought about writing greeting cards?" Rhys teased her as they drove toward the airport.

## CHAPTER TWENTY-FIVE

K atie saw Elise's car waiting in the loading zone when she approached the parking area. Elise jumped out with an umbrella and popped the trunk so she could load up her stuff. After a quick hug, they both ran to get in the car. Once they were in and underway, Elise looked Katie up and down. "Jesus Christ, you look like a hot mess. What did they do to you? Were you kept in a dungeon?"

"Shut up, asshole." They both laughed. "We had a bonfire on the beach last night and I ended up getting pretty wasted and then crying my eyes out all night in my friend Jennifer's room."

"Are you okay, sweetie?" Elise asked as they drove toward their mom's house for Sunday lunch. "Was it that bad?"

"I don't even know where to begin," Katie said.

"I don't suppose you met anyone who lived up to your standards?" When Katie was silent except for a shy smile, Elise let out a whoop and beat her hand on the steering wheel. "You have to tell me everything," she said as they pulled into her mother's driveway.

"I'm only telling this story once, so we'll talk after dinner. Right now I have to take a shower and get a little sleep before I pass out," Katie said.

"I'm giving you a pass because you look like shit, but after dinner the kids are going to watch a movie in the playroom and you're going to tell us the entire story, start to finish. I'm so glad you're home. I missed you." Elise gave her a much needed hug before they got out of the car and entered their mom's house.

Once inside, Katie was surrounded by her family who showered her with kisses and love before she excused herself to shower and take a short nap. The warm water was possibly the best shower of her life as she felt the stress, sand, and alcohol of the previous night wash away. Even though she hadn't talked to Rhys yet, she reassured herself that everything would to be okay. It had to be okay. She didn't want to believe she'd messed up her one chance at happiness because she was stubborn.

Two hours later, Andy woke her up from her nap with a warm cup of tea and a hug. "Hey, I missed you." He pushed her bangs from her eyes. "You smell better than you did when you first got here, but you still have a hint of whiskey clinging to you. It sounds like you had a hell of a time at that resort."

"You have no idea. I feel like I've been through a war." Katie put on her slippers and they walked downstairs to their waiting family.

Once dinner and the dishes were done, Katie and the other adults sat on the covered porch with cups of hot cocoa and watched the rain fall over the San Francisco Bay. "I missed you guys," she said, looking around at the people she loved.

"We missed you, too, but spill. What the hell happened last week?" Katie's mom pulled her chair closer to her so she didn't miss a detail.

Katie took a sip of her cocoa and let the warm sweet liquid heat her from the inside as she gathered her thoughts. "After Mom dropped me off I went into the dining hall and found a chair in the back. I was checking my email when a woman asked to sit with me." Katie spent the next hour telling her family every detail she could remember from the breakfast and dinners with Rhys to the dates with her and the other women. She explained to them how Rhys had been honest about how she felt and how Katie had resisted at every turn.

"I could just kick your ass, Katherine Elizabeth Fausch," her mother said.

"Geez, thanks, Mom. Give me a chance to finish." Katie wasn't sure if the end of her story made her look much better. "So the last date was with a woman named Jennifer at Safari West. We had an awesome time. She was a wonderful listener and she helped me understand what an idiot I'd been."

"I like this Jennifer already." Elise poked Katie's leg with her foot.

"Me, too. So anyway, after our date I knew I had to talk to Rhys and tell her how I felt, but unfortunately I couldn't get her away from that Addison chick. By the time I got to the bonfire last night, Rhys and Addison were already there. I knew I wasn't going to make it through the night without liquid courage, so I grabbed a bottle of whiskey and we all snuck off between the dunes to start our own fire and talk about the week. One thing led to another, and after we polished off the whiskey we started playing truth or dare with the empty bottle."

"Jesus, you guys are like high schoolers. I love it." Andy poured himself more cocoa and passed the carafe to their mom. "Please continue."

Katie filled her own glass when the carafe came to her and took another sip. The next part of the story was still painful so she leaned back against the couch cushions and took a deep breath to try to force herself to relax. "So we were playing truth or dare, and the bottle landed on our friend Carmen who dared Rhys to kiss me." When everyone gasped, Katie burst out in laughter.

"You guys are so easy," she said. "Addison perked up and didn't look happy at all, but Rhys came over and gave me a real, honest-to-goodness kiss that pretty much melted my insides and left me in a puddle on the sand. And then Addison freaked out and stormed off into the dunes so Rhys ran after her."

"I hate that Addison bitch," her mom said.

"Me too, although she probably doesn't really deserve that. She seemed like a perfectly nice girl except for the fact that she kept putting her hands all over my woman and calling her baby and sweetie and shit. It's my own fault for being so slow but still. Hands off, bitch." Katie took another sip of cocoa. "So Addison and Rhys ran off into the dunes. I was still a little dizzy and confused after that kiss and I knew I needed to get out of there, so I went to Jennifer's room. She invited me in and listened to me as I cried my eyes out. I finally fell asleep around four in the morning. Jennifer woke me up about thirty minutes before I was supposed to meet Elise. I rushed to Rhys's room only to find she'd left earlier because she was afraid the storm would get so bad she wouldn't be able to ride her bike across the bridge."

"Wait," Elise said. "She has a fucking motorcycle? Why didn't you lead with that? I really like this girl, Katie. Do you think she'll take me on her motorcycle?"

"Someone needs to get a motorcycle of her own, but also, yes, I'm sure if everything works out she'll take you on her motorcycle." Katie rolled her eyes at the look of excitement on Elise's face. "Back to my story. I'm just getting to the good part. So Rhys wasn't there and I was ready to just sit in the rain and cry when I found this letter that had been slipped under my door. Of course I stood on it dripping just enough to smudge some of the words including her God damn phone number, but here it is." She handed the letter to her mother and listened as she read it aloud. By the end there wasn't a dry eye in the room.

"What are you going to do, sweetie?" her mother asked, handing the letter back to her.

"First thing tomorrow morning, I'm looking all over the city until I find her and beg her forgiveness. I love her so much and I don't want to waste any more time not being with her."

"Oh, Katie." Her mom wiped the tears from her eyes. "I've waited so long to hear you say that."

"What time do you want me to pick you up, sis? I'll take you to track this woman down. Let's see if we can find something on the internet first so we at least have an idea of where we're going," Andy said.

Katie pulled out her mother's laptop and entered *Rhys Morgan* in the search box. The first link that came up was her bio on the Morgan Woodworks Company website. There was a little write-up with an adorable photo of her covered in wood shavings and a link to her gallery. She showed the photo to her family and then clicked the link. She was blown away by the sculptures she found there. Why hadn't Rhys told her what an incredible artist she was? Katie was speechless as she clicked through the photos and received oohs and ahhs as she shared them with her family.

"I hate to break up the party, but I better get to bed so I'm fresh as a daisy tomorrow. Want to just stay here tonight, Andy, since it's raining?"

"That sounds good. We'll go to her shop in the morning." He stood and stretched.

Katie's mom hugged her and planted a loving kiss on her forehead. "I'm proud of you, sweetie," she said. "Where are your clothes from last week? I'll wash them and have them ready for you to take home with you tomorrow morning."

"You don't have to do that, Mom," Katie said. "But I'll get my bag out of the back of Elise's car if you insist." They all laughed as she went to get the bag. She was happy to be home and with her family, but the anxiety of what would happen the next day left a lump in her throat. As she laid her head down to sleep that night, she swore she wasn't going to waste one more day not doing everything she could to make Rhys a part of her life.

## CHAPTER TWENTY-SIX

Katie woke up Monday morning in the warm embrace of her childhood room. Her mom hadn't changed anything since she'd left for college so the walls were covered in photos of teen magazine heart-throbs, unicorns, and posters of her favorite bands. She looked around and tried to remember what young Katie thought the real world would be like. Young Katie was much more open to the idea of love and all the magical things involved in belonging to someone. She wasn't sure if it was possible, but she hoped she could inject some of the idealism she'd felt as a child into her situation with Rhys. She wanted nothing more than to live happily ever after, but part of her still feared the potential pain loving someone could bring.

For the first time in her life she knew it was worth the risk. *Rhys* was worth the risk, and she wasn't going to let her fear control her and ruin her own fairy tale ending. With unfamiliar optimism in her heart, she jumped from the bed determined to do everything in her power to find her girl.

When she arrived in the kitchen Andy was eating the breakfast their mother had prepared for them. "Hey, guys." She picked up a pancake and stuffed it into her mouth. "Let's hit it, Andy. We're burning daylight."

"Someone's an eager beaver. Anxious to get laid?"

"Don't talk like that, Andrew Fausch," their mother said. "Show your sister some respect."

"Thank you, Mom." Katie smiled at Andy in triumph. "At least someone is looking out for me."

"I expect you to bring Rhys to lunch this Sunday."

Katie chocked on her pancake as Andy laughed. "Mom. I don't think we're at that point yet. I don't even know if she's going to want to see me again. I could have totally screwed up any chance I have and she wants nothing to do with me."

"That's nonsense. Of course she wants to be with you and we want to meet the girl who finally won our Katie's heart."

"Mom…"

"Don't whine, Katie. Go find that girl and make this right."

Unsure what to say that wouldn't dig the hole deeper for herself, she kissed her mom on the cheek and waved for Andy to follow her out the door.

"Good luck, sweetie," her mom called after her.

The moment they were safely alone in the car, Katie groaned in frustration. "Why is Mom so hot for me to bring her to lunch?"

"Why do you think? She wants to meet her, and she knows if we left this up to you, we won't meet her until your wedding."

"That's not true," Katie said with more conviction that it deserved. She wouldn't wait that long. Sunday lunch might not seem like that big of a deal to her mother, but to Katie, it was a really big deal. She hadn't taken Amber to lunch at her parents' for the first two years of their relationship. Amber had only gone a handful of times their entire relationship. If Katie was honest with herself, that was more Amber's doing than hers though.

Katie had wanted Amber to be more involved with her family, but she'd never been interested. The few times she went were extremely uncomfortable because Amber obviously didn't want to be there, and even though her family did their best to hide their opinions, it was clear they weren't impressed.

The idea that Katie would settle for someone who treated not only her family, but her with so much disrespect was ludicrous. She was so embarrassed about that part of her life and the person she'd allowed herself to become. Rhys wasn't Amber and the old Katie was gone. She would never tolerate that from someone anymore and she knew deep in her soul that Rhys would never be that person. It wasn't difficult to imagine Rhys in her life. She knew her family would absolutely adore her, and nothing about a relationship with Rhys would be like what she had with Amber. If she was ever going to move on, she needed to let go of the hurt Amber caused and allow herself another chance at a happy life with a partner who wanted to be with her for who she was.

"You okay?" Andy asked.

Katie smiled and slowly blew out a breath. "Yeah. I think I just might be."

"Good, now why don't you navigate us to where we're going, copilot. You have a girl to find and woo off her feet."

As they made their way across the bridge and into the city, Katie looked up the address of the Morgans' shop. After punching it into the GPS, she sat back and listened to the radio play Brandi Carlile. Her stomach was in knots thinking about what she would say when they got there. She stared out the window and watched the buildings pass by in silence. She somehow felt an overwhelming sense of loneliness she couldn't explain. What if Rhys told her she was too late? Would she beg? She'd beg if it came to that. She had no pride left as far as her feelings for Rhys were concerned. She'd do anything it took to convince her. Without a word, she felt Andy take her hand. She hadn't asked for it, but he knew she needed it. She loved that he knew.

Andy parked on the street outside the building and turned to her. "I'll wait here. Just shoot me a text if you're good and it's okay for me to leave. I love you, Katie. I know this is scary, but you deserve happiness. Now go get her."

Katie opened her door. "I love you, too. I really, really do. I'll let you know what happens. Thank you." She took a deep breath and climbed out of the car.

The reception area of the Morgan Woodworks Company was nice with a small couch, a couple of potted plants, and a water cooler. Katie walked up to the desk where she found a young woman on the phone who quietly mouthed "One sec, sorry." as she held her hand over the phone's mouthpiece. Katie sat on the couch and looked around the room. Several photos of sculptures she recognized from Rhys's online portfolio adorned the walls along with family photos. Katie stood to study them closer as she waited. Rhys definitely favored her father while the attractive woman she assumed was Max favored their mother. She felt her heart skip as she stared at Rhys's smiling face.

"I'm so sorry, how can I help you?" the woman asked when she got off the phone.

"Hi, my name is Katie Fausch and I'm a friend of Rhys Morgan's. Is it possible to talk to her?" Katie felt strange making a personal request in a business setting, but she couldn't think of how else to do it.

"I haven't seen Rhys today. Let me see if I can track her down." The woman picked up the phone and asked someone on the other end where Rhys was. When she hung up the receiver she asked Katie to have a seat and told her someone would be right with her.

A few minutes later, Max came into the office and immediately wrapped Katie up in a hug. Startled, she stiffened and looked up at her with astonishment. "Oh, God." She backed away. "I'm so sorry, that was totally inappropriate. Rhys is going to murder me for freaking out her girlfriend."

*Girlfriend?* Confused, Katie held out her hand as she introduced herself. "You must be Max. I'm Katie Fausch."

"You're exactly as she described. Rhys is going to be devastated she missed you." Max led her through a side door and into a hallway lined with offices.

"Is she not here today?" Katie asked as disappointment settled over her like a cloud.

Max led her into a comfortable lounge area that appeared to be a break room and invited her to sit on a black leather couch while she sat across from her in a chair. "She had to make a last-minute, unexpected trip to Alaska yesterday after she got back from the resort. She barely sat down before she heard the voice mail left by the director of some animal place that broke one of her eagle sculptures and desperately needed her to go up and fix it before their grand opening. She had to dump her dirty clothes out of her bag and pack warmer ones right away. We had lunch before her flight, and she gave me the rundown of everything that happened last week."

"Oh." Katie looked away in shame.

Max gave her a sympathetic smile as she stood and offered her a glass of water. "No, thanks," Katie said. "My brother is actually waiting for me in the car so I should get back out there before he thinks I've been kidnapped."

"Let me walk you out. I'm so sorry she wasn't able to be here. Disappointed won't even come close to how she'll feel when she finds out she missed you. If you don't mind me saying, I've seen her date a lot of women, but I've never seen her like this. I'm not trying to freak you out, but I want you to know that Rhys is the best person I know and she deserves someone who will appreciate and love her." Max smiled, but Katie could hear the message she was trying to impart.

"I've never felt this way about anyone," Katie said. "I don't know what our future holds, but I understand what you're saying. She's the best person I know, too, and I hope to have the chance to show her how much she means to me."

Beaming now, Max opened the car door for her as she climbed in. "Hi, I'm Max," she said.

"Hey, Max, I'm Andy. If Rhys is half as cute as her sister, you've scored, Katie." Andy gave Max the sexiest smile in his arsenal.

"Jesus, control yourselves." She knew Andy was bisexual, but it had been so long since he'd been with a woman she'd forgotten. She wasn't surprised Max would catch his eye. She was strikingly beautiful in a slightly more masculine way. Exactly Andy's type.

"It was a pleasure to meet you, Katie. I'm sorry Rhys wasn't able to be here, but I'm sure she'll look you up as soon as she's back." Max pulled out her phone. "Why don't you give me your number so I can have her call you?"

"Phone number. Can I get Rhys's number from you? The paper she gave it to me on was waterlogged and the number was smudged," Katie said.

"Totally." Max entered Rhys's number into Katie's phone for her. "Now what's yours?" She held her own ready to input the numbers.

Andy reached over Katie and took Max's phone from her hands to add his own number to her contacts. "I'll give you mine just in case you ever need anything I can help you with."

"Do you even know what the word subtle means?" Katie asked. Andy handed the phone to her so she could add her number as well.

"Wait," Andy said. "I think I was distracted by Max's smile and totally missed something. Rhys isn't here? Why don't we just wait? I wouldn't mind chatting with Max a little more."

"I'd like that very much," Max said, smiling at Andy.

"I've never been so uncomfortable in my life," Katie said. "Maybe I should call an Uber and leave you both alone."

"I'm sorry, you're right. Focus. This is about you. Where's your lady love?" Andy asked.

Max gave Katie an apologetic smile and explained to Andy where Rhys was. At that point Katie just wanted to go back to her apartment and bury her face in her pillow. What had started out as a hopeful day was turning into an exercise in frustration.

"Well, this is just silly. You've got a bag full of clean clothes thanks to our awesome mother so I'll take you to the airport. Do you know what hotel she's staying in, Max? There can't be that many hotels in Alaska, right?" Andy asked.

Max was obviously excited about Andy's new plan, but everything was happening so fast, Katie was having a difficult time keeping up. "Just fly to Alaska? Just like that?" she asked.

"Yes," Andy and Max answered in unison. "She's in Juneau at the Eagle Lake Nature Center," Max said. "I don't know what hotel offhand, but our receptionist would know. I'll go ask her and text you the details including her return flight so you can try to get a seat back with her. I'm going to keep this all a secret so she's surprised. When she realizes you've gone to Alaska to find her she's going to lose her shit. I'm so freaking excited."

"When you guys have babies, your first son must be named Andrew Max Fausch-Morgan after his aunt and uncle who made it all happen," Andy said.

"You guys are out of control." Katie tried to calm her heart and think about what she was going to do. Max and Andy quietly stared at her waiting for an answer until finally she realized there was only one thing she *could* do.

"Fuck it. Send me the flight information. Thanks for all your help, Max. It was a pleasure meeting you, and if all goes well, I'm sure we'll see much more of each other in the future," Katie said. Max and Andy winked at each other. "If Rhys doesn't think I'm stalking her by chasing her to Alaska, you'll see more of my twin, too."

"I would really like that." Max gave Katie a quick hug and shut the door so Andy could get her to the airport.

What the hell was she doing? This was by far the craziest thing she'd ever done but also nothing had ever felt so right.

## CHAPTER TWENTY-SEVEN

Rhys took a deep breath as she connected the eagle's wing to the prepared shoulder of her sculpture. Lucky for her, the break had been clean which allowed her to carefully flatten out the two pieces, drill holes for dowels, and glue the pieces back together. Tomorrow the glue would be dry and she would be able to do the finish work. With any luck, the seam of the break would be almost undetectable unless you knew it was there.

She put so much emotion into every piece it broke her heart to see one damaged, but she knew they were lucky it wasn't much worse. The moving company the director of the Eagle Lake Nature Center had hired to transport them from the airport to the center was picking up the bill to fly Rhys here to complete the repair.

She'd only been in Alaska one day, but it seemed like a lifetime because she'd spent it struggling to focus on her work and not Katie. Rhys wondered if Katie was back at work. She imagined her sitting at a desk, sketching ideas for greeting cards that would eventually be sold to someone and given for a graduation or birthday. She decided to google her when she returned to her room to see if she could find any of her designs. While waiting in Seattle for her connecting flight to Alaska, she'd done a brief search for "Katie Fausch," but she'd been so exhausted from all the travel she wasn't able to search very long before falling asleep in her chair.

"Hey, Rhys," Jeff, the director of the center, said as he checked her progress. "This looks great. I can't wait to see what it looks like when you're done. Both pieces are amazing, and we couldn't be happier with them. They're going to be perfect guardians on either side of the entrance to our visitor's center. Sorry we let it get broken."

Rhys wiped the little bit of glue that had seeped out through the seam when the pieces were pressed together. "No problem at all. I'm glad I was able to help. I had just come back from a week at a resort when I heard your message so I'm glad the timing worked out. I'll need to let this dry overnight, and tomorrow I'll work on making that seam disappear."

"Great. Hey, some of us are going to the pub tonight to get a beer and a little mediocre food. Are you in?"

Rhys put her tools away and cleaned her work area. "Thanks, but I think I'm going to head back to my room to watch some TV." Part of her wanted to go out. Jeff seemed like a really great guy, and the others she had met were nice as well, but she knew she wouldn't be much company with thoughts of Katie crowding her mind.

"You can't come all the way to Alaska and not have a duck fart and a Moosehead," Jeff said.

The distraction of being in a crowd of people might be just what she needed so Rhys decided she could allow herself a break from her moping for a few hours. "I'm a little afraid of this duck fart thing, but I guess I could be talked into one beer before I head back to my hotel."

"Awesome," Jeff said.

Rhys washed her hands in the utility sink and grabbed her coat. The bar was just down the road so they didn't bother driving. Since her hotel was across the street from the Nature Center, she looked forward to being able to have a couple of drinks without worrying about how she would get home.

They entered the bar through a set of old west saloon style swinging doors. Rhys did her best to take everything in as she looked from floor to ceiling at the craziness that was Alaska. A giant mounted moose head hung behind the bar surrounded by every oddity you could ever imagine. A giant mural of a mountain range adorned the back wall, and Rhys wondered if Katie enjoyed painting landscapes. She should have asked her when she'd had the chance. She sighed and shuffled behind Jeff into the crowded bar.

"We have a regular table," Jeff said as he led them toward the back of the bar. He waved at a waitress as they sat. Rhys was handed a menu and shook her head at the overabundance of options. She guessed when you lived somewhere without many restaurants, the ones you had probably offered as much variety as they could.

"Rhys, do you trust us?" Jeff asked.

"I'm not so sure, but why not? When in Rome, I guess," she said.

"That's the spirit." He smiled and took the menu from her hands. "Vicki, we'll need two smoked salmon flat breads, a basket of king crab legs, three baskets of cheese curds, three pitchers of Moosehead, and a round of duck farts. Our friend here is from California so we need to show her how Alaskans do it." Jeff patted Rhys on the back a little harder than she was expecting.

"I have a feeling I might regret agreeing to this little excursion."

"I hope you're wrong," the small raven-haired woman sitting next to her said.

Rhys turned to her and smiled. "I'm sure I'm just overly dramatic. I'm Rhys."

The woman blushed as she shook Rhys's outstretched hand. "I'm Vanessa and I know exactly who you are, Rhys Morgan. We've been following your work for years. Jeff was ecstatic when you agreed to do the eagle pieces for us. You're amazing."

"Really? You guys have been following my work? I've waited my entire life to hear someone say that. Thanks, Vanessa." Rhys beamed as she thought about what Max's reaction would be when she told her this story. She wasn't going to believe her so she was tempted to ask Vanessa to let her take a video of her saying it but decided that would be weird.

"I've seen photos of you on your site, but if I'd realized how hot you were in person I might have pushed Jeff to commission a sculpture from you even sooner."

There was a definite flirting vibe in Vanessa's tone, but Rhys wasn't exactly sure how to react under these circumstances. "Well,

I'm glad he finally did. This is my first visit to Alaska and even though I haven't been here very long, it has exceeded my expectations." Rhys didn't miss the hopeful glint in Vanessa's eyes. Oh shit. That may have sounded flirtier than she had intended. "The little bit of scenery I've seen has been unbelievably beautiful."

"Oh really?" Vanessa purred.

"The mountains and stuff, and the ocean. I wish I had more time and I'd thought to bring my camera." Rhys was digging herself a deeper hole and she had no idea how to stop so she turned toward to the person on the other side of her, hoping to give Vanessa the hint that she wanted to talk to other people, too. Of course the person on the other side of her was Jeff and he was in the middle of a conversation with someone else. Ugh.

Vanessa lifted Rhys's hand from where it sat on her thigh and turned it so she could study her palm. "Very interesting," she said as she traced a line along a crease with her finger.

"Does it say I'm going to die someday?" Rhys joked, begrudgingly turning back to her.

Vanessa's seductive smile would have pulled Rhys in if she'd met her a month earlier. She was a gorgeous woman. Stunningly gorgeous. But that was before. Rhys worried in that moment she might not ever fully get over something she'd never even had with Katie.

"Do you want to know what I'm reading?" Vanessa's voice brought her back to the moment.

"Sure." Rhys tried to pull her hand away with no luck.

Vanessa leaned closer than Rhys was comfortable with and whispered in her ear. "It says you're going to get laid tonight."

Rhys managed to pull her hand away and stick it safely in her jacket pocket. "Well, that's something my palm would surely know."

With her lip extended in a pout, Vanessa tried to pretend she wasn't as hurt as Rhys suspected she was.

"I'm sorry," Rhys said. "Under normal circumstances I would jump at the opportunity to spend the night with a beautiful woman like you, but unfortunately I'm in a weird space right now."

"I get it," she said. The scowl on her face had eased into embarrassment. "Sorry, I didn't see a ring so I thought I would take a chance."

"I'm flattered, but we're going to have to just be friends."

When the waitress returned she was followed by two busboys helping her with the food and drinks. "Here you go, guys. I'll be right back with the duck farts and third pitcher of beer."

A couple of minutes later, Vicki returned with a tray of tiny little yellow plastic ducks. She handed one to each person at the table and winked at Rhys before tucking the tray under her arm. "Good luck, California. These fools will have you stumbling home after midnight if you let them."

Rhys took a moment to study the plastic duck sitting in front of her. It appeared to be a normal toy duck except for the hole cut in the top to allow liquid to be poured in. "What am I getting myself into?" she asked.

"It's one part Kahlua, one part Baileys Irish Cream, and one part whiskey," Jeff explained. "Put that little duck ass to your mouth and pucker up."

Rhys laughed when she realized a hole had been drilled into the ass end of the toy big enough to suck the alcohol from. "Holy shit, you guys are a weird bunch." Rhys placed the toy to her lips and sucked.

"Huzzah." Everyone cheered as they followed her lead.

Jeff ordered another round of shots and two more pitchers of beer when the food arrived. Having grown up in San Francisco, Rhys was no stranger to crab, but she'd never had anything like the crab in Alaska.

"Jesus Christ, this is amazing."

Vanessa wiped a stray bit of food from Rhys's chin. "You're adorable."

It would be so easy to just allow this woman to ease her troubles. It wasn't like Katie had wanted her. At this point she doubted she'd ever see Katie again, and she couldn't lock herself away in a tower, never to feel the touch of a woman again. Jesus, she was being dramatic. Rhys smiled at Vanessa and held up the tiny plastic duck containing the liquid that would help her forget her broken heart.

"To duck farts and new friends."

Vanessa tapped her duck's bill to Rhys's as if giving it a kiss.

"To new friends."

They both sucked down the shot, quickly chased with almost an entire pint of beer. The buzz from the alcohol allowed Rhys relax a little but didn't do anything to ease the pain she felt in her chest. God, what a freaking sad sack she was. Was it natural to feel physical pain from a broken heart? She'd never experienced anything like this. She thought she'd been heartbroken before, but nothing compared to the damage done by a woman she'd only known a week. Rhys felt pathetic.

"Let's do another shot with a Moosehead chaser," Jeff said.

Rhys held up a hand in surrender. "I can't. Thank you guys so much for introducing me to your weird ass Alaskan customs, but I have to call it a night or I'll never get up in time tomorrow to finish the eagle."

Jeff stood and hugged Rhys. "Thanks so much for helping us and for coming out with us tonight. I'll see you tomorrow, but if I forget to say it, we're honored to have your sculptures here at the center. They're truly amazing."

Rhys felt her cheeks warm with blush. She'd never been comfortable accepting compliments, and this trip had been full of them. To be honest, her ego had taken such a beating over the last few days the appreciation was very welcome. "Thanks, Jeff, it's been my honor and I hope to come back someday when I can spend more time exploring your amazing area."

"You're welcome any time. Do you need help getting back to your room?"

Jeff was a kind man and Rhys really did hope to visit again someday. "I'm good. I think I stopped the duck farts before I hit the point where I can't find my way home. You guys have an amazing night."

Everyone waved good-bye before going back to their own conversations, but Rhys noticed Vanessa slide out of the booth and walk toward her.

"Hey," Vanessa said when she caught up to Rhys.

"Hey, Vanessa. It was really nice to meet you." Rhys held out her hand to shake.

Vanessa wrapped her arms around Rhys's and squeezed. "If you ever work through whatever has you holding back, come back to see us. To see me." Before Rhys was able to reply, Vanessa kissed her on the cheek and jogged back over to her friends. Rhys knew the attention should have made her feel good, but at the moment, it only made her feel even lonelier than before. She couldn't go on like this without at least talking to Katie. As she walked back to her hotel room she decided that as soon as she got back home she'd find her and ask her out for coffee. It wasn't everything that she wanted, but she missed her so much that at this point she was willing to only be friends if that's all Katie wanted. Anything to just have her in her life.

## CHAPTER TWENTY-EIGHT

Katie was a nervous wreck as she sat in her room waiting for Rhys to return. She had arrived in Juneau around five in the evening and headed straight to the hotel thinking Rhys would either be there or would at least arrive soon. Not exactly sure what she should do and not wanting to make embarrassing assumptions, she checked in and got her own room across the hall.

Once she dropped off her bags and freshened up a little, she took a deep breath and knocked on Rhys's door. When there was no answer, she knocked again. Realizing no one was there, she went back to her room and waited. A half hour later, she knocked again but still no luck. By eight she was hungry so she headed down to the hotel restaurant and had dinner. When she was done, she knocked again and still no one answered. Finally, she decided she was probably driving their neighbors crazy so she wrote Rhys a letter.

*Dear Rhys,*

*Enclosed you will find the crisp one-hundred-dollar bill I owe you for losing the bet we made on the day we met. You were right, I met someone at the resort that I adore, but I'm such a huge idiot I may have let her get away. I spent the week trying to convince myself I needed to stick to these stupid rules and restrictions, and in doing so I completely ignored what my heart so clearly knew from the start.*

*I belong to you, Rhys Gwyndolyn Morgan. I feel as if I've belonged to you since the day I was born and the universe is finally catching up. I've never in my life felt the way I feel when I'm with you, and it took me too long to admit to myself how much I liked it. How much I need you. I can be stubborn, and sometimes it takes me a minute to see what's right in front of my face. You said in your letter that you're holding out your hand and I just have to reach out and grab it. I'm grabbing it and I'm jumping off this cliff with you. Sink or swim, I can't not try.*

*If your offer still stands, you can find me across the hall in room two-seventeen waiting for you. Please give me a chance to show you how much you mean to me.*

*Your loving and devoted Katie Bear.*

Katie folded the paper around the one-hundred-dollar bill, then rummaged through the drawers in the desk and found an envelope with the hotel's logo on the front. Once everything was safely tucked inside, she kissed it and slid it under Rhys's hotel door. When the envelope was out of her hands and inside Rhys's room Katie felt equal amounts panic and relief. It was out of her hands now and all she could do was wait. If she was a religious person she would probably pray, but since she wasn't, she'd have to settle for watching late night reruns of *The Golden Girls* in an attempt to distract herself.

Every time she heard someone padding down the hallway or opening a door, she thought it might be Rhys. Around nine thirty, the knock Katie had been waiting for finally came. She took a deep breath to steady her rapidly beating heart and opened the door. She couldn't help but smile at a disheveled, but still adorable Rhys standing in the hall.

"Hi," Katie said. A million scenarios had crossed her mind of how their meeting would play out from the moment she read Rhys's letter, but now that the time had come she felt frozen with fear. "Please, come in."

Rhys awkwardly stepped into the room and folded her arms over her chest as if she wasn't quite sure what to do with her hands. "I got your letter." She leaned back against the entryway wall for support. "I went out for drinks with some friends so I'm trying to figure out if I'm drunker than I thought or if you're really here."

The distance between them in that moment seemed so much more than only a couple of feet. Katie didn't know what she'd expected, but she knew it was her own fault and she had to proceed with caution. If Rhys was ever going to believe she was sincere, she owed her a massive apology, even though what she really wanted to do was take her to bed and make love to her. Katie held her hand out, and Rhys allowed her to guide her into the room to sit on an uncomfortable couch that looked like it had seen better days. "Come sit with me and we'll talk. Can I get you some water?"

"I'm not crazy drunk or anything," Rhys said. "I have my wits about me, but I feel like there's a chance I'm drunker than I think and I'm dreaming all this. Am I dreaming this?"

The confused look on her face broke Katie's heart. "You aren't dreaming, baby." Katie reassured her with a kiss on the cheek. "Everything has happened so fast it feels a little dreamlike to me, too. I haven't had a drop to drink since the bonfire night, which, by the way, may have caused me to swear off drinking for the rest of my life, so I can confidently say this is really happening."

Katie stood to get Rhys a glass of water. "I'm sorry to just show up like this," she said. "I promise I'm not stalking you or anything."

Rhys took the offered glass when Katie returned and drank half the liquid in one gulp. "I really needed that, thank you."

"I think maybe I made a mistake." Katie was more and more anxious as time passed.

Rhys sat on the edge of the cushion and took Katie's hand in hers. "No," she said. "I'm so excited that you're here. I'm trying to get my slightly fuzzy brain to understand what exactly this means. I mean, I read your letter and I know what you said and I know what I hope it means, but part of me feels like it's too good to be true. So good in fact that I'm not sure how to react."

The immediate reaction her body had to the simple contact of holding Rhys's hand made Katie smile. "I know. It's my own fault I've made you feel this way. I'm so sorry, Rhys. My only excuse is I'm an idiot."

Rhys smiled and scooted a little closer to Katie on the couch. "You aren't an idiot. You're stubborn and sometimes frustrating but not an idiot."

The sound of a group of people returning to their room from a night out on the town distracted them for a moment. "Can I ask you a question?" Rhys asked.

"Of course," Katie said.

"Why now? What happened to change your mind?"

Katie thought about the question and what to say. She knew her answer meant everything and the pressure to get it right, to say the right thing, only made her feel more vulnerable. She knew that was what this was all about, though. Vulnerability. She'd stopped allowing herself to be vulnerable when Amber walked out the door, and in the process, shut herself off to the chance to love or be loved by someone else. She couldn't and wouldn't allow that to happen with Rhys anymore. This was the universe giving her another chance, and she wouldn't fuck it up this time. "Would it be terribly forward of me to ask if we can get under the covers and snuggle? I missed you and our time together on the beach and I just want to be close to you."

"Nothing would make me happier," Rhys said as she removed her shoes and walked toward the bed.

"Let's take off our pants so we can get comfortable. It's taking everything I have not to just rip your clothes off and explore every inch of your body right now, but I do think it's better if we talk first." Katie removed her jeans and crawled under the covers.

Rhys removed her own pants and crawled in next to her with a smile on her face. "You have the absolute best ideas."

They lay on their sides facing each other for a few minutes before Katie finally spoke. "I missed you." She reached out to slip her fingers between Rhys's. "I don't think I realized quite how difficult it was going to be without you until you were already gone."

"I'm sorry Kat—" Rhys started, but Katie gently pressed an index finger to her lips to stop the apology before she was able to speak it.

"No apologizing. You didn't do anything wrong, and after what I put you through last week I'm lucky you're speaking to me at all. I jerked you around like a total asshole, and I promise to spend as much time as it takes to show you I realize how stupid I was. I was scared and I let my fear control me. I promise to be better." Katie scooted closer.

"You never answered my question. Why now?" Rhys asked.

"Why this dramatic change? To tell you the truth, I'm almost scared to believe it's true."

Katie slid even closer and rested her hand on Rhys's hip. "Is this okay?"

"Yes," Rhys said.

"I spent the entire week trying to convince myself the feelings I had for you weren't real. I think the tipping point was our date Thursday in Chinatown. When we came back to the resort and you went to your room, I had dinner with Carmen and Brooke. They said we acted like lovesick teenagers when we were together," Katie said.

Rhys leaned forward to place a gentle kiss on her lips. "Lovesick teenager pretty much describes how I've felt since I met you," she said when she pulled back.

Katie was slightly stunned by the contact and wasn't exactly sure how to proceed. The part of her that wanted to climb on top of Rhys and do really dirty things was battling the part of her that knew she needed to give Rhys time to get her bearings.

"I realized I felt like a lovesick teenager myself and I needed to talk to you about it. I went to bed that night planning to talk to you the next day, but things happened so fast that morning and then when you ended up bringing Addison to dinner I didn't have the opportunity."

"Addison." Rhys sighed as she leaned back and stared at the ceiling.

"What happened with her? I never saw you after that kiss at the bonfire."

Rhys placed her hand over her face and covered her eyes. "I'm so embarrassed. She is a really nice girl and didn't deserve me being such a dumbass. We'd talked before the bonfire so it wasn't like we were dating or anything, but she'd asked me if I had feelings for you and if that had anything to do with why I wasn't going to date her. I told her my feelings didn't matter because you weren't interested, and then the kiss happened and I think she felt like I'd betrayed her. I was an ass. I ran after her after I made a fool out of myself with that kiss and apologized, but the damage was done. She was understandably upset. She was very aware of my feelings for you and apparently thought you felt the same."

"I would say I'm sorry for my part, but I can't say I'm sad she's not in the picture anymore. She's not in the picture anymore, is she?"

"Oh no, she's long gone although I wouldn't be opposed to a friendship with her if she contacts me. She was a really cool chick, but even if my heart hadn't already been claimed, it wouldn't have worked. Her family owns a farm in Petaluma that she can't leave, and I'll never leave my family in the city. I'm not into long-distance relationships so I would have had to put on the brakes after the week anyway."

Katie rested her head on Rhys's shoulder and wrapped her arm around her middle to snuggle closer. "I wanted to punch her in the mouth when she was all over you like that, but I can't fault her for wanting to touch you. You're pretty touchable."

Rhys wrapped her arm around Katie and squeezed. "Where do we go from here? Just so you know, I'm all in. Whatever you're comfortable with, I'm totally on board for. I think about you to distraction, and the thought of having to live my life without seeing you again was torture. I can't tell you how happy I am right this moment."

Katie leaned on an elbow and brushed Rhys's bangs from her eyes with her free hand. "I almost realized too late how much I needed you in my life. I've never felt like this about anyone before and it took me a beat to wrap my head around it, but now that I have, I'm all in too. Will you be my girlfriend, Rhys Morgan?"

Katie couldn't help but giggle when Rhys rolled them over so she was hovering above her. "I would love to be your girlfriend, Katie Fausch. I think I'm starting to remember how this works."

"How what works?"

"This." Rhys gently planted kisses all over Katie's face before pressing her incredibly soft lips to hers. Katie didn't believe there could ever have been a kiss as good as this one in the vast history of kisses. Gentle, yet demanding, she felt completely possessed and wanted nothing more than to give Rhys everything she needed and more.

She pulled away for a breath and buried her face in the pillow next to Katie's head. "I'm pretty fuzzy, but I'm not sure if it's from the alcohol or my hormones at this point."

"Do you need us to stop?" Katie asked the question but prayed she would say no.

Rhys leaned down and gently pressed her lips to Katie's again. "A week's worth of pent up sexual energy is about to demand it be released. I'm not sure my heart could take stopping."

Katie's head spun as she felt Rhys slide a hand into her shirt and unhook her bra. The release of the restrictive clothing was a relief. "Did you just undo my bra with one hand? You seem like you have lots of practice with this."

"I'm just cool like that," Rhys said. "Do you really want to talk about how much practice I've had removing women's bras?"

"Not particularly, now kiss me, you fool."

Rhys sat up and pulled her own shirt and bra over her head, leaving her in only a pair of boxer briefs.

"God, baby, you're so fucking sexy." Katie trailed a sharp fingernail from Rhys's collarbone, between her breasts and down to the waist of her boxers. Touching Rhys's muscular body like this sent a flood of wetness to her center. "I can't believe I'm here, and I'm actually getting to do things I've been fantasizing about since I pulled my head out of my ass and admitted to myself how much I want you."

Rhys helped Katie remove her shirt. "Holy fuck." She steadied herself on the bed and looked at Katie's body for the first time.

"Are you okay there, chief?" Katie asked with a hint of real concern.

"I'm okay. I'm going to have to take this so much slower than I normally would."

"We can wait," Katie said. "We should wait until you're sure."

Rhys straddled Katie's hips and leaned down for a kiss. "I may be a bit clumsy and slower than usual, but this is for sure happening." Her kisses continued down Katie's body as she made her way toward the last remaining piece of clothing.

"Poor baby," Rhys said when she finally reached the juncture of her thighs. "Someone's panties are all wet. Is that because of me?"

None of Katie's previous lovers were talkers in bed so the question threw her off for a minute but also made her pussy ache with need. "That's all you." She tilted her head back in a gasp when she felt Rhys's finger trace the elastic band of her panties before slipping under the cloth and pulling the damp garment aside.

"You have a beautiful pussy, my love." Rhys leaned down to kiss her mound. "May I taste you?"

"Yes," Katie moaned as her head dropped back onto the pillow. "I'm so fucking hot for you right now I feel like I'm going to pass out."

Rhys slipped her arms under her legs and scooted closer. "Don't do that. I like my woman to be fully aware of the orgasms I'm about to give her."

"You're a cocky little sucker, aren't you?"

"Let me show you why."

Katie felt Rhys's warm tongue run up one side of her slit, then down the other. She tentatively pushed it between her folds. With a moan, she gently pulled her labia into her mouth and used her tongue to caress the sensitive tissue.

"Holy fuck, you feel so good," Katie said. She'd had great oral sex before, but she'd never felt worshiped like she was in that moment. Rhys seemed to be in no rush. Katie ached for more but luxuriated in the thorough attention she was getting.

Feeling a low level heat build, Katie reached down and threaded her fingers through the hair on the back of Rhys's head, gently grinding her face a little deeper. The rumble of Rhys laughing at her obvious need sent a shock to her clit.

"You taste so good," Rhys said as she moved up to suck Katie's clit into her mouth, rubbing it back and forth with her tongue. "I've thought about what your pussy would taste like all week."

"I hope I live up to your fantasies."

"You are so much more than I ever could have imagined," Rhys said as Katie's moans grew louder and her hips began to pump up and down. "May I put a finger or two inside? You're so wet and I promise to be gentle."

"Yesss," Katie hissed as Rhys ran a finger around her opening, gathering wetness along the way. "Please fuck me. I need you inside of me. Please, baby." With the desperate request, Rhys slowly inserted first one and then two fingers into Katie's core. She could feel the slight stretch of her walls as Rhys's fingers slowly pistoned in and out.

"I can't believe I'm inside you, baby. Your pussy is so tight it can barely take my fingers. Does it feel good?" Rhys asked. "Do you like it when I finger fuck you?" Rhys slid up Katie's body, and pulled a nipple into her mouth. She gently sucked while she continued the exploration with her fingers, using her thumb to rub her clit.

Katie was being consumed by pure pleasure. So many things felt good she was losing focus. Rhys's fingers plunged in and out in a steady rhythm Katie couldn't distinguish from her own heartbeat. "I love having you inside me," she said, remembering she hadn't answered Rhys's question.

One deep plunge brought Katie right to the edge of release. "Oh fuck."

"There it is," Rhys moaned. "I knew I'd find it."

Rhys released her nipple with a pop and moved up Katie's body to kiss her lips while she continued to fuck her with her fingers. "Are you ready to come, sweetie?" she asked with a sly smile.

"Rhys, I'm so close."

"It's okay, sweetheart. I'm going to make you come now. Hold on to me tight."

Katie fought the fog of lust to understand what Rhys was saying. It seemed as if Rhys had taken complete control of her body and Katie could do nothing but surrender. Every nerve felt hypersensitive as Rhys adjusted herself on top of her and looked deep into her eyes. "Here we go, come for me, baby." Rhys fucked her deeply and rubbed the same area that had brought Katie to the edge before. This time it pushed her right over and she came in wave after wave as Rhys whispered encouraging words to her. The pleasure was so intense Katie finally had to reach down and push the invading arm away before she came apart at the seams.

When her heart started to beat again and the haze cleared, she opened her eyes to find a very cocky looking Rhys staring down at her. "You okay?" Rhys asked as she lazily ran her wet fingers around the outside of Katie's slit.

"Fuck, woman." Katie tried to make sense of what just happened. "I've never felt anything that intense before in my life."

"We're just getting started." Rhys gently dipped her finger between the folds to lightly touch the still sensitive clit.

Katie jumped and pushed Rhys's hand away. "Hold on there. I need a minute to recover before we start doing that again. Oh, my fuck. That was so fucking good. I'm saying fuck a lot. It's the only word that comes to mind right now."

Rhys settled back on the bed next to Katie. "Just wait until I have time to map out all the areas of your body that bring you pleasure. I'm like a treasure hunter."

"I'll say."

Katie could see Rhys was having a difficult time keeping her eyes open. She ran her fingers through her hair as they held each other. "You okay, baby?" she asked. "I want to make love to you, but you look like you're exhausted."

"I can't believe I'm saying this and turning down that offer, but I don't think I can stay awake any longer." The sad, sleepy look on her face was adorable.

"I'm sorry, sleepyhead. I'm fading fast, too."

"I have to get up tomorrow and finish my sculpture." Rhys got up and set her alarm for six in the morning. "I've got about three hours to sleep."

"Let's get to bed then. I don't want my girlfriend chopping something off trying to work with big tools on very little sleep." Katie turned to face away from Rhys and pushed herself back so she was snuggled up to her as tight as possible. She felt an arm drape around her as soft sounds of sleep whispered in her ear.

## CHAPTER TWENTY-NINE

The sound of her alarm pulled Rhys from a deep sleep. After hitting snooze, she snuggled up to Katie next to her. When the alarm went off again a few minutes later, Rhys forced herself to sit up and turn it off. She rubbed her face to clear her eyes and turned to look at Katie as she slept. The reality of what had happened the night before hadn't truly sunk in, but as she watched Katie's steady breathing, an ache gripped her chest. Not a bad ache. An ache that came from being so happy she thought her heart would explode.

Rhys wasn't sure if she should wake her up or wait until after her shower, but before she could decide Katie rolled over and stretched.

"Good morning, sweetie." Katie reached out to rub her arm.

"Good morning. You look adorable when you sleep."

"I'm glad you think so. I liked sleeping next to your little furnace of a body so you may see a lot of me in the mornings."

"I can't think of a better way to start the day." Rhys leaned down to give her a kiss. "What are your plans for today?"

Katie checked her phone for messages. "No real plans other than some emails I have to return. What time will you be done with your work?"

"I can't imagine it'll be more than a couple of hours at the most. My flight leaves at three in the afternoon. When are you going home?" Rhys asked.

"Same flight as you. I was able to get a middle seat right next to you."

"It just occurred to me, how in the world did you know where I was?" Rhys stood and starting pulling clean clothes from her bag.

"Well, when Elise picked me up at the resort I was a wreck. I was soaking wet and dripped all over the letter you left me, and of course of all things, your phone number smudged where I couldn't read it. We drove to my mom's for Sunday lunch and Andy offered to take me to your shop the next morning so I could talk to you. I can't believe it was only yesterday morning. I spoke to Max and after she and Andy shamelessly flirted with each other, it was decided I should just come here and make a grand romantic gesture. They promised me it wouldn't seem at all like stalking even if that's exactly how it feels."

"You're so freaking cute when you blush." Rhys rubbed her thumb across Katie's red cheek before giving it a quick kiss. "You have an open invitation to stalk me as much as your little heart desires, Katie Bear. Also, I'm not surprised that Max was flirting with Andy. If he is even half as cute as you, she wouldn't be able to resist."

"I don't know why, but I was surprised Max was straight for some reason."

"She's bisexual but typically dates more women than men. I thought Andy was gay."

"I've never heard him label himself, and he usually dates men but he has dated women before so I guess he would probably consider himself bisexual as well. He's very picky about the people he dates, and he was certainly into Max so I would be surprised if they haven't been texting each other since I left."

"Well, Max is a great gal and is going to make someone a great partner someday, but she's so focused on her job I worry about her."

"I like that your family means so much to you," Katie said. "My family is everything to me and one of my hang-ups with relationships has been it's difficult to find people who understand that. Other than insisting I find someone to love and don't die alone in my apartment, my family isn't in my business, but we do spend lots of time together. Most people don't want to spend time with their girlfriend's family that much."

Rhys crawled back into bed and gave Katie a lazy kiss on the lips. "I think both our families are part of the package. I wouldn't want to be with someone who had a problem with me spending time with my family, and the fact that you feel the same makes me like you even more."

"You better get in the shower if you're going to finish up in time for the grand opening." Katie gently pushed Rhys in the direction of the bathroom.

"Care to join me, Ms. Fausch?"

"Do you have time for that kind of shenanigans this morning?"

Rhys checked her watch and did a quick calculation in her head before reaching out a hand to help Katie out of bed. "If we start now I think I can squeeze in a long shower."

"You get the water warm and I'll be right there."

Rhys purposefully gave her an exaggerated shake of her hips as she sauntered into the bathroom and turned on the shower. She stepped into the stream of water and let the warmth surround her as she washed off the lingering smell of alcohol and sex from the night before. How in the world did she get here? Did she just actually spend the best night of her life having sex with the most beautiful girl she'd ever seen?

She looked around the empty bathroom and worried for a moment it was all a dream. Maybe she wanted this so much she had only convinced herself it happened and now that she was showering and waking up, the illusion had washed away.

Before Rhys could fall too far down that rabbit hole of despair, the door opened and a naked Katie shyly stepped into the room. "Is the water warm?"

Rhys blew out a relieved breath. "I didn't make you up."

"What?"

"I was starting to think my alcohol addled brain from last night might have made you up and you weren't actually here. I'm really glad I was wrong."

Katie pulled the shower door open and stepped in, cuddling up to her under the warm spray. "I'm cold. You have to warm me up."

"I'm starting to feel like me warming you up is going to be a running theme in our relationship."

"Aww, poor baby." Katie smacked Rhys lightly on the butt cheek.

"Oh really?"

Katie's giggles turned into a gasp when Rhys pulled one of her arms behind her back and reached down to take a nipple into her mouth. The nub immediately became hard as Rhys dropped to her knees in front of her and replaced her mouth with her fingers, lightly twisting the sensitive nipple as she kissed down her naked body.

"You are so fucking hot, Katie. You make me so wet."

"Are you sure that isn't the shower?"

Rhys gently swatted Katie on the ass for the comment and chuckled. "Yes, I'm sure it isn't the shower. I want you so bad I feel like I can't focus."

"Easy, baby, you're doing just fine," Katie said as she reached down to thread her fingers through Rhys's hair and gently guide her mouth toward her center.

"Hold yourself open for me." Rhys kissed around the trimmed blond mound in front of her. When Katie used her fingers to part her pink lips, Rhys reached out with her tongue and licked.

Katie held onto the wall for stability as Rhys gently inserted two fingers and began to rhythmically slide them in and out of her tight hole. Sensing Katie was struggling to stay upright, Rhys guided her to the bench in the corner of the shower stall.

"Sit here and let me properly thank you for coming all this way."

"Fuck, we could have been doing this for the last week. What the hell was I thinking?"

Katie's hips lifted to pull her mouth even closer.

"Keep going, baby. Such a good girl licking my pussy like that."

Rhys moaned into her pussy as she doubled her efforts, curling her fingers to put pressure where she knew it would push Katie over the edge.

"Fuck yes. Fuck yes, baby. Just like that. I'm going to come. Don't stop."

Rhys could feel Katie's tight channel get impossibly tighter when she came with a scream. The sound echoed through the tiled bathroom, and Rhys had no doubt the neighbors were going to know exactly what they had been up to.

When the contractions eased, Rhys slowly pulled her fingers free and kissed the inside of Katie's thighs. "That was beautiful, baby. I could do that every day for the rest of my life." In the fog of post coital bliss, the words were out before she thought about their implication. "I'm sorry, I wasn't trying to freak you out. I don't mean—"

Katie cut her rambling off by sliding off the bench to sit next to her on the shower floor. The bluest eyes Rhys had ever seen looked at her with nothing but love. "We'll figure this out as we go. Don't be afraid to tell me how you feel. This is all new and I'm not ready to make huge commitments, but I'm for sure ready to see where this leads. I've never met anyone like you before. I've never wanted something so much in my life which freaks me the hell out on one hand but excites me on the other. I'm scared but I'm ready to give it my best if you are."

"I can work with that." Rhys helped Katie to her feet and wrapped her arms around her. "I hate to say this, but I need to get down to the center and finish up my eagle friend. Want to meet me down there when you're done and we can grab a bite to eat before we have to catch our plane?"

"That sounds perfect. I'm going to wash all remnants of the amazing sex from my body and then I'll be right behind you. Thank you, Rhys."

"You don't have to thank me for sex, you crazy woman. It's my pleasure, believe me."

"Not for the sex, dork. Thank you for opening that door even after all the shit I put you through this week. You didn't have to and I realize now what I would have missed out on. I'm an idiot."

"You're not an idiot. You were afraid. I get it. You came to your senses in the end."

"Finally." Katie rolled her eyes. "Hey..." Katie paused and Rhys watched as a slow smile spread across her face.

"Hey, what?" Rhys asked.

"This is it. In some weird way I know this is the beginning of the rest of our lives."

Rhys was confused but optimistic. "I'm hoping that's a good thing?"

Katie smiled and kissed her one more time. "It's a really good thing. What are you doing this coming Sunday?"

## EPILOGUE

Just once more around the block," Elise begged when Rhys parked her motorcycle in the Fausches' driveway and pulled off her helmet.

Katie rolled her eyes and tugged on the motorcycle jacket Elise had borrowed for the ride. "No. Leave my girlfriend alone and get your own motorcycle."

Rhys steadied the bike as Elise got off. Six months' worth of Sunday lunches, and every single time Elise begged Rhys to take her for a ride on her motorcycle.

"You're selfish, Katie," Elise teased her.

"Whatever, I found her first. Hands off." They walked toward the house with Rhys right behind them. The day had been everything Katie could have hoped it would be. Her family adored Rhys, maybe a little too much, and Rhys seemed to like them, too. In that moment she couldn't remember why she'd ever hesitated to invite Rhys into her life, but now that she had, she was even more in love with her.

"How was the ride, girls?" Katie's mom asked when they entered the house.

"Amazing," Elise answered. "I think we should keep Rhys."

Katie rolled her eyes. "She's not a puppy, Elise. Besides, I've already decided to keep her."

Rhys smiled from ear to ear. "That's a relief," she said.

"We have to get home," Katie said as she hugged her family good-bye. "Andy and Max should be back from Italy tonight. I hope everything goes okay with their flight."

"I'm sure it will be fine," Rhys said. "You always worry when people are away from home."

"She's always been like that, Rhys," Katie's mom said. "She likes having everyone close."

Katie pouted. "I can't help it. I love you guys so much."

"We love you, too, baby." Rhys kissed her and then wrapped Katie's mom in a hug. "As always, thank you for an amazing lunch, Liz."

"You are very welcome, Rhys. When are you going to make an honest woman out of my daughter so you can start calling me Mom?"

The silence in the room was deafening.

"I—" Rhys started.

"Mom, please stop harassing my girlfriend." Katie quickly waved good-bye and rushed Rhys toward the door. She loved her mother, but sometimes she wanted to strangle her. Why would she ask something like that? They'd only been dating six months. They weren't anywhere near ready for marriage. Where they? She'd been with Amber for four and a half years and never felt as sure about their relationship as she did with Rhys, but did that mean she wanted to marry her. So soon?

The entire way home from her mother's house, Katie analyzed her feelings and where she thought they were in their relationship. She had no doubts that Rhys was the one she wanted to spend the rest of her life with, but did that mean they should get married after only six months? That seemed awfully soon. Was her fear only remnants of her past hesitation or was it legitimately crazy to think they should get married?

They weren't even technically living together. Not technically. Katie still had her own apartment even though it had become more of a storage facility since she spent almost every night with Rhys. Marriage would definitely be skipping a few steps.

Katie squeezed Rhys as they rode the motorcycle across the Golden Gate Bridge toward home. Would Rhys even want to live with Katie? She knew the answer to that question was yes. Even though Katie was completely sure about being with Rhys, her instincts were to take things slow. She hoped Rhys didn't take that as an indication she wasn't sure about being with her. Katie could see how her holding onto her apartment might seem like she wasn't confident about their future. Katie knew she needed to make sure Rhys understood how serious she was.

Rhys pulled the bike into the warehouse and they both climbed off. Katie's heart swelled when Rhys removed her helmet and her hair stuck up in that adorable way in the back that made Katie smile every time. She truly loved her.

"Take me upstairs and make love to me, stud."

The grin on Rhys's face made Katie smile. "You got it, you sweet talker, you." Rhys took Katie's hand and quickly led her upstairs to her loft.

The smell of warm cinnamon greeted them when they entered the room. Rhys had made homemade cinnamon rolls for breakfast that morning, and the memory of sharing them in bed made her smile. In that moment she had no doubt she would marry Rhys if she asked. Katie knew she could always ask, but she'd always dreamed of being proposed to so she would just be patient.

Rhys turned on the lights and dimmed them to their lowest level. "Music?" she asked.

"Yeah, something romantic."

"Alexa, play classic jazz station," Rhys said which was followed by the sound of Etta James singing "Sunday Kind of Love."

"Perfect," Katie said as she leaned into Rhys's arms.

Rhys kissed her and slid her hands into Katie's shirt, lifting it over her head to be tossed onto the floor. "Mmm, you didn't wear a bra today."

Katie pulled the snaps on Rhys's shirt, exposing her toned body. "Nope, it's free boob Sunday."

"Free boob Sunday?" Rhys picked Katie up, encouraging her to wrap her legs around her waist while she carried her to the bed. "I like it. I think you should make it a weekly thing."

"I just might do that," Katie said as she was gently set down on the mattress. Katie sat up on the edge of the bed and kissed Rhys's stomach. The warmth of her skin only heightened Katie's arousal.

Her fingers worked the buttons of Rhys's jeans as she methodically released them one by one. "Baby?"

"Yes, my love." The control it took for Rhys to go slow was evident in her strained voice.

"Do you have a strap-on?" Katie asked.

Rhys froze and Katie feared she'd freaked her out. "We don't have to—"

"No, no, no," Rhys said, bending down to kiss Katie's lips. "I for sure want to, and yes, I certainly do. I've been trying to figure out how to ask you if you'd be interested in doing that, but I wasn't sure how to broach the subject."

Katie helped Rhys pull her pants the rest of the way off, leaving her in very sexy boxer briefs. "Why would you be afraid to talk to me about it?"

Rhys climbed into bed and pulled Katie with her. "I don't know. I really have no idea other than I had a bad reaction from a previous girlfriend that made me a little hesitant."

"What kind of a bad reaction?" Katie asked. The look of embarrassment on Rhys's face broke Katie's heart. "Talk to me, baby."

Rhys let out a breath and gave Katie a gentle kiss on the lips. "It wasn't anything major, but it was embarrassing. Do you remember that Stacy girl I told you I dated a few years ago?"

"The chef?"

"Yep, that's the one. Anyway, Stacy worked late nights and she was usually really horny when she was done with her shift so she'd come over here, we'd have sex, and then she'd go home."

"So, she used you for sex?"

"Pretty much, but don't feel sorry for me. I wasn't really into her other than for sex either so it was fine," Rhys said. "One night after we'd dated for a couple months, I decided to surprise her by being naked in bed wearing a cock when she came over. It all seemed really hot to me, but I should have discussed it with her first. I'd been with so many women who were totally into it that I just wasn't thinking."

"What did she do?" Katie asked.

"She freaked the fuck out, that's what she did. We got into a huge argument and she told me I was a presumptuous asshole for assuming she'd be into that and if she wanted a cock, she would be with a man. It wasn't good and it ended whatever thing we had going between us. She stormed out and I never saw her again. I was horribly embarrassed and have been scared to suggest it to a girl ever since."

Katie climbed on top of Rhys and straddled her narrow hips. "Rest assured, I'm into it and it doesn't mean I want to be with a man. That's the miracle of strap-ons. All the pleasure of being fucked with a cock without having to be with a man."

Rhys smiled and flipped them around so she was on top. "I'll be right back."

Katie watched as she slid off the bed and jogged into the bathroom. She hadn't had strap-on sex in a while, and the last time she did it hadn't been that great, but she wanted this with Rhys. Katie slid her fingers into her panties and checked to see if she was as wet as she thought she was. She swirled her finger from her center and up to her clit, transferring the wetness.

When Rhys walked back into the room she moaned when she found Katie pleasuring herself while she waited. "Couldn't wait for me, sweetheart?" Rhys asked as she climbed onto the bed.

Katie reached out and took Rhys's cock in her hand. "I've never seen a harness like this before," she said. Rhys wore a tight pair of red underwear that held the cock in place.

"It's a million times better that those old leather harnesses they used to have. So much more comfortable, and I think it gives me more control."

"It's sexy as hell."

Rhys leaned down and kissed Katie on the lips. "Thank you."

"Do you have a vibrator in your underwear?" Katie asked when she heard the soft buzz coming from Rhys's crotch.

"I do. I tuck a bullet vibrator in there. I can come without it, but it just makes it even more pleasurable for me." The bed dipped as Rhys slid down Katie's body and draped her legs over her shoulders. "Let's get you nice and wet for me, sweetheart."

Katie sighed as Rhys brought her to climax twice with her mouth before climbing back up to lay beside her. "I don't know if I can take anymore, Rhys."

Rhys pulled a nipple into her mouth. "Do you want me to stop?"

"No," Katie said with more conviction than she intended. "Please, I want you inside me."

An almost feral growl escaped from Rhys as she positioned herself above Katie and lined up the tip with her center.

❖

Before Rhys slipped inside, she noticed Katie was tense. She looked at her face and realized she was holding her breath and her eyes were closed.

"What's wrong, sweetie? Are you okay?" Rhys worried she might have hurt her or maybe she wasn't as into this as she had originally said.

Katie slowly opened her eyes and gave Rhys a shy smile. "Yeah, I'm sorry." She draped her arm over her face in an attempt to hide the blush that spread across her cheeks.

Rhys scooted back and sat on her feet. "Honey, we absolutely don't have to do this if you aren't into it. I don't need this to be satisfied. It's something I enjoy but not something I need if it makes you uncomfortable."

She removed her arm from her face and pulled herself into a sitting position with her back against the headboard. "Baby, no, I'm totally into this. I promise. I just…"

Her hesitation to share her feelings made Rhys feel terrible. Had she rushed this? "Let's get rid of this and go back to licking your pussy. It's totally fine, and licking your pussy is my fav—"

"Rhys." Katie placed a hand on her arm to stop her from getting up. "I want this, very much. I just haven't done it in a while, and the last time I did it was with someone who didn't take the time to get me ready first. You absolutely have, and then some. I'm plenty ready, but the memory of the last time is hard to push away. I know once we start, it'll totally be fine and I'll forget all about the last time. I'll only have good memories of you being inside me." Katie got on her hands and knees in front of Rhys and slipped her lips over Rhys's shaft, sliding down to take much more than Rhys ever imagined she could.

"Oh...fuck." Rhys knew her dick wasn't real, but she was pretty sure all the blood in her body had collected in that area. Possible or not, she felt herself get harder as she watched Katie's blond head bob up and down. "Jesus, Katie, I—"

Katie lifted her head enough to lick the tip. "Shhhh...let me take care of you."

It was almost too much for Rhys to process. Her heart was beating out of her chest as she placed a hand over the back of Katie's head and threaded her fingers through the silky strands of her golden hair. "Fuck, baby, suck my cock."

"Mmm..." Katie moaned and sucked even harder. Rhys was lightheaded listening to the quiet sound of Katie's lips as they slid up and down her cock.

"God, Katie, fuck, I'm close. Don't stop, baby."

Katie sped up her effort and reached down to push the balls of the dildo against Rhys's center, effectively pressing the bullet vibrator harder against her clit in a rhythm that matched the bob of her head.

"Oh fuck, yes, yes, like that. I'm coming, baby."

Katie lifted her head enough to smile up at Rhys for a moment. "Come in my mouth, baby," she said in the sexiest voice Rhys had ever heard.

She slipped her mouth back onto the dick and moaned when Rhys's body stiffened and she came with a roar. Katie pulled her back onto the bed and snuggled into her side as Rhys struggled to catch her breath. "You okay, baby?" Katie asked.

Rhys smiled and nodded as she reveled in the post orgasmic euphoria that was so much stronger when you were completely in love and in awe of the person who got you there. "I'm beyond excellent. Are you okay? I didn't hurt you, did I?"

"Pretty sure I was the aggressor that time."

Rhys chuckled and traced a finger along Katie's swollen lips before kissing her. When she pulled back, they were both out of breath. "We may need to get an insurance policy on this." Rhys pointed to her mouth and smiled. "Or maybe a bodyguard. Maybe I need to hire a bodyguard that will protect my new favorite thing in the entire world."

Katie pouted and took Rhys's finger from where it rested on her lip to slowly drag it down to her breast. "What about these? You like my mouth more than my breast? I thought you were into boobs?"

Rhys moaned and leaned forward to take a puckered nipple into her mouth and suck. "You're right. I'm an idiot. Do you think Ethel will ever forgive me?"

"Ethel?"

Rhys smiled. "Yeah, Lucy," she pointed toward Katie's left breast, "and Ethel," she said, pointing to the right.

"You're a nut and you aren't naming my breasts Lucy and Ethel. You're going to have to come up with something much better than that."

"You're right. Besides," Rhys rolled her tongue around the hard point of her nipple before kissing the underside of her breast and continuing down to leave a trail of kisses down her body toward the patch of neatly trimmed hair at the juncture of her legs, "I would be an idiot to choose anything over the most beautiful pussy I've ever seen."

She pulled the glistening folds apart with her thumbs and lovingly studied every inch of Katie's pussy. "You're so fucking beautiful, Katie. I'm not just saying that because I'm hoping you let me play with it for the rest of my life." Rhys looked up at Katie and winked.

"It's all yours, baby." Katie brushed Rhys's bangs from her forehead and smiled down at her. "For the rest of our lives."

Rhys smiled before leaning down to suck her labia into her mouth. "Damn, your pussy is seriously sweet. It's amazing."

"I eat well and drink a lot of water."

"Really, that's why?" Rhys slipped a single finger into her core before popping it into her mouth. "Mmm…that's amazing."

"I'm glad you approve." Katie smiled down at her before giving her a mock stern look. "Now get back to work. That pussy isn't going to lick itself."

"Oh God, I'd never leave the house if they could do that." Rhys giggled.

"Rhys."

"Sorry." Rhys lowered her head and sucked the labia back into her mouth, giving them a gentle pull with her lips.

"Fuck, yes. So good."

The encouragement made Rhys push her chest out with pride even though no one could see her do it. Katie squirmed beneath her and pushed Rhys's face harder into her core as she moaned. When she thought Katie was wet enough, she slipped first one, then two fingers inside. She kept them completely still for a moment to allow her time to adjust, but soon Katie was moving her hips up and down, fucking herself.

"More," Katie groaned. "Please, Rhys, more."

"More fingers?" Rhys asked.

"Yes, baby, please."

Rhys moaned and doubled her efforts on her clit before pulling out and sliding back in with three fingers this time. It was a tight fit, but she took her time to allow Katie a chance to get used to the new intrusion before she moved.

"Fuck, yes." Katie arched her back and reached down to pull Rhys's fingers deeper inside. "Yes, fuck, yes…"

The cock, still strapped to Rhys, pushed against her clit as her hips pistoned up and down against the mattress. "Katie, you feel so fucking good."

"I want your cock, Rhys, now."

The command took a minute for Rhys to register. Did Katie just demand—

"Rhys, fucking now, baby, please. I want your cock inside me. I need you to come inside me."

Rhys scrambled up the bed and tucked her hips between Katie's thighs. "Are you sure?"

"Now, baby, please."

The cock was hard in Rhys's hand as she stroked herself a couple times before lining up the tip with Katie's warm, wet center. "I'll go slowly. You'll let me know if I hurt you, right?"

Katie nodded, threw her head back, and parted her lips in a gasp when Rhys pushed inside. She suspected it was bigger than anything Katie had ever taken, and she worried she would do something to hurt her and make this a bad experience.

"Rub your clit for me, sweetheart. Relax as much as you can. I know it's big and I want it to feel good for you," Rhys said. Her arms shook as she held herself over Katie's body, too afraid to push deeper but too excited to stay still. "Katie, I need—"

"More, Rhys. Please give me more. I'm not going to break."

Rhys smiled. "Sorry, I'm a little overprotective."

Warmth spread through her body when Katie smiled and gently placed her hand on Rhys's cheek. "It's okay, sweetheart. I'm okay. I'll let you know if it's too much, but right now, I need you to take what you need from me. You did an excellent job of getting me ready for your gigantic, hard dick." Katie winked at her and gave Rhys a gentle smack on the cheek. "Let's get going, big boi, you've got a woman to please."

"Yes, ma'am." Rhys was quite sure she'd never been so happy in her life. How in the hell had she stumbled upon the absolute perfect woman at a singles resort. Surely the newspapers would want to hear of this story. It was a one in a billion chance. Maybe not one in a billion, but she certainly never expected it to actually turn out this way.

With a gentle push of her hips, she sank deeper into Katie's body before slowly pulling out until just the tip remained. She looked down to find Katie's natural lubrication covering the cock and the sight took her breath away. She never wanted this moment to end. Before she could overthink things, she pushed back in, slightly deeper this time.

The drag of her cock as it slid in and out was an indication of just how tight Katie was and how much of an effort it was for her to take her like this. "You're so fucking tight, baby. You're squeezing my cock so tight I'm not sure how long I'm going to be able to last."

"Don't you dare stop. I'm not done with this." She reached down and wrapped her small hand around the cock as it was pulled from her core. "You need to make me come before you're allowed to spill inside me, understand?"

"Yes, yes, ma'am." Rhys knew this was going to be a challenge because she was already so close, but she was more than willing to give it the old college try. "Let's get you turned over so I can get deeper." "I'm pretty sure you've gone as deep as you can." The protest was mumbled, but Katie allowed Rhys to pull out and flip her onto her belly. Rhys pulled her up onto all fours and pushed her head down against the pillow.

"Scream into the pillow if you need to." Rhys chuckled but was only partly joking as she slid back into Katie's pussy and started a steady rhythm, driving deeper every time she pushed.

"Oh fuck, Rhys. You're so fucking deep. You're hitting me right…fuck."

Rhys angled her thrusts to bump the tip of her cock against the front wall of Katie's pussy, she hoped it was right where her g-spot was.

"Yes, I'm gonna come, baby."

"That's it, Katie. Come on my cock, baby. Squeeze my dick and milk it dry."

Katie went silent for a moment other than the faint sound of air escaping from her lungs before she grabbed the sides of the pillow her face was buried in and screamed. Rhys grabbed her hips and pumped faster as Katie pushed back against her, trying to get her even deeper.

She could feel Katie's pussy contracting on the cock nestled so close to her body, and it sent her quickly spiraling toward the edge. Rhys bit the inside of her cheek in an attempt to stop the impending flood. "Katie, baby, I'm—"

"Come inside me, Rhys. Please, baby, push your come so deep inside my pussy then you can watch it drip out of me and onto my thighs."

"Fuck, yes, take my cock. I'm going to come. Get ready."

"I'm more than ready, baby. Please come inside me."

Rhys jerked Katie's hips against her and roared her release. The contractions from her orgasm almost seemed like her cock was actually pumping Katie full of her essence, and the experience was emotionally overwhelming.

When her body began to relax, she gently pulled her cock from Katie's pussy and collapsed onto the bed. She wiped the tears as they streamed down her face.

"Oh, shit, baby, are you okay? Did you hurt yourself?"

"No." Rhys coughed and did her best to rein in her emotions. "I'm such a loser. I can't believe I'm freaking crying."

Katie brushed a tear from Rhys's cheek and gently kissed her lips. "Tell me what you're feeling."

"It's way too early for that."

"Okay..." Katie draped an arm and leg around Rhys's body as she snuggled tightly into her side. "How about I tell you how I'm feeling?"

"Okay."

Katie cleared her throat and leaned up on an elbow so she was looking down into Rhys's eyes. "I love you, Rhys Morgan. I love you and I'm really excited about our future together."

Rhys couldn't stop the smile as her heart lifted in joy. "Really?"

"Really."

"I love you, too. A bunch."

"Really?" Katie asked, giving her a quick peck on the lips.

"Really."

"Well, do you love me enough to ask me to move in with you?" Katie asked.

"Seriously?"

"That's up to you."

Rhys's body vibrated with happiness. "Will you move in with me?"

"Yes," Katie said and tickled Rhys's side which made her squirm and giggle like a girl.

"I'm so freaking happy." Rhys rolled over and held herself above Katie. She couldn't believe how quickly things were happening, but she wasn't scared. For once in her life she felt like she belonged to someone and they belonged to her. She knew this was forever.

# About the Author

Angie Williams, winner of a third grade essay competition on fire safety, grew up in the dusty desert of West Texas. Always interested in writing, as a child she would lose interest before the end, killing the characters off in a tragic accident so she could move on to the next story. Thankfully, as an adult she decided it was time to write things where everyone survives.

Angie lives in Northern California with her beautiful wife and son, and a menagerie of dogs, cats, snakes, and tarantulas. She's a proud geek and lover of all things she was teased about in school.

# Books Available from Bold Strokes Books

**Bet Against Me** by Fiona Riley. In the high stakes luxury real estate market, everything has a price, and as rival Realtors Trina Lee and Kendall Yates find out, that means their hearts and souls, too. (978-1-63555-729-9)

**Broken Reign** by Sam Ledel. Together on an epic journey in search of a mysterious cure, a princess and a village outcast must overcome life-threatening challenges and their own prejudice if they want to survive. (978-1-63555-739-8)

**Just One Taste** by CJ Birch. For Lauren, it only took one taste to start trusting in love again. (978-1-63555-772-5)

**Lady of Stone** by Barbara Ann Wright. Sparks fly as a magical emergency forces a noble embarrassed by her ability to submit to a low-born teacher who resents everything about her. (978-1-63555-607-0)

**Last Resort** by Angie Williams. Katie and Rhys are about to find out what happens when you meet the girl of your dreams but you aren't looking for a happily ever after. (978-1-63555-774-9)

**Longing for You** by Jenny Frame. When Debrek housekeeper Katie Brekman is attacked amid a burgeoning vampire-witch war, Alexis Villiers must go against everything her clan believes in to save her. (978-1-63555-658-2)

**Money Creek** by Anne Laughlin. Clare Lehane is a troubled lawyer from Chicago who tries to make her way in a rural town full of secrets and deceptions. (978-1-63555-795-4)

**Passion's Sweet Surrender** by Ronica Black. Cam and Blake are unable to deny their passion for each other, but surrendering to love is a whole different matter. (978-1-63555-703-9)

**The Holiday Detour** by Jane Kolven. It will take everything going wrong to make Dana and Charlie see how right they are for each other. (978-1-63555-720-6)

**Too Hot to Ride** by Andrews & Austin. World famous cutting horse champion and industry legend Jane Barrow is knockdown sexy in the way she moves, talks, and rides, and Rae Starr is determined not to get involved with this womanizing gambler. (978-1-63555-776-3)

**A Love that Leads to Home** by Ronica Black. For Carla Sims and Janice Carpenter, home isn't about location, it's where your heart is. (978-1-63555-675-9)

**Blades of Bluegrass** by D. Jackson Leigh. A US Army occupational therapist must rehab a bitter veteran who is a ticking political time bomb the military is desperate to disarm. (978-1-63555-637-7)

**Guarding Hearts** by Jaycie Morrison. As treachery and temptation threaten the women of the Women's Army Corps, who will risk it all for love? (978-1-63555-806-7)

**Hopeless Romantic** by Georgia Beers. Can a jaded wedding planner and an optimistic divorce attorney possibly find a future together? (978-1-63555-650-6)

**Hopes and Dreams** by PJ Trebelhorn. Movie theater manager Riley Warren is forced to face her high school crush and tormentor, wealthy socialite Victoria Thayer, at their twentieth reunion. (978-1-63555-670-4)

**In the Cards** by Kimberly Cooper Griffin. Daria and Phaedra are about to discover that love finds a way, especially when powers outside their control are at play. (978-1-63555-717-6)

**Moon Fever** by Ileandra Young. SPEAR agent Danika Karson must clear her werewolf friend of multiple false charges while teaching her vampire girlfriend to resist the blood mania brought on by a full moon. (978-1-63555-603-2)

**Quake City** by St John Karp. Can Andre find his best friend Amy before the night devolves into a nightmare of broken hearts, malevolent drag queens, and spontaneous human combustion? Or has it always happened this way, every night, at Aunty Bob's Quake City Club? (978-1-63555-723-7)

**Serenity** by Jesse J. Thoma. For Kit Marsden, there are many things in life she cannot change. Serenity is in the acceptance. (978-1-63555-713-8)

**Sylver and Gold** by Michelle Larkin. Working feverishly to find a killer before he strikes again, Boston Homicide Detective Reid Sylver and rookie cop London Gold are blindsided by their chemistry and developing attraction. (978-1-63555-611-7)

**Trade Secrets** by Kathleen Knowles. In Silicon Valley, love and business are a volatile mix for clinical lab scientist Tony Leung and venture capitalist Sheila Graham. (978-1-63555-642-1)

**Death Overdue** by David S. Pederson. Did Heath turn to murder in an alcohol induced haze to solve the problem of his blackmailer, or was it someone else who brought about a death overdue? (978-1-63555-711-4)

**Entangled** by Melissa Brayden. Becca Crawford is the perfect person to head up the Jade Hotel, if only the captivating owner of the local vineyard would get on board with her plan and stop badmouthing the hotel to everyone in town. (978-1-63555-709-1)

**First Do No Harm** by Emily Smith. Pierce and Cassidy are about to discover that when it comes to love, sometimes you have to risk it all to have it all. (978-1-63555-699-5)

**Kiss Me Every Day** by Dena Blake. For Wynn Evans, wishing for a do-over with Carly Jamison was a long shot, actually getting one was a game changer. (978-1-63555-551-6)

**Olivia** by Genevieve McCluer. In this lesbian Shakespeare adaptation with vampires, Olivia is a centuries old vampire who must fight a strange figure from her past if she wants a chance at happiness. (978-1-63555-701-5)

**One Woman's Treasure** by Jean Copeland. Daphne's search for discarded antiques and treasures leads to an embarrassing misunderstanding, and ultimately, the opportunity for the romance of a lifetime with Nina. (978-1-63555-652-0)

**Silver Ravens** by Jane Fletcher. Lori has lost her girlfriend, her home, and her job. Things don't improve when she's kidnapped and taken to fairyland. (978-1-63555-631-5)

**Still Not Over You** by Jenny Frame, Carsen Taite, Ali Vali. Old flames die hard in these tales of a second chance at love with the ex you're still not over. Stories by award winning authors Jenny Frame, Carsen Taite, and Ali Vali. (978-1-63555-516-5)

**Storm Lines** by Jessica L. Webb. Devon is a psychologist who likes rules. Marley is a cop who doesn't. They don't always agree, but both fight to protect a girl immersed in a street drug ring. (978-1-63555-626-1)

**The Politics of Love** by Jen Jensen. Is it possible to love across the political divide in a hostile world? Conservative Shelley Whitmore and liberal Rand Thomas are about to find out. (978-1-63555-693-3)

**All the Paths to You** by Morgan Lee Miller. High school sweethearts Quinn Hughes and Kennedy Reed reconnect five years after they break up and realize that their chemistry is all but over. (978-1-63555-662-9)

**Arrested Pleasures** by Nanisi Barrett D'Arnuck. When charged with a crime she didn't commit, Katherine Lowe faces the question: Which is harder, going to prison or falling in love? (978-1-63555-684-1)

**Bonded Love** by Renee Roman. Carpenter Blaze Carter suffers an injury that shatters her dreams, and ER nurse Trinity Greene hopes to show her that sometimes love is worth fighting for. (978-1-63555-530-1)

**Convergence** by Jane C. Esther. With life as they know it on the line, can Aerin McLeary and Olivia Ando's love survive an otherworldly threat to humankind? (978-1-63555-488-5)

**Coyote Blues** by Karen F. Williams. Riley Dawson, psychotherapist and shape-shifter, has her world turned upside down when Fiona Bell, her one true love, returns. (978-1-63555-558-5)

**Drawn** by Carsen Taite. Will the clues lead Detective Claire Hanlon to the killer terrorizing Dallas, or will she merely lose her heart to person of interest, urban artist Riley Flynn? (978-1-63555-644-5)

**Every Summer Day** by Lee Patton. Meant to celebrate every summer day, Luke's journal instead chronicles a love affair as fast-moving and possibly as fatal as his brother's brain tumor. (978-1-63555-706-0)

**Lucky** by Kris Bryant. Was Serena Evans's luck really about winning the lottery, or is she about to get even luckier in love? (978-1-63555-510-3)

**The Last Days of Autumn** by Donna K. Ford. Autumn and Caroline question the fairness of life, the cruelty of loss, and what it means to love as they navigate the complicated minefield of relationships, grief, and life-altering illness. (978-1-63555-672-8)

**Three Alarm Response** by Erin Dutton. In the midst of tragedy, can these first responders find love and healing? Three stories of courage, bravery, and passion. (978-1-63555-592-9)

**Veterinary Partner** by Nancy Wheelton. Callie and Lauren are determined to keep their hearts safe but find that taking a chance on love is the safest option of all. (978-1-63555-666-7)

**Everyday People** by Louis Barr. When film star Diana Danning hires private eye Clint Steele to find her son, Clint turns to his former West Point barracks mate, and ex-buddy with benefits, Mars Hauser to lend his cyber espionage and digital black ops skills to the case. (978-1-63555-698-8)

**Forging a Desire Line** by Mary P. Burns. When Charley's ex-wife, Tricia, is diagnosed with inoperable cancer, the private duty nurse Tricia hires turns out to be the handsome and aloof Joanna, who ignites something inside Charley she isn't ready to face. (978-1-63555-665-0)

**Love on the Night Shift** by Radclyffe. Between ruling the night shift in the ER at the Rivers and raising her teenage daughter, Blaise Richilieu has all the drama she needs in her life, until a dashing young attending appears on the scene and relentlessly pursues her. (978-1-63555-668-1)